RED DELICIOUS DEATH

RED DELICIOUS DEATH

SHEILA CONNOLLY

WHEELER
CHIVERS

This Large Print edition is published by Wheeler Publishing, Waterville, Maine, USA and by BBC Audiobooks Ltd, Bath, England.
Wheeler Publishing, a part of Gale, Cengage Learning.
An Orchard Mystery.

The text of this Large Print edition is unabridged.
Other aspects of the book may vary from the original edition.
Set in 16 pt. Plantin.

LIBRARY OF CONGRESS CATALOGING-IN-PUBLICATION DATA

Connolly, Sheila.
    Red delicious death / by Sheila Connolly. — Large print ed.
      p. cm. — (An orchard mystery) (Wheeler Publishing large print cozy mystery)
    ISBN-13: 978-1-4104-2797-7 (pbk.)
    ISBN-10: 1-4104-2797-8 (pbk.)
    1. Women—Fiction. 2. Orchards—Fiction. 3. Cooks—Crimes against—Fiction. 4. Large type books. I. Title.
PS3601.T83R43 2010
813'.6—dc22   2010016370

BRITISH LIBRARY CATALOGUING-IN-PUBLICATION DATA AVAILABLE

Published in 2010 in the U.S. by arrangement with The Berkley Publishing Group, a member of Penguin Group (USA) Inc.
Published in 2010 in the U.K. by arrangement with the author.

U.K. Hardcover: 978 1 408 49219 2 (Chivers Large Print)
U.K. Softcover: 978 1 408 49220 8 (Camden Large Print)

Printed in the United States of America
1 2 3 4 5 6 7 14 13 12 11 10

*In honor of
Alice Waters of Chez Panisse
and
Michael Pollan,
who both changed the way
I look at food*

ACKNOWLEDGMENTS

As always, this book could not have happened without the combined efforts of my agent, Jacky Sach of BookEnds, and my tireless editor, Shannon Jamieson-Vazquez.

Getting acquainted with the local foods community has been a pleasure. I owe thanks to the Chefs Collaborative in Boston and several of its members, particularly Justin Melnick, executive chef at Tomasso Trattoria & Enoteca in Southborough, who let me tour his kitchen and who answered my questions about finding and using local products (and thanks to Sister in Crime Gail Clark, who introduced me to his fine restaurant), and Jamie Bissonette, who demonstrated how to reduce a pig to dinner.

Thanks again to Sisters in Crime and the fabulous Guppies, who provide boundless encouragement, and to my family, who dutifully accompanied me to restaurants near

7

and far and suffered through many excellent meals for the sake of this book.

Bon appetit!

1

"They're all dead."

"What?" Meg Corey dragged her gaze from the orderly rows of apple trees that marched over the hill. Almost all were past bloom now, and some of them had what even a novice farmer like Meg could identify as apples. Small, maybe, but it was a start. She turned her attention to Carl Frederickson, her beekeeper. Until this morning, Meg hadn't even known she *had* a beekeeper, but it seemed like every day since she'd inherited the orchard, something — or someone — new she hadn't known about turned up. "Who's dead?"

"The entire hive. See?" Carl held up a wooden frame with what she recognized as honeycomb filling the middle section. Carl was wearing a beekeeper's outfit, including gloves and headgear. Meg was not, so she decided to stay where she was. But even from a safe distance Meg could see that the wax looked shriveled and discolored.

"What happened?" Meg asked. Poor Carl sounded like he was about to cry. It was abundantly clear that he loved his bees; when he pulled off his headgear, the look on his face made Meg even more convinced he was devastated.

Carl had shown up at her door early on this bright June morning. "I'm here to check your hives," he had announced.

Meg had had a wild flash of an image of this good-looking stranger checking her out for a rash. He had the face of an angel, if the angel was middle-aged and had spent a lot of time gazing at the sun, although his wreath of brown curls suggested a younger man. Then she realized he must mean beehives. She had beehives?

"Um, okay. What does that involve?" she asked.

Carl could apparently sense her confusion. "You *are* Meg Corey, right? That's your orchard up there?" He waved vaguely up the hill beside her house.

"Yes. But I didn't realize I had beehives."

"You do," Carl said. "Fifteen. Technically they're not yours, though — you lease them from me. Christopher Ramsdell had a contract with me, but when we talked about renewing for this year, he said I should ask

10

you about it."

"Oh." She had no idea that one could lease bees. Rent-a-bee? One more thing Meg didn't know. Luckily, she trusted Christopher Ramsdell, the professor who had been using her orchard as a university research site for years. "If Christopher's happy with your arrangement, I'm not going to argue. But isn't the season over?"

"Just about. But the contract ran through this bloom, and we'd have to renew for next year — if you're interested. Right now I'm just checking on the hives, to make sure everything's all right. Haven't you seen them?"

She thought for a moment, and was embarrassed to realize she hadn't been paying attention. "I'm sorry — I'm kind of new at all this. So you figure out how many bees I need, and you come around to make sure they're happy and healthy?"

"That's about it. I can show you the hives now, if you've got the time."

"Why not?" It was a beautiful day, and Meg hadn't visited the orchard for, oh, at least three hours. Something might have changed, as it seemed to do all the time. It really was fascinating, watching the bare trees bloom and leaf out, and then seeing apples appear. Meg was looking forward to watching them become a real crop in a few short months. "Lead the way."

Carl climbed straight up the hill and headed for the far side of the orchard, toward a wooden box about three feet high, painted white. Meg had noticed it and the others like it scattered through the orchard, but hadn't given them much thought. Before approaching, Carl pulled on his protective gear.

"Do I need to wear something like that, too?" Meg asked.

"No, not unless you're opening up the hive. You should be fine. This is a second-year hive — it has two tiers, and the frames hang inside the tiers. That's where the bees build the wax chambers." He carefully lifted the lid off the box, and then pulled out a vertical frame. A few bees, annoyed, flew away, but otherwise there was little activity. Meg could make out the yellow of the wax, and the deeper gold of what must be honey in a good number of the cells. And, she realized, even from where she stood, she could hear a constant low humming. How had she missed the sound of all those bees?

"Do you collect the honey?" Meg asked Carl.

"I do, and I sell it, too — though I can let you have it, if you want, for a fair price."

12

"I'll think about it. But if you've got buyers lined up, that's okay."

"Thanks. But later you might like to watch how I harvest the honey, if you've never seen it before."

Nope, Meg had never seen a honey harvest. It was only one of a long list of agricultural events she had managed to miss during her previous career as a banker in Boston. She was catching up fast, out of necessity: the orchard she had inherited was supposed to provide her with a steady income, now that the banking job had gone away. "I'd like that. You said I have fifteen hives?"

Carl carefully replaced the honey-filled frame in the hive, and closed the top again. "Yup. One per acre is the standard. Sometimes we can go with fewer — depends on what else is around you, what other pollinators you've got." He led the way to the next box, some fifty feet away.

As they approached, Meg could read the change in Carl's body language. If he'd been a cat, his ears would have pricked up. Then she noticed the silence — this time there was no hum coming from the hive. And when Carl lifted off the lid, nothing moved.

He stared sadly into the silent hive. "They

13

were fine just a couple of weeks ago."

"So we got through pollination all right?"

"I think so. I hope so. Listen, this really isn't your problem. The contract says you get fifteen healthy hives, and if some of these have crashed, I'll need to replace them. But it's getting harder and harder to find healthy hives, and it takes a while to start up new ones."

"What do you mean, it's getting harder? What's happening to the bees?"

"I don't know. Nobody knows what's killing them off, not even the guys over at the university. Best guess, it's a virus or something that's been passed around from country to country, but we don't know how it spreads from hive to hive, why it takes some and not others. And without knowing that, we don't know how to stop it either." He shook his head. "I'll have to see what I've got to replace this hive for you. Sorry, Meg."

"Hey, don't apologize — it's not your fault, is it?" Meg made a mental note to ask Christopher or Bree Stewart, her new orchard manager, about this whole bee death phenomenon. She'd heard it mentioned in the class she had audited at the university this spring, but she hadn't expected to witness it up close.

Carl glumly surveyed the rest of the

orchard. "No, I guess not. Most people around here have had problems with it. Look, you don't have to stick around for all of these. I'll take care of swapping the rest of 'em out."

"Thank you, Carl — I'll let you handle it."

Carl sighed. "No problem. Good to meet you, Meg."

"Same here," Meg said. "I hope you find that most of them are all right."

"So do I," Carl said mournfully.

As she made her way down the hill, Meg could hear her phone ringing through the open windows. It was nice, after the long New England winter and grudging spring, to finally be able to air out the house, let it breathe. The phone had stopped by the time she let herself in the front door, but when she checked her messages, she saw her friend Lauren's name on the missed call log. Lauren still worked at the bank that had nudged Meg out the prior year, in what seemed to Meg like a different universe. She called Lauren back.

"Hey, farm girl!" Lauren's cheerful voice greeted her. "How's it going?"

"Oh, fine." Meg wasn't about to mention the dead bees, which would mean nothing to city girl Lauren. "When are you coming out to see the place? Better hurry, or I'll make you pick apples for your keep."

"Promises, promises. Listen, I called because I've got kind of an odd request."

"Okay, what?"

"I know these people — I mean, they're not exactly friends, but sort of friends of friends, if you know what I mean?" Lauren was apparently in a talkative mood, so Meg tucked the phone under her chin and searched through her refrigerator for something cold to drink as her friend went on. "Anyway, they both graduated from a cooking school in Rhode Island — Providence, I think — and they got married right after, and they've been working in Boston for a couple of years and now they want to open a restaurant."

"I hope you've told them they're crazy? From everything I've heard, it's not easy, and most restaurants go broke in the first year." And those were the statistics in a strong economy — who knew what the odds were now? "Do they have money? Or someone backing them?"

"So they say — apparently one of their daddies is footing the bills. And they claim that they've studied the financial side of the business, so they know what they're getting into."

16

Meg suppressed a snort. Like anybody knew what they were getting into with a new venture — just look at her.

Lauren was still talking. "They knew they didn't have a prayer in Boston, between the cost and the competition, so they decided to look at other areas, and they really like the Pioneer Valley — that's what you call your neck of the woods, right? Did I mention they're into local foods? Anyway, they've done some looking around there, but I think they were kind of shocked by how expensive space was in Amherst and Northampton."

Meg settled herself in her chair, and her cat, Lolly, immediately jumped into her lap. Meg rubbed her head idly. "From what I've seen, there are a lot of pretty intense foodies there, too, so lots of competition. Well, good luck to them. But why are you calling me?" Meg could sense a request for a favor coming.

"I'm getting there. I remembered that you lived out there in the country, and I wondered if you had any ideas about a good place in the area to set up a new restaurant."

Meg suppressed a laugh. She could count on the fingers of one hand the times she had eaten in a real restaurant since she had moved to western Massachusetts. "Lauren,

I've been here less than six months, and I don't know a whole lot about the restaurant scene. But . . ." Meg stopped as an idea sprouted. "What about here in Granford?"

"What about it? I thought it was a flyspeck of a place."

"It's small, but it's an easy drive to both Amherst and Northampton, where the foodies lurk, and there's no competition in town. And I know there *are* a lot of farmers around, so they'd have suppliers on hand."

"Interesting idea. I can run it by them. What kind of sites might be available?"

"I can't tell you offhand, but I know a real estate agent in town who'd love to help." Frances Clark had hoped to sell Meg's property, and since Meg had decided to stay rather than sell, she felt an obscure obligation to help her would-be real estate agent out. "You want me to call her?"

"Sure. Of course, the kids will have to see the place, do some homework, but it's a start."

"The kids?"

Lauren sighed. "Between you and me, they seem awfully young, even though they've got to be close to twenty-five."

"And we're ancient, right?" Not quite a decade older.

"Some days it feels like it. Anyway, I knew

you'd have some good ideas. Let me talk to them, and you talk to your real estate person, and we'll see if we can get them all together."

"Sounds like a plan."

"Thanks, Meg. Oh, by the way, they want to open by September first."

Meg choked on her drink. "You're kidding! That's less than three months away!"

"I know. I told you they were young. They'll find out fast enough. Oh, hey, how's that plumber guy of yours?"

"Seth? You'll have to come see for yourself. He's moving his office into my backyard." Seth lived just over the hill, on land the Chapin family had owned for centuries. He had gone into the family plumbing business, but recently he had decided to follow his true passion, renovating old homes. Since the building that had housed the original plumbing business had been razed to accommodate the new shopping center on the highway through town, Meg had offered to let Seth take over some of the space in her outbuildings that she hadn't planned to use. She thought she was getting the better deal: with the problems that plagued her eighteenth-century colonial house, it was handy to have a plumber on the premises. Meg hadn't decided whether the fact that she and Seth had a . . . something blossoming between them made his constant presence a plus or a minus.

"That's pretty convenient. Okay, let me check my calendar and I'll see when I can break loose. And I'll send the kids out your way. Talk soon!" Lauren hung up.

Meg sat, stroking Lolly, turning over what Lauren had told her. Granford really could use some decent food, although she had no idea what kind of menu these young chefs would be considering. Local foods sounded like a promising concept, and had been getting good media buzz. And there were probably plenty of providers around who would be happy to get the business. But whatever kind of food the fledgling chefs offered, they'd have to be able to attract people from outside of town, because Granford's population of thirteen hundred or so would not keep a restaurant in business very long.

Well, one step at a time. First they would need a location. Meg dislodged a protesting Lolly and retrieved her phone book so she could call Frances.

Frances answered on the first ring — not surprising, considering the abysmal state of the local real estate market. "Hi, Meg! You ready to sell?"

Meg laughed. "No, not yet. I'm just getting to know the orchard. But I've got a possible lead for you. A friend just told me about a couple of chefs who want to open a restaurant, and I gather they can't afford Amherst and Northampton. Do you know of any places in town here that might work?"

Frances snapped into business mode. "Square footage? Seating capacity? How much build-out expense can they handle?"

Meg laughed again. "Hey, I don't know! I just heard about this. Let's assume they're not looking for a fast-food joint on the highway, but something more upscale, to compete with the fancier places in the bigger local towns. Anything promising along those lines?"

"Let me think about it, but I'll bet I can come up with some possibilities. When are they looking to do this?"

"Immediately or sooner. My friend says they want to be up and running by fall."

Frances gave a short bark of laughter. "Yeah, right — in their dreams. But who am I to discourage them? If they buy the building, it's their problem. Let me check my listings."

"Terrific."

As Meg hung up, she realized she felt quite pleased with herself. She had done a good deed for her friend Lauren; she had given Frances a lead on some potential business; and she might just have helped score a decent restaurant for Granford. Not bad work, for under half an hour. And maybe Seth could help with the build-out, since he was a plumber; and he could help with zoning and licensing requirements, since he was a town selectman. Better and better.

She stood up, dislodging the cat. "Well, Lolly, I guess I'd better get back to work."

2

Meg had known Brian and Nicole Czarnecki for two hours and didn't know whether to pat them on their heads or strangle them. Short and comfortably rounded, Nicole's dark curls danced around her face, which telegraphed every emotion she felt — and there were many. She would have been a disaster in a poker game. Brian — taller, broader, and definitely quieter — followed his wife with what looked like sincere adoration. They seemed to communicate almost telepathically, with a quick exchange of glances or a passing touch.

Lauren had warned Meg that the chefs were young, but she hadn't mentioned that they were extremely sure of themselves, and predictably naive. They had shiny new degrees from a prestigious culinary academy, a couple of years of cooking experience under their belts, and they were certain that they knew all they needed to about fitting out and running a restaurant. Right. But it was hard to squash Nicole's obvious enthusiasm, and Meg found she didn't have the heart to try. It was too hard not to like them.

Meg knew making this sale was important to Frances. A single woman maybe ten years older than Meg, Frances supported herself with her real estate sales, and they had been few and far between lately. Frances had lined up four sites for their inspection. The first three had been flops across the board, and Meg had been reminded of Goldilocks: one had been too big, one had been too small, but so far nothing had been "just right." Meg wasn't really sure how she had been roped into accompanying them; she had called Lauren as soon as Frances had lined up some viewings, and somehow Lauren had told the baby chefs that Meg was going to show them around the neighborhood. As if she knew much, after a scant six months. But she thought she should be polite to potential neighbors, and she wanted them to see Granford in a good light, mainly for selfish reasons: she really did want a restaurant in town. At least Granford was looking pretty these days, in the first full flush of summer. The sloping green at the heart of town was lush with grass, and the white church rose strong and true against the blue June sky. From this distance you couldn't tell it needed a coat of paint — badly.

Meg exchanged a glance with Frances as they made their way up the front walk of the last place on the list, and Frances winked at her.

"Now, Nicole, Brian, I've saved the best for last," Frances said. "Let's take a minute to look at the exterior before we go in."

They were standing in front of a square, solid brick building, once painted white, with a generous wraparound porch, perched like a setting hen at the higher end of the Granford town green.

Frances went on. "You've got a terrific site overlooking the town — you can't miss it when you're coming along the highway from the west. Imagine it lit up in the evening."

Nicole and Brian looked out over the green. "Kind of small, isn't it?" Nicole said.

"Granford? Yes, but we're close to bigger towns, with easy access. South Hadley's that way, Northampton and Amherst that way." Frances waved at the two-lane roads that intersected in the middle of Granford. "You're just far enough off the main road so that it's quiet, with plenty of space for parking here, on the right side. What do you think?"

Nicole turned to Brian, who nodded. "Can we see the inside?"

"No problem. Listen, I can get you a really good price on this one. It's been in the same family for years — the old couple living here wanted to stay in the family home, but they died recently and the heirs can't be bothered with it. I think they'll accept any reasonable offer."

"They didn't die in the house, did they?" Brian asked.

"No, of course not. In the hospital at Holyoke, a week apart. Kind of sweet, if you think about it. And they kept the place in really good condition — didn't add too much either. So you won't have to undo a lot." Frances strode up the porch steps on the side and fished out a bunch of keys. "Ready?"

"Okay." Brian and Nicole followed her in, with Meg trailing in their wake. She was looking forward to seeing the inside of this house herself. She'd been driving by it for months, and had noticed the "For Sale" sign out front, but she had more than enough to keep her busy at her own place, between the renovations she was slowly doing by herself — which would accelerate now that the weather was nice — and the work needed in the orchard. Meg listened to Frances's spiel with half an ear while she studied the house. Nice square rooms, with reasonably high ceilings. Long windows opening onto the broad front porch. She tried to visualize the rooms filled with linen-draped tables, candlelight, muted conversation, and the subdued clink of glassware and china: yes, it might work. It would be intimate and warm in winter, and there would be a nice breeze through the windows in summer. For the first time since they had set out today, Meg felt a surge of optimism.

She tuned in to what Nicole and Brian were saying. "How many tables, do you think? What about the flow? I'd kind of hoped for a single space, not a couple of rooms. Brian, you're going to be front — what do you think?"

He shrugged. "Smaller rooms might be more intimate. Frances, where's the kitchen?"

"Oh, right — kitchen. I didn't even think about that," Nicole burbled. "I'm an idiot. I hope it's not a dark hole in the back?" She looked inquiringly at Frances.

"Nope," Frances replied promptly. "It's in an L of its own, with plenty of space. Not much in there now, but lots of potential."

As Meg followed the three toward the kitchen, she watched the chefs. They seemed to be thinking seriously about the site — they hadn't even bothered to look at the kitchen in one of the places they had already visited. "How much were you thinking of investing in remodeling?" Meg asked.

Brian and Nicole turned to her, looking as though they had forgotten her existence. Nicole answered, "We won't have a whole lot, after we buy a place. And we're going to need to fit out the kitchen first — I want real quality appliances and all, you know?"

"Maybe you should talk to a professional. I know someone who does both plumbing and renovation, and I'm pretty sure he'd give you a good deal. That is, if you're serious?"

They glanced at each other, then Brian turned back to Meg. "Maybe. But we could do a lot of the work ourselves. I'm pretty handy with a sledgehammer."

"Why don't you two check out the kitchen and I can give him a call, see if he can come over now. If you're interested, that is."

"Okay, sure," Brian said, then followed Frances and his wife into the kitchen.

Meg turned away and hit Seth's speed-dial number on her cell phone.

"Chapin Plumbing — oops, Renovation.

Hi, Meg. What's up?"

Meg walked over to one of the windows overlooking the green. "Are you doing anything right now?"

"I'm always doing something, but I'm in town, if that's what you're asking. What do you need?"

"Frances is showing some potential buyers the house at the top of the green. They're looking for a restaurant site, but they're probably going to have to put together a whole new kitchen. I thought maybe they could use a professional opinion before they got too carried away."

"The Stebbins place? Great building, but you've got to be careful with that old brick. I can be there in five."

"Bless you."

Meg shut the phone and followed the sound of voices toward the kitchen, off to one side of the building. Even Meg could tell that some major changes would be needed to fit it out for restaurant cooking.

Frances was talking rapidly. "Sure, you'd have to tear all this out, but it's great space, isn't it? And set off from the dining areas, which will cut down on noise and odors. And the plumbing hook-ups are already in place."

Meg cleared her throat. "I've asked that

friend of mine to come over and take a look — he can probably give you a good idea of what would need to be done."

"Cool," Nicole said. "And thanks. What's upstairs?"

"Three bedrooms — well, technically four, but the fourth one was probably the nursery when the place was built," Frances said. "One bath. You have plans for the upstairs?"

"We thought if there was enough space, we could live in the restaurant building, at least in the beginning, while we're getting set up. Can you show us?"

"Sure. Meg, you coming up?" When Meg shook her head, Frances went on, "Let us know when Seth gets here. Come on, you two — there's a back set of stairs, which is perfect for what you want."

While the trio clattered up the uncarpeted stairs, Meg wandered around the downstairs rooms. Even with a solid structure, it was a pretty safe bet that the house would need a major overhaul to turn it into a business — which meant a major outlay of capital. Did the kids have a clue what they were getting themselves into? And had they given any thought to zoning, permitting, a liquor license? Or did they only have pie-in-the-sky ideas about opening a nice place to eat?

Meg wasn't sure whether she envied them their youthful optimism, or pitied them for the rude awakening that undoubtedly awaited them.

"Hello?" Seth called out from the front of the building.

Meg went out to greet him, and watched as he approached, the usual spring in his step. She always thought that he looked like the original town settlers would have looked: compact, solid, competent. That wasn't surprising, since the Chapins had been among those founders. And if anyone could steer the Czarneckis in the right direction, Seth could.

"What's the story? Are they really interested, or just looking?" he asked her.

Meg shrugged. "I can't really tell. They saw a couple of other sites, but even I could tell they wouldn't work. I think they like this place, and Frances is giving them the pep talk. And as a plumber, you can tell them what they'll need to do in the kitchen, which is pretty much a blank slate at the moment. And as a selectman, you can tell them about permitting."

Seth held up a hand, grinning. "Whoa! First we'd better figure out if they're serious. You think they'd be a good fit for Granford?"

"You're asking me? I think they make me feel old." Meg sighed.

Seth laughed. "Can it, Meg. You've taken on a lot of new things recently, so I don't think you're too stodgy yet. Let's see what they've got to say."

As Frances, Nicole, and Brian made their way down the stairs, Seth stepped forward to greet them. "Hi, I'm Seth Chapin — Granford resident, contractor, plumber, and selectman. You name it, I've probably done it. You're thinking about using this place as a restaurant?"

Nicole's eyes were brighter than they had been when she went up the stairs, Meg noticed.

"Well, it's not definite, but it's the nicest place we've seen, if we can get a deal we can afford. We know we've got a lot of expenses coming. Can you take a look at the kitchen?"

"No problem." Seth led the young chefs back toward the kitchen, leaving Meg and Frances in what must once have been the front parlor.

"What kind of funds have they got?" Meg said in a low voice.

Frances grinned. "Enough. From what they've said, Nicole's dad gave them a nice check as a wedding present, and they've been saving their pennies since. I'll get them a good deal, if they go for it. I know the owners pretty well."

"Are there restrictions on what you can do with a historical structure in Granford?"

"Some. We'll see. I hope Seth doesn't scare them off."

"He'll be fair. I'll bet the selectman side of him would want this to work, but I don't know if that talks louder than the plumber-renovator side."

Nicole emerged from the kitchen alone. "Guy stuff. They're talking about drains and venting."

"You both plan to cook?" Meg asked.

"Oh, yes! We both love it — although Brian took more business courses than I did. And we've got another friend — he couldn't make it today because he had some stuff to finish up in Boston, but he could be here by next week. He's our sous chef. So Brian will take care of the build-out, and then later, the front of the house. I'll handle planning menus and do most of the cooking, and Sam will deal with the vendors and prep work. We've got it all planned out."

Seth and Brian emerged from the rear, still deep in conversation. Apparently male bonding extended to pipe chases and grease filters. "What's your schedule for the job?"

Seth asked.

"We're aiming for September first. Are we nuts?"

"Depends. It's doable, but it might be tight."

Brian looked relieved. "Hey, you're the first person who even thinks it's possible. And Sam and I can do a lot of the unskilled stuff, if you'll let us."

"I could use the help," Seth replied. "When are you going to decide on the site?"

Nicole and Brian exchanged a long look before Brian spoke again. "Cards on the table? We like this place. It has a good feel, and it's in our price range. Let me talk to our mortgage broker, and maybe we can make an offer, say, tomorrow?"

They might be naive, Meg thought, *but at least they're decisive.* Frances looked like she was ready to weep for joy, and Meg had to wonder how many deals she had closed lately.

"You won't regret it," Frances said. "It's a great town, good people. You do this right, and you can attract business from the whole area. You let me know when you're ready to make a deal, and I'll talk to the owners."

"Thanks, Frances. And Meg, you, too — you've been a big help, and now you've put us in touch with Seth. I think we're going to like it here."

Meg waited on the porch as Frances escorted Brian and Nicole back to their car, talking a mile a minute. She was admiring the view when Seth came up behind her.

"Think they can make it work?" she asked over her shoulder.

"Maybe. I won't say no. And the town will be happy to have them."

"They've got a pretty tight timetable. Are they going to be able to get all the permits and permissions and whatever?"

"From the town, sure — one of the benefits of small-town government. They'll have to take care of the liquor license, assuming they want one, and the state board of inspection, but I can probably walk them through that. Speaking of government, are you coming to the selectmen's meeting?"

"I guess, if you want me to. What is it you think I can do?"

"You know something about municipal finance — maybe you can give us some ideas on how to generate revenue."

"Don't you have finance people in place? A treasurer?"

"Of course we do, but they don't have your kind of experience. Please?"

"I said I'd come, didn't I? And I'll admit I'm curious. Most of the issues I've worked with have been for larger towns and cities. I'm not sure what will apply to a place this size."

"Numbers are numbers — just whack a few zeroes off what you're used to and it'll be fine. Can I pick you up?"

"Sure. You want me to feed you first? Even though it won't be up to Boston restaurant standards."

"Sounds good. See you at six."

3

Back at her house, Meg spotted her orchard manager — and housemate — Bree's car in the driveway, but she wasn't in sight.

"Bree?" Meg called up the stairs.

"Be right down," came a voice from the back of the house.

Since graduating from UMass with a degree in agriculture at the end of May, Briona Stewart had taken on the official job of orchard manager for Meg. Bree might be untested, but she clearly knew a lot more about orchards than Meg did. Meg was still getting used to the idea of having someone else living under her roof full-time, but since the salary she could afford was pitifully small, she'd hoped that offering room and board would help. Bree guarded her privacy jealously, and there had been a few bumps along the way, but they seemed to have settled into a routine in the past month.

Meg went to the kitchen and opened the

refrigerator, looking for ideas. The sound of the refrigerator door prompted Lolly to appear, and she wrapped herself around Meg's ankles. "No, silly cat, it's not dinnertime yet, and you've still got food in your dish. I'm trying to feed *people* here." Meg reached down to scratch behind Lolly's ears, and after accepting her due, Lolly strolled back toward the dining room. Meg pulled out a package of chicken breasts.

"Yo, Meg — you wanted me?" Bree clattered down the back stairs that led from her room above to the kitchen.

"I just wanted to know what your dinner plans are. I asked Seth to come by and eat, because we're going to the selectmen's meeting after dinner."

Bree grinned at her. "That makes, what — three times this month already? You two are moving right along, hmm?"

"We're moving at our own pace, thank you very much. Anyway, he's here, I'm here — it just makes sense to eat together. Heck, you've eaten with us most of those times," Meg blushed despite herself. "Besides, we're both busy. How about you and Michael? You've been spending a lot of time together lately," Meg parried.

"We're fine. Point taken." Bree didn't volunteer any more.

Meg didn't want to pry, so she changed the subject to plans for the harvest. "How's the hiring going? Will we have the same crew as last time?"

"Looks like."

"Did you have any trouble getting them to sign on?" Meg knew that when he had been running the show, Christopher had usually employed Jamaican pickers, as did many of the orchard growers in the area, but she had had some concerns about Bree handling the crew of mainly older men. Bree had Jamaican parents herself, but she was also young and female, and Meg hadn't been sure how well the men would accept her.

Bree shrugged. "Not really. A few made some comments, but my auntie set them straight. She knows them from way back."

"Good. Then we're all set?"

"As soon as we have apples. You decided who you're selling them to?"

"Um, I'm working on it." In fact, Meg had fallen behind in her marketing plans. At first it had seemed unreal that her bare trees would produce a crop. And then she had wanted to be sure she understood the ins and outs of selling her apples: Supermarket chain? Local cooperatives? Setting up her own farm stand? The end result was that she hadn't done anything yet, but she knew she couldn't put it off much longer. The first apples would ripen in less than two months.

"How's the barn build-out coming?" Meg asked instead. Seth had promised to fit out the climate-controlled holding chambers she would need when her crop ripened, and that date was approaching fast.

"We'll get there. Seth's got a lot going on — trying to put his offices together, handling your orchard stuff, and making a living besides. That's one busy man."

"Tell me about it. Plus he's a selectman, which eats up more time."

"No wonder he doesn't have any time for romance, eh?" Bree grinned wickedly.

Seth arrived promptly at six. He still knocked, rather than walking right in, which Meg thought was both sweet and silly, given how much time he spent at the house. But he was always careful not to intrude. "Hi, Meg, Bree. Something smells great."

"Bree offered to do the cooking," Meg said. Bree waved and turned back to stirring something. "So, who's going to be at the meeting tonight? I don't know if I've met them all."

"There are three members of the Board

of Selectmen: me, Tom Moody, who you should know from the Town Meeting, and the redoubtable Mrs. Caroline Goldthwaite. Then there's Jeannine Crosby, the selectmen's secretary, who keeps the minutes, and Jack Porter, the town treasurer. I don't think Jack's coming, though."

"What about a finance committee?" Meg asked.

"Five members, appointed by the selectmen. They meet separately. Tonight is just a regular working meeting."

"Who handles zoning?"

"Sally Thayer — I don't think you've met her either."

"Should we be talking about the restaurant deal if it's not finalized?"

"I think we can talk about it in general terms — there are a lot of details to be worked out, things that the town, or at least this board, hasn't considered before. Even if Brian and Nicole don't go for it, it's still a good idea, so maybe we need to open up that can of worms."

Meg made a face at him. "That's a lovely image for a restaurant. You know, if we want the town to support this, then they have to be able to afford a meal there. If it's too upscale, the people of Granford will get annoyed."

"Agreed. But we're a long way from that yet."

The Granford Selectboard met in a room in the Victorian town hall on the green — which had a convenient view of the proposed restaurant site. Meg wasn't sure what her role at the meeting was: she had some small legal standing as a resident, albeit one of less than six months, but she had a limited knowledge of the inner workings of the town. And what little the town's citizens knew of her was not exactly positive, after she had disrupted the last town meeting in a rather spectacular way.

"Hi, Tom — you remember Meg Corey, don't you?" Seth began, guiding Meg over to Tom Moody, seated at the end of the long oak table. He stood up promptly and offered his hand.

"Hard to forget her, don't you think?" He softened his statement with a smile. "Welcome, Meg. You don't plan to drop any bombshells tonight, do you? Because I'd like to get home in time to watch the Red Sox game."

Meg returned his smile, relieved by the warmth of his reception. She had seen him before, at the last town meeting, but now she could see he was close to Seth's age, and outweighed him by at least twenty pounds, in the wrong places. "You don't have to worry. Nice to see you again, Tom, under happier circumstances," Meg replied.

"Meg, this is Mrs. Caroline Goldthwaite, our third selectman — or maybe we should be saying 'selectperson'?" Tom gestured to a woman already seated at the big oak table. She was probably past seventy, her silvered hair neatly set, carefully dressed in a pressed blouse and tailored skirt, and wearing pearls. Meg promptly felt shabby in her jeans and shirt.

Mrs. Goldthwaite didn't rise, but waited for Meg to approach her before she extended a slender hand; when Meg took it, it was cold and dry, despite the warmth of the June evening. " 'Selectman' will do fine, Tom. I don't hold with this feminist silliness. Meg, I'm happy to meet you at last. Your reputation precedes you."

"I'm happy to be here, Caroline." When a faint cloud passed over the woman's face, Meg quickly added, "Mrs. Goldthwaite. But I'm here mainly as an observer, and maybe as a consultant. I'm happy to listen and learn."

Once everyone had settled themselves in chairs, supplied with bad coffee from the office pot, Tom Moody declared the meet

43

ing open. The three board members ran through a number of business items, which Meg had little interest in, so instead she studied the participants. Seth brought his usual enthusiasm to the discussion; Tom was more laid-back; and Mrs. Goldthwaite frequently looked as though she smelled something objectionable, although her comments showed that she knew quite a bit about the articles under discussion — and disapproved of most. This was an elected group, wasn't it? Meg reflected. Did Caroline Goldthwaite represent a sizable constituency in Granford?

"Meg, do you have an opinion?" Seth's voice interrupted her musings.

"Oh, sorry. What was that?" Great: now she'd been caught wool-gathering.

"Why don't you explain what your area of expertise is, as a start?"

"Of course. Before I moved to Granford, I was a municipal bond analyst for a Boston bank. That means I evaluated the underlying credit strengths and weaknesses of the issuer, reviewed the issuer's financial history, that kind of thing. I left when my bank was bought out by another one, and my position became redundant. That's when I decided to move here and take over the house and orchard on County Line Road."

44

"The Warren place," Mrs. Goldthwaite sniffed. "It's a shame what's been allowed to happen there over the years. Absentee owner."

Meg refused to apologize. "Yes, my mother inherited it some years ago, but she hasn't been here since. I'm planning to rectify the neglect, and I'm running the orchard now."

Tom broke in, "Well, I for one am happy to have you here, now that that other little mess has been cleared up. Granford can use some new blood, and the fact that you're smart is a plus." He smiled at her. "Has Seth filled you in on Granford's dismal financial state?"

Meg nodded. "The broad outlines. The bottom line is, the town has no dependable revenue sources, and we're losing a lot of the working population, which eats into our already shrinking tax base. The new development on the highway will help, and may even keep current residents or attract some new ones, but it may not be enough to stem the tide."

"That about sums it up." Tom nodded. "Eroding tax base, growing expenses — fits Granford and most of the small towns in the state, or even the country. Makes you wonder just why we keep asking to be elected."

Mrs. Goldthwaite spoke stiffly. "I consider it a privilege to serve this community, as my ancestors did before me. And surely you exaggerate the problems. This town has survived since the eighteenth century, and I'm sure it will continue to do so."

Meg watched as Tom and Seth exchanged an exasperated glance over Mrs. Goldthwaite's head. Apparently this was not a new debate.

"That doesn't mean we can't do something to improve conditions, Mrs. Goldthwaite," Seth said. "In fact, there's one piece of new business on the table, and we owe it in part to Meg. There are some potential buyers looking at turning the Stebbins place into a restaurant." At the look of utter dismay on Mrs. Goldthwaite's face, Seth hurried to add, "A nice one, of course, not a fast-food place. It's not a done deal yet, but I think in principle it's a good idea, and there are a number of municipal issues we should consider, in the event that this does go forward. I believe the buyers will need some approvals from the town, at a minimum, and we should be prepared for that request."

"I for one am appalled," Mrs. Goldthwaite said imperiously. "That lovely house on the green? You want a car park, and nasty cooking odors, and trash blowing about? Surely there must be a private buyer who would love it as it is."

"Mrs. Goldthwaite," Tom began, trying to swallow his exasperation, "that place has been on the market for close to a year without even a nibble, and you know Frances Clark has been working her tail off to sell it. So we should at least consider this option. Seth, what are your concerns?"

"We'd have to check the zoning — we might need a variance. Structurally the building is sound enough, but they'd need a whole new kitchen and I'd have to be sure it's up to code. I can handle that. What I know less about is permitting, liquor licenses, all that stuff. We need to know what hoops the town has to jump through to get this up and running. And the buyers want it all to happen yesterday."

"You've met them?"

"I did, with Meg. In fact, it was a friend of Meg's who pointed them toward Granford, and I think we owe her a vote of thanks. It's a good idea, and a good opportunity for Granford."

Mrs. Goldthwaite gave an audible sniff but said nothing.

Tom ignored her. "I agree with Seth — seems like the perfect setting, and we sure could use some decent food in this town. We can ask Fred Weatherly — he's the town counsel, Meg — to look into the legal details, and talk to the assessor's office. All just in preparation, Mrs. Goldthwaite."

Caroline Goldthwaite sat rigid in her chair. "I shall reserve judgment until I have seen the details, but I want to go on record that I think it is a poor idea."

And what, Meg wondered, *would you consider a good idea?* Yankee thrift was well and good, but the town needed an infusion of cash from somewhere, and this seemed like a relatively benign solution. Meg was startled to hear her cell phone ringing in the depths of her purse. She pulled it out: Frances. "Excuse me, but this may be relevant." She stood up and walked over to the window overlooking the green, where the Stebbins house was bathed in evening light. "Frances?" she answered.

"They did it! Offer made and accepted — assuming you get the folks at Town Hall on board. First real sale this year!" the real estate agent crowed.

"That's great, Frances. I'm at Town Hall now, so I'll pass on the news. Thanks for letting me know."

"And there's more! I got the owners' permission to let them go ahead and move in as soon as tomorrow while the paperwork clears, but they've already done the credit check and all that, so there shouldn't be any problems. I owe you a bottle of champagne, lady!"

"I'll take you up on that! See you."

Meg turned back to the others. "The buyers have made an offer, and the sellers have accepted it. Granford will have a restaurant — if we can make it happen."

Seth grinned at her, Tom applauded, and Mrs. Goldthwaite sat silent, her eyes empty.

4

Nicole Czarnecki knocked on Meg's front door the next morning, holding a covered plate of something that smelled of cinnamon. Her dark curls were barely restrained by a colorful kerchief that had several floury fingerprints on it.

Meg's mouth started watering immediately. "Nicole, if you're looking to bribe your way into my house, you've come prepared. Come on in."

"Nicky, please! I don't mean to bother you so early, but I really wanted to thank you for finding the house for us, so I brought you some scones. We're so excited! I can't wait to get started."

"Can you stay to eat some with me? I'd love to hear how things are going. Where did you even find a place to cook them? I thought the old kitchen was a mess." Meg left the door open to catch the morning breeze and led the way back to the kitchen.

"Heck, a good cook can produce a meal with a campfire and one pan. This was almost luxurious."

Bree was seated at the kitchen table, leafing through the paper, and looked up when Meg and Nicole came in. "Hello."

"Bree, this is Nicole Czarnecki. She and her husband just bought that house at the top of the green and want to open a restaurant. Nicole, this is Briona Stewart, my orchard manager."

Nicole smiled widely. "Can I call you Bree? And I'm Nicky. My husband's Brian. You want a scone?" She slid the plate onto the table and removed the wrapping.

"Sure, Bree's fine. Those look great." Bree helped herself.

Meg poured coffee all around, and then joined the others at the table. "So, Nicky, you've really moved fast. You've settled in the place already?"

"Well, we kind of fell in love with it, you know? It was funny — we had to try real hard not to look too excited when Frances showed it to us, because we thought maybe she'd hike up the price."

Meg had a ballpark idea of what the house had sold for, and wondered just how big Daddy's wedding check had been. "I'm sure Frances has been fair to you. I always heard

51

that starting a restaurant was expensive. You've got to remodel the building, buy equipment and all the stuff for the front, supplies — and you've got to have some cushion for your start-up period, until you're established. Are you ready for all that?"

Nicky laughed. "You sound like Brian. He's the numbers guy, and he says he's looked at all of that. You know — lots of spreadsheets and estimates. I know we've got to be careful, but I'm *so* looking forward to this! I've been cooking since I was a kid, just messing around with recipes. I've got lots of ideas! And I'm really thrilled to be in a place that's a lot closer to the food. I grew up in New York, and then we went to school in Providence, and we worked in Boston — so I never saw a lot of real fields, you know?"

Bree snorted, and Meg glared briefly at her. "I know what you mean," Meg said. "I'm pretty new to this kind of thing myself, and here I find myself running an orchard, with Bree's help. I still don't recognize half the things I see planted in the fields around here." She hesitated a moment: she hated to rain on Nicky's parade, but she didn't want to see her going off in the wrong direction. "You know, there are some great restaurants around here, in Amherst and Northampton.

What are you going to do to stand out? Do you have a menu planned?"

"We're working on it," Nicky said cheerfully. "Oh, and you haven't met Sam yet. He just arrived from Boston, and he's going to be staying at the house, too. He's looking into suppliers. Isn't it great that we're here at this time of year, when there's so much to choose from? And Seth is terrific, isn't he? Does he live here with you and Bree?"

Bree swallowed what sounded like another snort, and Meg hurried to say, "He lives just over the hill. But his office is at the end of the driveway there. He'll do a good job for you — he really cares about old buildings."

"It's going to be great to clean up the place a bit." When Nicky saw Meg's expression, she added quickly, "Don't worry, we don't want to destroy it. It's got charm, and Seth says it's pretty sturdy. And we haven't got the money for fancy designers, so mostly we're going to settle for paint and polish. I like your place here — did Seth do the floor?"

Meg smiled proudly. "He helped, but it was mostly me. So I know what you're getting into, and I don't envy you. Still, I think strong and simple should appeal to people, especially around here. As long as you don't tart it up with chintz and wooden chickens."

Nicky let loose a delighted giggle. "No way! Besides, I don't want anything to distract people from the food. So, Bree, you from around here?" Nicky asked.

"Born and raised," Bree said. "I just graduated from UMass, in Amherst. If you're asking, my parents are Jamaican."

"Ooh, I'll have to get some recipes from you. Can you get the ingredients you need around here?"

Bree relaxed slightly, and Meg wondered if she had been braced for an insult of some kind. "Most — there's actually a pretty big Jamaican population around here. You said you're from New York?"

"Manhattan, mainly, 'til I went to Providence. Daddy didn't much like me going to cooking school — he thought I should get what he calls a 'real' degree and do something serious — but he came around, and now he's really behind me. He says he always liked my cooking — but then, he would, wouldn't he? And Brian's great, too, of course. He likes to cook, but he's much more into running things."

"You met at culinary school?"

"Yes. Sam, too. We're kind of like the Three Musketeers, you know?"

"Are you partners, officially?" Meg asked.

54

"We're friends. We don't have a legal agreement or anything, if that's what you mean. And we've all put in what we could, except I could do a little more than them, because Daddy's helping."

Nicky seemed completely open and sunny, even about the financial side of the situation. The delicious scones showed that she could cook. But how good would she be at running a business?

Meg was surprised to find that she cared. From what she'd seen so far she liked Nicky, innocent though she might be. She wanted to see their business succeed, for a variety of reasons. But it wasn't up to her to babysit this project; she had enough on her own plate with the orchard. Still, the next couple of months would be crucial to Nicky and Brian — maybe she could break free a little time to make sure they were on track. If Brian was the financial brains behind this, maybe she could sound him out discreetly and find out if he knew what he was talking about.

"You know, UMass has a pretty decent hospitality program," Bree was saying.

"Oh, I know. Brian told me all about it. He thought we could probably find some graduates to hire, in the future, maybe."

"You need staff? I still know a bunch of

students who'd be happy to have the work, and maybe some of the pickers' families."

"Great! I love this town already! Everybody has been so helpful — Meg, Frances, Seth, and now you, too, Bree. I just know this is going to work." She beamed at them, and at the world in general.

Meg hoped she was right.

Nicky pressed on, "Can we go talk to Seth now? We've got to start making real plans, and the clock is ticking!"

"Seth's not always around, you know. His business keeps him running around a lot." When Nicky's face fell, Meg added, "But I know he wants to help you. Why don't you call him and set something up?"

Nicky bounced out of her chair and pulled out a cell phone. "Excuse me a sec." She went into the dining room.

Meg and Bree exchanged a glance. "High energy, isn't she?" Bree said in a whisper.

"You've got that right. I hope she knows what she's doing," Meg replied in the same tone.

Bree shrugged. "Who knows? Enthusiasm helps. I wonder how many people say no to her?"

Nicky came back. "He's coming by the place at three. You guys want to come, too?"

"I've got some stuff to do," Bree said, "but

not anything you need to be here for, Meg."

Meg wavered. She thought she ought to know what Bree was doing, if it was related to the orchard, but she also wanted to be sure that Nicky and crew got off on the right foot. What could a couple of hours hurt? "Sure, I'd love to be there."

"Oh, good. Hey, before I say something stupid, are you and Seth, like, together? 'Cause I kind of got that vibe."

Meg could feel herself blushing. She hadn't really decided how to define their relationship, whatever it was. "Sort of. We haven't known each other long."

"Hey, cool. Listen, I'd better get back and make sure Brian and Sam are making progress, but I'll see you later!" She scooped up the plate she had brought the scones on, now empty except for crumbs.

"Why don't we go out this way?" Meg led her toward the kitchen door. Outside, she pointed. "That's Seth's space, and the barn is mine — that's where the apples are going soon."

Nicky actually held still long enough to take in the view. "It's pretty here. It sure is different than New York City. But I like it. Thanks again, Meg. It's great to be making friends here so fast. See you later!"

Inside again, Meg sat down to finish her

coffee. "What do you think?" she asked Bree, who was tidying up.

"I like her, I guess. I don't want to see her fall flat on her face."

"I don't either. I hope she's sincere about this, and it isn't just the whim of the moment. I'll have to scope out this Sam guy, too. You really think you can find staff for them?"

"Sure, no problem. Plenty of people around here looking for work these days."

Meg pulled up to the Stebbins house at three and found that Seth had arrived before her — and he had brought Bree. Meg parked and greeted them. "Hi, you two. Bree, I thought you weren't coming."

"Seth grabbed me — he stopped by the house. I finished up my stuff early, and — okay, I'll admit it — I want to see what they're doing."

"You and me both."

"Told you — I bet nobody says no to Nicky," Bree muttered as they approached the open front door.

Brian greeted them in the vestibule. "Welcome, welcome! Sorry I can't offer you refreshments, but we did scrounge up a bottle of champagne. You'll join us? We want to start off right."

He looked so pleased with himself that Meg couldn't turn him down. "Of course."

Brian had bought plastic glasses, and he set them on the stairs to pour. When he had filled the glasses, he called out, "Nicky? Sam? Our first customers."

"Coming!" Nicky called out. She appeared a second later with the person Meg assumed was Sam, in tow. "Hi, Meg, Bree, Seth," she said breathlessly. "And this is Sam."

"Sam Anderson," Sam said, offering his hand. He looked as though he could be Nicky's big brother. He was broad but not fat, with a thick mop of curly dark hair in need of a cut, and an amiable, handsome face. "Thanks for coming by. Nicky's told me about all your help with this. I'm going to be sous chef, and help plan the front of the house."

Brian distributed glasses, and then raised his. "May our stomachs always be full, and our plates empty."

Everyone drank, at least a token sip. Then Seth said, "Listen, we've got a lot of planning to do before we start construction. You want to tell me what you're thinking?"

"I'll let you guys handle that," Nicky said to Brian and Sam. "I want to tell Meg and Bree about the layout."

"Seth, let's go into the kitchen and we can talk," Brian said. He led Seth and Sam into the kitchen at the side, leaving Nicky, Bree, and Meg in the front.

"Tell me what you had in mind, Nicky," Meg began. "You've got the central hallway — are you going to use the rooms on both sides as dining areas?"

Nicky drifted around the room, running her hand over the walls and woodwork. "I'd love to open this up — just one big, airy room. Can't you see it? Watching the glowing lights of the town, with maybe a fire here in the fireplace, candles on the tables. But Seth says the building would fall down if we took out the walls."

Meg looked out the window and reviewed the visible buildings: the small library (no lights at night), the church (the same), the Historical Society (ditto), and the small general store slash pharmacy (maybe that would stay lit after dark?). The nearest residential buildings were currently screened by summer foliage, but Meg doubted they'd be very visible even in winter. The Stebbins house, perched on the low hill, its windows glowing with warm light, would actually be a nice contrast to the otherwise dark town, and would be an attractive beacon to anyone passing along the main highway.

"A hearth fire could be very welcoming, and it would probably be cozier for diners if you keep the rooms intimate anyway, rather than opening them up. You'll have to check if the chimneys are okay, though, if you want to use it. Do you plan to have a bar?"

Nicky shook her head emphatically. "I wouldn't waste the space. This place is about the food, not about drinking. Although we've got room for a great wine cellar, when we can afford one."

"Where's your setup space? Powder rooms? Supplies for the tables?" Bree broke into Nicky's raptures with surprisingly practical questions. When Meg raised an eyebrow at her, she said, "I used to waitress. And I know what a pain it is if your staff keeps tripping over each other trying to do their job because of a lousy layout, or running into customers trying to find the loo."

Nicky waved an airy hand. "I'll let Brian and Sam worry about all that. I want to think about food. And menus. Meg, I haven't had time to visit all the good restaurants around here. What're they like?"

Meg laughed. "I've eaten at about three restaurants in the time I've been here. I'm a working farmer, and I'm broke, so I'm the last person you should ask. Maybe I should ask you: what clientele do you want to attract?"

"I want to bring in people who appreciate good food, beautifully prepared. No prepackaged garbage. There should be enough sophisticated people at the colleges around here, no? And visiting parents?"

At last Nicky had come up with a practical point: parents whose kids attended the local colleges probably wanted to eat at a nice place — if they had anything left after writing whopping tuition checks. Maybe Nicky had given this some thought after all.

"Okay, but that's seasonal. Are you going to do anything targeted toward Granford residents?"

"How many are there? Do they even eat out?"

Meg took offense at Nicky's dismissive tone, even though she knew what she meant. "I don't know. You'd do better to ask Seth — he's lived here all his life. Or Frances."

"Do you know the other farmers around here? Because I'd really like to know where to get vegetables and fruits. What kind of apples do you grow?"

Bree answered, rattling off a list. "For starters, Gravenstein, Spartan, Cortland, Northern Spy. They'll start ripening about mid-August, if we get a good summer. I bet

Michael would know some other vendors. You into organic, Nicky?"

"Who's Michael? Your boyfriend?" she asked. When Bree nodded curtly, Nicky went on, "Yes and no. I don't think we could qualify as an organic restaurant — there are all sorts of guidelines we'd have to meet. But I support the principles, and I think organic food just plain tastes better. Why would Michael know vendors?"

"He heads this organic nonprofit group in Amherst," Bree said. "He knows the area pretty well. I'll ask Michael, then. He knows lots of people around here. You about done here, Meg? I need a ride back to the house."

The men emerged from the kitchen, and Meg saw that Seth had a clutch of paper towels with scribbles on them. At least he'd graduated from the paper napkins he'd been using at her house to plan the barn. "Let me work these up and give you some estimates. I can make time to start next week, if that's good with you."

"Thanks, Seth — you've given me a lot to think about. And thanks for your input. I probably would have knocked the house down." Brian looked relieved, Meg thought. *What had he been expecting?*

Nicky gravitated to Brian's side, and he slipped an arm over her shoulder. She fit very neatly under it, Meg noticed. "You guys figure out what you needed?"

"Wait 'til you see the plans," Sam said. "The flow will be terrific."

"Sounds good. And I found you a lead on suppliers — Bree's boyfriend, Michael. So everybody's good, right?"

The setting sun poured in the west-facing windows in the front, bathing Nicky, Brian, and Sam in golden light. They looked young and happy, and Meg felt a pang. Had she ever been that eager and hopeful? She shook herself: after all, she *had* just embarked on a new venture, or maybe it was a new adventure, with the orchard. And she had Seth — although not quite the way Nicky had Brian, who looked down at his wife with something like adoration.

Meg jumped when Seth came up behind her and laid a hand on her shoulder. "You heading back?" he asked.

"I guess," Meg said. "Bye, you all, and good luck. Thanks for the tour. I'll look forward to seeing what you do with the place."

"Thanks again for everything, Meg. And you, too, Seth. I can just feel this coming together! And we're going to have so much fun! I'll call you about staff, okay, Bree?" Nicky called. Bree raised a hand without turning and kept moving.

Meg and Seth managed to escape Nicky's enthusiasm and made their way to the parking lot. Bree climbed into Meg's car, but Meg tarried a moment to talk to Seth. "How do the plans look?" she asked.

"I think I managed to talk them out of doing anything really stupid. They don't know a lot about old buildings. And I pointed out that they needed a few things like at least one bathroom downstairs, and figuring out where they want electric outlets, because those aren't going to be easy to install in brick walls."

"They've certainly got a lot of enthusiasm, don't they?"

"More enthusiasm than sense, you're implying? Hey, at least they were smart enough to ask for help from me and you."

"Me? I don't know anything about restaurants. Not even the budgeting, except to know that profit margins are pretty slim even for the best-run places."

"Sure, but at least you've seen something of the wider world, right? Eaten in some fancy places?"

"Well, of course, back in my banking days, but that's not what they need here in Granford. Is it?"

Seth looked out at the green and the surrounding buildings. "No, not really. But give them a chance. First they've got to get the structural stuff done, and then get equipment in. *Then* they can worry about names and napkin colors and menu fonts."

"And they can get to know some of their new neighbors, which should help tone down whatever it is they're thinking."

"Exactly. See? It'll all work out."

"Seth, you are an eternal optimist."

"I try."

5

The speed with which time flew past alternatively thrilled and terrified Meg. According to Bree, the orchard was thriving — enough sun, enough rain, and Bree and Christopher had handled what little (and nontoxic) spraying they recommended. Meg felt like an anxious mother, checking on the growth of her apples nearly daily.

On a late June day she felt too restless to sit in the house — where far too many tasks confronted her — and decided to do an inventory of the outdoor projects she should tackle before it snowed. The roof was going to have to wait a while longer, and she didn't have the cash to pay for painting the body of the house, nor did she have the time to do it herself — one more project on the waiting list. But the trim she thought she could handle, and maybe puttying some of the leakier window sashes. She was standing in the yard looking up at the front of the house when her cell phone rang, and she pulled it out of her pocket and flipped it open.

"Hello?"

"Hey, babe! How's it going?"

Lauren. "Terrific. Fabulous. I'm contemplating scraping paint at the moment."

"And you like that why?"

"It's not that I like it, but that I have to do it or the whole house might crumble into dust. Houses seem to have this built-in urge to self-destruct, and we hardy homeowners must battle constantly to prevent it. Hence the painting."

"This is why I rent," Lauren said smugly. "How are our child chefs doing?"

"Better than I expected, actually," Meg replied. "They've finished ripping stuff out of the building, and now they're beginning to put other stuff back in. At least they haven't given up yet. Are you going to come check it out?"

"Once they've got tables and chairs and stuff like food, probably. And of course I want to see you — I still can't picture you in overalls and a straw hat."

"More like jeans and a baseball cap. But I am now the proud owner of a pair of muck boots."

"Do I really want to know what those are?"

"You aren't going to need any in Boston, but around here they're essential. It can get pretty muddy. Did you have a reason for calling, or did you just want to make fun of me?"

"Who, me? I'm just touching base." Lauren hesitated a moment. "I miss you, you know? It's no fun around here anymore."

Meg thought briefly of the life she had left behind in Boston. Did she miss it? A few things: movies, good food, music. And a few — a very few — friends like Lauren. The rest of it, all the deadlines and the pressure and the in-house politics, she was happy to forget. "Lauren, you love your job, and you love beating out the competition."

"I guess," Lauren sighed. "But come back and visit me sometime, will you?"

"After the harvest, when I'll have more time." At least four months away.

"Okay. Take care, and send me an invitation to the restaurant opening."

Meg promised to do so. As she hung up the phone, she saw an unfamiliar car pull into her drive, and Sam Anderson climbed out. Meg hadn't seen much of him since his arrival, or of Nicky and Brian either, although Seth provided regular updates on their progress at the restaurant. She could only imagine how busy they must all be, with their self-imposed deadline of September first. "Hi, Sam," she called out. "What brings you my way?"

Sam grinned shyly. "Hi, Meg. I'm exploring. Getting the lay of the land. Or something like that."

"Were you a city kid, too, like Nicky?"

"More or less. Closest I got to any farms was visiting the grandparents in Maryland. But farms are where the good food is, and that's what matters. I can learn."

"I know what you mean. You want to come in and have something to drink?" Meg asked.

"If it's no trouble. I can't stay long — I'm still trying to find my way around Granford. We've been so busy working on the building that I haven't looked around as much as I should."

"Come on in." Meg led the way to her kitchen door. Inside, she poured them both glasses of iced tea, added some mint she had found growing outside the kitchen door, and sat across from Sam at the kitchen table. "So, it sounds like the three of you have a real plan. What kind of food supplies are you looking for?"

"You must have heard about slow food?

The whole locavore movement?" Sam said hopefully.

Meg didn't have the heart to disappoint him, so she hedged and said, "I think so. But can you tell me what I should know?"

"Well, I'll give you the short answer. There's been a lot of interest in farmers' markets for, oh, the past twenty-five years, first in California. Don't get me started on the evils of corporate farming, but at least there are people trying to fight back, by growing healthy food and not shipping it halfway around the world, but selling it quickly to people who appreciate it. And preserving heirloom species that otherwise might be lost forever." Sam's eyes shone with fervor, and Meg could see why Nicky was so fond of him.

"You should talk with Christopher Ramsdell, over at UMass," Meg said. "He managed this orchard for years. He also gets very worked up about apple varieties, and the evils of commercialism."

Sam nodded vigorously. "Good, good. Well, the slow food movement is part of that, too, and Alice Waters at Chez Panisse — she's been a real role model for years. Thank goodness it's catching on. So what Nicky and I want to do is cook with the freshest food possible, and remind people just how good it can taste. And it's healthier for them, too — no preservatives, no added salt. Just good honest food."

"You're making me hungry. Do you know what you need, and who to talk to?"

"Bree's friend Michael has been helping, and Seth knows a lot of people. But like I said, I haven't had a lot of time to follow up yet. I'm just getting started. Can we count on you for apples?"

"Of course. Except I'd better warn you, I have no idea what I've got out there. Bree, my orchard manager — you met her at the restaurant — would know better." Meg sipped her iced tea. "So, you three are all living upstairs?"

"Yeah. Saves us money, even if the bathroom gets a little crowded sometimes. And there's plaster dust everywhere."

"That won't last forever. Are you still on track for the opening?"

"I think so, if everything goes right." Sam downed the last of his drink and stood up. "Well, I don't want to keep you. I just thought it was rude to pass by and not stop to say hello. Let me know if you have any other ideas."

Meg escorted him to the door. "I'll do that. And your food ideas sound wonderful."

Sam grinned shyly again. "Thanks. See you!"

As he pulled out of the driveway, Bree emerged from the depths of the barn. "Was that Sam?"

"Yup. He said Michael's given him some good leads."

"Good. Hey, wanna see your new tractor attachment?"

"I didn't know I had a new one. What's it for?"

"It's a forklift — you need it to lift the big apple boxes and move them from one place to another. Come on, I'll show you."

Meg obediently followed Bree into the dim barn. Bree strode up to the elderly green tractor and patted the new addition proudly. Meg looked bewildered. "But it's in back."

"Has to be — those boxes are heavy when they're filled. Your engine's in front, and then you add these counterweights, too" — Bree nudged a pile of oddly shaped metal objects with one foot — "so you don't tip over backwards."

"If you say so. You'll show me how all this works, right?" Meg said dubiously.

"Of course. And we've got time to practice. You're still a month or more away from needing it. So Sam's scouting out vendors?"

"So he says. I can't help much, but I'm glad Michael's working with him. Thanks for setting that up."

"Hey, it's just business — everybody wins."

"What's the story on this local foods movement? Is it more than just the fad of the moment, like oyster foam or steak ice cream?"

"Let's hope so! Corporate farming has all but destroyed small farmers like you, across the country, with some help from the government. But finally people are trying to bring back healthy food. You're already part of that movement."

"Good for me," Meg said, laughing. "It's a real challenge to try to balance economics, politics, and healthy eating all at once, isn't it?"

"You bet, but somebody's got to do it. You need me for anything else today?"

"Not that I know of. I was thinking about painting the trim, if I have the time."

"Better now than next month," Bree said. "Well, I'm off to Amherst. See you later."

As Bree drove off, Meg ambled over to talk to her goats. "You having fun, watching all this coming and going?"

The goats nodded. Or maybe they were just pulling up tufts of grass — Meg was still learning goat language. She checked out their pen: yes, fence still secure, plenty of water, and the grazing was holding up. All was well in the goat world, at least. She turned back to look at the house. The body was white, the sills black, as were the sashes. Ergo, she needed some black outdoor paint, which meant another trip to the home store. At least she had reduced her trips there to only two a week.

Now Seth appeared from his office space between the house and the barn. Really, this was like Whack-a-Mole, with people popping up from every hole.

"Hi, Seth. I didn't know you were here."

"I'm not, actually. I'm supposed to be in at least three other places, but I had to pick up some paperwork. What are you looking at?"

"I'm thinking of painting the trim, before I get sucked into the harvest. You have any recommendations?"

"Scrape well. Prime the bare wood. Then a good coat of oil-based paint, maybe two, depending on the condition of the wood. You need scrapers, sandpaper, decent brushes, and a good brand of paint."

Meg sighed. "And I thought this would be simple."

"It is, relatively. Were you planning to rehang the window sashes? Because that might make them easier to paint." When Meg looked blank, he went on, "You know — sashes, hung on cords, with weights?"

"You lost me, but I suppose I can look it up online. Maybe I should wait until next year?"

"Don't worry, you'll get the hang of it fast enough. I can show you how to do the first one, and then you can do the rest."

"Okay, I guess. So I'm off to the home store — again. Oh, Sam stopped by — he's starting to talk to local growers."

"Oh, right. Nice guy."

"They're all nice. And I love the way they talk about food. But that doesn't mean they know what they're doing on the business side."

"Hey, don't borrow trouble. So far everything has gone smoothly, knock on wood. Well, I've got to go meet a building inspector. See you later."

And Seth in turn pulled out. She watched him go, marveling at his endless energy. He made her feel like a slacker, as he juggled multiple jobs, including building out his office space, her apple storage, and the restaurant, and handling his responsibilities as a town selectman. But he never complained — he just kept moving. And so should she.

She went back into the house to retrieve her wallet and keys, so she could buy tools and paint for the latest of her long list of projects.

6

A few days later Meg was painting a window frame when Seth called out from the barn door. "Meg? Come take a look."

Meg climbed carefully down from the ladder and wiped her hands on her already-stained painter's pants. She'd finished the windows on the west side and was working her way counterclockwise around the house. Four windows on one side, nine across the front, four on the east side — not including all the others on the kitchen L. But she had to admit that once she fell into a rhythm, the work went quickly, and she could keep an eye on the orchard and the barn while she worked. "They're ready?" she called back.

She joined Seth at the barn door and gazed dubiously at the pair of large, ugly, boxlike structures that had been shoehorned inside. "You sure this is what I need?"

Seth looked offended. "This is a pair of a

state-of-the-art, computer-regulated, climate-controlled apple storage chambers. Don't judge them by the outside — the insulation looks ratty, I know. But inside they're great: new concrete floor, everything plumb and level, nice wide access to get your equipment in and out. All your controls are convenient and easily accessible, right here on this wall panel. All you need now is apples and you are good to go."

Meg felt contrite — he really had worked hard on these, delaying finishing his own offices in the adjacent shed, which in an earlier century had been a carpenter's shop. "I'm sorry, Seth. I don't mean to sound ungrateful. I mean, you finished construction on time and under budget, which is remarkable, considering everything else you're doing."

"I promised you this would be ready."

"You did, and you delivered. Thank you." She stepped forward to deliver what she had intended to be a quick peck on the cheek, but which somehow developed into something else that was even better. Finally she sighed and leaned against his chest, her eyes shut.

"You're welcome," he said, putting his arms around her. "You're worried about the whole harvest thing, aren't you?" he asked.

She pulled back and looked up at him. "Of course I am. Shouldn't I be? I mean, six months ago I didn't even know I had an orchard, and now I'm supposed to run it as a profitable operation? I'm terrified. There's so much I don't know!"

"Meg, you've got Bree to help, and you've got me. You're doing fine. Besides, if the crop's a total failure, you and Bree can go waitress at the restaurant."

"Don't even joke about that. How's construction going over there anyway? I haven't seen it for a while." For the first couple of weeks, Nicky had called Meg every time a new item was finished. Meg thought it was sweet, but she couldn't exactly drop everything she was doing on the spur of the moment to go check out the new wall finish or stove or shipment of dishes. Still, she admired the real progress that the Czarneckis had achieved. The kitchen L had been gutted and rebuilt to accommodate the larger-scale stove, ovens, freezer, and refrigerators, and separate dry-food storage had been framed in. There was another area set aside for plates, glassware, silverware, and other front-of-the-house supplies. Seth had even managed to carve out space for a tiny lavatory under the stairs, although he hadn't done more than rough it out the last time she had seen it.

"It's looking good. The schedule's holding, anyway."

"That is nothing short of amazing. You do good work, Mr. Chapin."

"Thank you, ma'am. I try." A muffled phone rang. "Hey, is that yours or mine?" he asked. Meg patted down her pockets; Seth did the same.

"Mine," she said. "It's Nicky." She flipped it open. "Hey, we were just talking about you."

"Sam's dead," Nicky's teary voice whispered without preamble.

Meg stiffened. "What? Sam? What happened?" Seth was watching her face with concern.

"I don't know. The police called — they wanted us to come identify him, but I couldn't, so Brian . . . Can you come over? Please?"

"Of course. I'll be right there." Meg shut the phone and looked at Seth.

"What's going on?" he asked.

Meg took a deep breath to steady herself. "Apparently Sam is dead, and Nicky's all alone at the restaurant. She wants me to come over."

"I'll drive."

Meg felt relieved before she even realized

81

she'd been dreading it. She had no idea how to comfort Nicky. It would be a lot easier with Seth there to back her up. "Thank you. Let me grab my bag in the house."

By the time she had retrieved her purse and locked up, Seth was waiting in the car with the engine running.

"What happened?" Seth asked as he took the back road toward town, avoiding the highway.

"She didn't say — I don't even know if she knows. Just that Sam was dead, and Brian had to go ID him."

"Not at the restaurant, then?"

"I guess not. Thank goodness. But . . . no, there's no point in getting ahead of ourselves. Right now Nicky needs some support, and we'll just have to wait for details."

It took no more than five minutes to arrive at the center of town. Seth pulled into the parking area next to the restaurant, and Meg beat him to the front door. Nicky opened it before they could knock. She'd obviously been waiting, and she threw herself into Meg's arms, sobbing. Meg held her for a few moments, then said gently, "Maybe we could go inside?"

Nicky nodded without speaking, and somehow they shuffled their way into the hall, with Nicky clinging to Meg. Seth followed, pulling the door closed behind him.

It took a while for Nicky's storm of tears to pass. Her sobs slowed, then stopped. Finally she stepped back from Meg. "I'm sorry. I didn't know who else to call."

"That's what friends are for, Nicky. Do you know what happened?"

Nicky shook her head. "No. I don't know anything. Brian and I were here working most of the morning, and Sam said he was going out to talk to some local growers. He didn't say which ones. He's been doing that a lot lately, all over the place — you know, talking to people, finding out what's available. And then we get this call from somebody, I guess the police, who found him dead, and that's all I know. Poor Sam, he was so happy here! Maybe it was a car accident — he doesn't know all the local roads . . ." Nicky started sobbing again, but when Meg reached out, she backed away, then crossed the room, wrapping her arms around herself. "No, I'll be all right. I just have to get a grip. Brian's going to be upset, too, and I need to be there for him." She gazed out the window, her back to Meg and Seth, as if she was expecting to see Brian right then.

Meg and Seth exchanged a wordless, helpless glance. Meg had no idea what she was supposed to do, but they didn't have long to wait: after a few more minutes, Brian's car appeared, followed by a Granford police cruiser. Both pulled into the parking area.

When Brian opened the front door, Nicky flung herself into his arms and he grabbed her, murmuring into her hair.

"Hi, Art," Seth said to the man who followed Brian in: Art Preston, Granford's chief of police. Meg was reassured by his solid presence: Art looked ideally suited for the job of small-town officer, with his broad build and permanently sympathetic expression. "What happened? Was it an accident?"

Art looked briefly at the young couple, still entwined, then tilted his head toward the adjoining room. When Seth and Meg followed him there, he spoke in a low voice. "No, it wasn't. Mr. Anderson was found in Jake Kellogg's back field, where he keeps his pigs."

"What was Sam doing there?" Meg asked, keeping her voice low as well.

"I have no idea. I was hoping these folks could tell me." He nodded toward Nicky and Brian in the adjoining room; they remained oblivious.

"How'd he die?" Seth asked.

"Don't know yet. No wounds on him, as far as I could see, but I didn't mess with

84

the body."

"Was it an accident?" Seth pressed.

Art leaned toward them and lowered his voice even further. "Maybe. Maybe not. But it's a suspicious death, so we have to investigate. I left an officer there to wait for the ME and the detectives from Northampton."

Damn. Meg had hoped she'd seen the last of Detective William Marcus of the state police. "Was it the pigs?"

Art shook his head with a grim smile. "That's an urban legend, I'm afraid. How much you know about raising pigs?"

"Exactly nothing," Meg admitted.

"Well, Jake's got a good setup there — nice tidy pig houses, and plenty of room for his animals. Pigs need a couple of fenced acres, a house for shelter, clean water and food. They keep their, uh, elimination in one separate place, and in hot weather they like a mud wallow. The wallow's at the lowest part of the field, near a dirt lane with a ditch. Your man was found facedown in this pig wallow, just inside the fence. I won't guess whether he fell or was pushed or dumped, or whether he was dead or alive when he went in there. I'll leave that for the ME." Art paused and checked again on Nicky's rate of sobbing, which seemed to be declining again. "I should head back out

85

there. I just wanted to get Mr. Czarnecki back here, and get some background on Mr. Anderson."

"Who found him?"

"Jake. He went out to feed the pigs, and bang, there was a body. Gave him a scare."

Meg couldn't remember if she'd met Jake Kellogg. She wasn't even sure where the Kellogg place was. Was he one of the vendors Nicky had mentioned? Had Sam gone out there to look over the pigs, with an eye toward future dinners? But if so, why hadn't he asked Jake to show him around? Wandering through someone else's property, even in this rural area, was at best considered rude, and at worst, an invitation for a load of buckshot. Sam couldn't have been that naive, could he? How deep was a pig wallow? Could a man fall in and be unable to get out? Meg realized that her mind was wandering, and was surprised to find Seth's arm around her shoulders.

She glanced over at Brian, who looked like he was coming out of a fog himself. He and Nicky finally pulled away from each other, and Brian said, "Hey, could I make everyone coffee or something?"

Art nodded. "Good idea."

With evident relief, Brian fled to the kitchen. Apparently Art decided that Nicky had finally wept herself out. "Mrs. Czarnecki? Can I ask you some questions about your friend?"

Nicky ran her hands through her tangled hair, then wiped her cheeks. "Nicky, please. Of course, I'll tell you anything I know. What happened to Sam?"

"I'm afraid we don't know for sure yet. He was found in a field on the other side of town. Was he in the habit of hiking? Taking long walks in the country?"

Nicky straightened her back and sniffed. "No, he was a city boy. But he's been talking to local farmers about supplies for the restaurant. That's what he said he was doing today."

"Did he happen to tell you where he was going?"

"No. He's keeping track of all that by himself. I just tell him what I'd like him to look for, and off he goes."

"You're not open for business yet, are you?" Art said, looking around the empty room strewn with construction debris.

"Not yet, not until September — we hope. But Sam wanted to find out what there was to work with, so we could map out a seasonal menu. He really seemed to be enjoying it, too. He's been going to the local farmers' markets as well. Sort of reconnoitering."

"Where was he from originally? Boston?"

"No, we met in Providence, a few years ago, but his family's from Maryland."

"The state police can look into that. This was his current residence?"

"Yes, we've all been living here, upstairs, to be closer to the restaurant and to save money. There's so much going on, with the construction, and stuff getting delivered, we thought it made sense to stay here. Do you want to see his room?"

"I'll wait. The detectives from Northampton will have my hide if they think I tried to interfere with their investigation. I just wanted to get the rough outlines for my own sake, since this town is my responsibility. You don't happen to know if he had any enemies, do you?"

"No! He's one of the sweetest men I know. Knew. He loved what he was doing, he loved working with us. He's a really good cook, too. Oh" — Nicky's face fell — "now we'll need a new sous chef." Tears loomed again. "How'm I supposed to train a new sous chef? Sam and I worked so well together . . ."

Luckily Brian emerged from the kitchen with a tray laden with coffeepot, cups, and accessories, to divert the storm. "I'm sorry we don't have chairs yet — they're on order," Brian said.

Once they'd all awkwardly gulped down their coffee, it fell to Seth to break the impasse. "Sorry, guys, but I've got a job lined up in Springfield today, so I've got to go. Meg, do you need a ride back home?"

Meg looked at Brian, who said, "We'll be okay. Thanks so much for coming when Nicky needed you."

"I'm happy to help. Art, you'll let us know what you find out?"

"Don't I always? Go on, before Detective Marcus shows up."

Meg turned back to Nicky. "Nicky, you can call me any time. And I'm sure there's a simple explanation for what happened to Sam."

"Thanks, Meg," Nicky said damply. "You go ahead. Brian and I will do . . . whatever needs doing."

Meg and Seth hurried to Seth's car. Once on the road, neither said anything until Seth pulled into Meg's driveway and turned off the engine. "Well," he began.

"Well indeed," Meg replied. "Chalk up one more sudden death in Granford." When Seth nodded, Meg continued, "I suppose we could hope he had a long-standing heart problem or something? An allergy to pig manure? No, that's cruel — I shouldn't be joking about this. After all, he's dead. He seemed like a nice guy, what little I saw of him."

"I agree, and I spent more time with him than you did. Smart, funny, knew the business. I wonder how the kids will manage now? I gather it takes a team to handle a restaurant, and the three of them had things pretty well worked out between them. Hard to drop someone new in, at this late date."

"What do you think they'll do now?"

Seth shrugged. "I don't know them well enough to guess. I know they've sunk a lot into the building, and I don't know what they'd get back if they walked away now."

"I wonder," Meg began, then stopped.

"What?"

"It's just . . . Sam seemed too young and healthy to just keel over like that. Although I know it happens. Maybe he ate nothing but butter and his arteries just closed down on him. Poor Sam. What a way to go — in a pigsty."

"You've got that right. I have trouble believing this was any kind of accident. But I'll leave the detecting to Marcus."

"Amen to that. And thanks for coming along, Seth. I don't know why Nicky thought of me first."

"Because she knew she could count on you to help. That's a good thing, Meg."

"I'll accept that as a compliment. You must be rubbing off on me, Seth. And I'm glad Nicky and Brian have each other; they're going to need someone to help getting through all this. It won't be pretty."

Back at her house, Meg watched Seth pull away, and wandered over again to check on her goats, in their enclosure on the other side of the driveway. As usual, they trotted over to greet her. She felt guilty that she still hadn't named them. "Hi, goats. Yeah, I know, I really need to name you two. But I wanted to get to know you first, okay?"

She looked around her. This pen couldn't be too different from Jake Kellogg's pigpen, could it? She tried to imagine a body toppling into it. No doubt, her goats would've come over to check out any interesting addition to their space. What would pigs do? She had no idea.

Shaking her head, she bade good-bye to her goats and retrieved her paintbrush. How many more windows were there?

7

Bree came in the back door as Meg was trying to figure out how to combine the ingredients in her refrigerator into something resembling dinner. Too bad the restaurant wasn't open yet. Would it ever be now, with Sam's death hanging over it?

"Something moving in there?" Bree asked.

"No, I was just looking for inspiration. Did you hear about . . . ?" Meg wasn't sure what to say about Sam's death. She still harbored the hope that it had been some kind of sad accident. Sam had tripped and hit his head on a really hard pig? *Stupid, Meg, stupid.*

"Hear what?" Bree was rummaging in a cupboard looking for a snack.

"Sam Anderson was found dead in a pig wallow."

Bree shut the cabinet door and turned to face Meg, leaning against the counter. "No kidding? That's terrible. He was a nice guy.

What happened?"

"I don't know yet. Apparently he was found facedown in the mud, and the police asked Brian to identify the body. Nicky called me, and Seth and I went over to the restaurant to comfort her, but nobody knew anything yet. They were there with Art, waiting for the state police and the ME when we left."

"Not that Marcus creep again?"

"Probably. I don't like him either, but he's what we've got. And he's not stupid, even if he is a jerk," Meg admitted. She'd had more experience in the past than she'd wanted with the unpleasant Detective Marcus.

"Are the cops thinking accident?"

Meg shrugged. "I don't know. We can ask Art, once the state guys finish. And before you ask, the pigs didn't do it."

"Of course they didn't. Pigs don't kill people."

"Maybe he committed suicide by mud? Sorry, that seems kind of flippant."

"Don't worry about it — making jokes is one way of dealing with bad stuff. But suicide? I don't think so. Sam seemed like a real happy guy. Loved his job, really got excited about food, you know?" Bree said.

"That was my impression, too, although I didn't spend much time with him. Had he made any friends in town?"

"Can't say. Those three were so wrapped up in fixing up the restaurant, I don't think they had a lot of time to get out and meet people. Although I think I saw him in Northampton once or twice."

"Checking out the competition?"

"Maybe." Bree gave Meg a sidelong glance. "You do know he was gay?"

Meg stared at her. "No, I did not. It never occurred to me, but it's none of my business. Are you sure?"

"No, but I got that vibe, and then Michael and I saw him going into a couple of places in Northampton that lean that way."

"You think that's what he was doing in Northampton? Cruising, or whatever you call it?" Meg asked.

"Well, I'd guess the pickings are pretty slim in Granford. But Northampton — there's something for everyone there. Think the cops know?"

Meg shrugged helplessly. "They just found the body — I don't think they've investigated his personal life yet. But I suppose it could have something to do with his death, if he got involved with the wrong person. Nicky and Brian would probably know."

Bree agreed. "It would be kind of strange if they didn't. They all seemed pretty tight.

94

I don't know how well it would have gone over in Granford, though."

"Do you have a problem with the people of Granford?"

"No. I haven't met many of them. But this is Hicksville, right? Everybody's been here since day one, and they've married a lot of cousins. The smart ones leave town and don't look back."

"Bree!" Meg was honestly shocked at the younger woman's apparent hostility. "That's insulting. I've met plenty of decent people here. You can't just label them a bunch of inbred cretins. You've got to live with them, too, you know. Why are you so bent out of shape about Granford? Have you had problems yourself here?"

"Sorry — no, I haven't had a problem with anybody from around here. It's just that I know what it's like to be on the wrong end of discrimination. But as long as the Granford folk stick to business, I'm good with them. You find anything that looks like food yet?"

Meg noted the quick change of topic. "I was just thinking I wished the restaurant was open, because I really don't feel like cooking, and I don't feel like driving anywhere just for some lousy fast food."

As if in answer to her prayers, Seth

knocked at the back door with a couple of grocery bags in hand. Meg could see Art, out of uniform, pulling into the driveway behind him. "Thought we could throw some burgers on the grill, if that suits."

"Sounds great — except I don't have a grill," Meg said.

"You do now." Seth pointed toward Art: he was wrestling a portable barbecue out of the trunk of his car. "And I brought all the fixings. Hi, Bree."

"Hi, Seth. Art going to dish about what happened to Sam?"

"He might be persuaded, not that he's really in the loop. Meg, you have mustard, ketchup, that kind of thing?"

"Of course. That much I can handle," said Meg indignantly, while mentally scanning her cupboards and hoping she wasn't wrong. She turned to Art and greeted him. "You certainly came prepared. But won't your wife be missing you?"

"Nope, she's got some kind of meeting tonight, and she told me to fend for myself. So here I am."

Half an hour later they were assembled in hastily commandeered chairs around the new barbecue, burgers sending tantalizing smells into the still evening air. Meg's goats kept an eager eye on activities. "I'm going to have to get some lawn chairs, aren't I?" Meg remarked to the world in general.

"You should. You'd better enjoy it out here now, before mosquito season begins."

"Hey, don't spoil it for me, Seth. Let me enjoy the moment. Art, isn't it time to flip those burgers?" It was kind of fun, ordering the chief of police around.

"Yes, ma'am." Art complied. Smart man: he had brought not only the barbecue, but also charcoal, fire starter, and basic tools. Obviously he knew his way around a grill.

Meg leaned back in her chair. "You know, I could get used to this kind of thing, where someone else brings the food and cooks it for me. But I have a sneaking feeling I won't have this kind of time once the orchard starts producing."

"You've got that right," Bree agreed. "Hey, Chief, those about done?"

"Coming up," Art replied, sliding the burgers onto a large platter, along with buns. He set the tray on an over-turned bushel basket. "Dig in."

After a suitable interval during which several burgers with condiments disappeared quickly, along with ample helpings of a potato salad Seth had brought and a few bottles of beer, Art finally said, "You ready to hear what I know, or would it spoil your digestion?"

"Does it involve pig manure?" Meg asked.

"No, I promise."

"Are you breaking any laws by filling us in?"

"Nothing big, and I trust you three to keep quiet, right?"

Meg sighed. "Okay, hit us with it. What happened?"

"Preliminary findings show that Samuel Anderson died from suffocation, facedown in the mud."

Prepared though she was, Meg shivered at the news. "What an awful way to go. But how did he end up in that position? Was he unconscious? Did somebody knock him out?"

"No sign of any blows, and the preliminary tox screen was clean — no alcohol or drugs." Art hesitated a moment, then said, "It looks like someone held him down."

"What? That's terrible. But how? I mean, Sam was a pretty big guy, young, in good shape."

"Hard to tell, but nothing obvious. Of course, they'll run a more complete tox screen. That might turn up something, though Nicky and Brian swear he didn't do drugs. No signs of a major struggle. No bruises or other marks on the body, as far as I know. As I said, no blow to the head. But there was one significant piece of evidence — a big muddy footprint on the back of his shirt."

Art's statement met with a few seconds of shocked silence.

Finally Seth said, "So someone shoved him into the muck and held him down until he suffocated?"

"Oh, God, Art," Meg whispered. "That means it *is* murder. How awful."

Art's face was grim. "Exactly. I don't have to ask you to keep this quiet, do I? I shouldn't be telling you this, but you knew the guy and his friends. In fact, you're probably about the only people in town who did."

Meg, Seth, and Bree exchanged wary glances. "Damn!" Meg said. "Does that mean that Marcus is going to want to talk to us?"

Art sat back in his chair, his shirt buttons bulging. "Maybe. Depends on how he wants to handle things. I think he'll probably downplay the whole murder angle, at least for now. The press is going to be all over this, you know. And it doesn't make Granford look good."

Seth asked, "He wasn't killed somewhere else and dumped there, was he?"

"Doesn't look like it. Footprints were kind of messed up, but his car was found a mile or two away — of course, the state police are checking that out. No obvious tire tracks, although the lane to the piggery was pretty dry — the only muck was along the verge and in the pen itself, so maybe tire tracks wouldn't show. But I don't think anyone could have carried him — he had to run a good 220 pounds. Most likely he died on that spot. Any idea what he might've been doing out there?"

Meg finished the last of her beer, now lukewarm. "Nicky said that he was looking for suppliers, remember? I suppose that included pigs — pork. What kind of operation does the farmer run? I don't know anything about raising pigs."

"Jake Kellogg's got a real nice setup," Seth volunteered. "A couple of acres, maybe a dozen pigs at a time. I think he sells to a couple of local restaurants. Anyway, his pigs live in little huts in a field, at least in warm weather, and they can roam around. He feeds 'em real well, too. All pig operations smell, but this one's well sited, and there's nobody downwind to complain."

"What's Jake like?" Meg asked. "I don't think I've met him."

"Probably not. He's not the most sociable

guy. He's got to be fifty-odd now, but he's in good shape. He and his wife raised four kids there — the youngest is still at home. The rest live in-state, but they aren't interested in the farm."

"Is he the type to overreact to trespassers?" Meg asked.

"Nah, not Jake," Art responded. "He's pretty easygoing. Besides, nobody's going to wander along a back lane and walk off with a pig, are they? And before you ask, I don't think physically he could have hauled Sam around himself . . ." Art finished dubiously.

"Jake had a hernia operation a couple of months ago," Seth added. "I'd wager he saves the heavy lifting for pig food."

"Seth, how do you know everything about everyone?" Meg asked, half-admiring, half-baffled.

"I talk to people, that's all. And Mom took them over a casserole, when he got out of the hospital. She's known him forever, and his wife."

Art interrupted, "Maybe you all can tell me more about Nicky and Brian? Seeing as they're newcomers. You folks and Frances are probably the only ones who've spent much time with them."

"You think they might have killed their business partner? Who was also their friend?" Meg bristled at Art's implication: suspect the outsiders. Of course, Sam was an outsider, too. It certainly would be much tidier if they had kept it in their little outsider circle.

Art was still talking. "You're the one who brought them to Granford, right, Meg?"

Meg nodded reluctantly. "A friend of mine from Boston knew them. She called me and said that a young couple was looking for a place out here to open a restaurant, using local products. They'd checked the obvious places, Northampton and Amherst, and decided they couldn't afford either of them, so I told Frances Clark, and she found some places in Granford for them to look at. They loved the Stebbins house as soon as they saw it, and the deal went through quickly."

"Was Sam Anderson part of the deal?"

"You mean, did he put money up? He was a working partner, at least. I think Nicky said he chipped in what he could, but I don't know whose names are on the deed. I gather most of the money came from a wedding present from Nicky's father. I just did a friend of a friend a favor, putting them together with a real estate broker. And I thought Granford could use a decent restaurant." Meg was having trouble controlling her voice. Sam, dead? He had seemed so vital, so enthusiastic, when he had stopped by.

"Meg," Seth said gently, "Art isn't accusing you of anything. You acted with the best of intentions, and I'm sure everything was aboveboard."

"Sorry," Meg said, contrite. "I guess I'm feeling kind of defensive."

"Meg, I didn't mean to point any fingers at you," Art said. "Or at Nicky and Brian. They seem like good kids. I'm just trying to get the lay of the land here. And I'm sure Detective Marcus will be asking the same kinds of questions."

"And I'm sure he'll find an excuse to badger me," Meg replied. "For the record, as far as I know, Nicky, Brian, and Sam are exactly what they say they are: nice young people who want to start a business in a small town, a town that can really use the business. I have no idea why Sam is dead, or who would have wanted to kill him." Meg glanced briefly at Bree, who gave her a small nod.

Bree had been quietly following the conversation, until now. "Chief, Sam was gay," Bree said flatly. "I saw him around a couple of Northampton bars I've heard about. I don't know if he hooked up with anybody — he's only been here a couple of weeks, right? But that's not a motive to kill anybody around here, is it?" Bree challenged the police chief.

Art responded, "Of course not, but that's something to check out. Not that Anderson was killed because of his sexual preferences, but it's possible he got mixed up with the wrong person over there. Could he have been meeting someone out at Kellogg's? He wouldn't have a lot of privacy, living over the restaurant with Nicky and Brian."

"So he went looking for a nice private field?" Bree scoffed.

Meg intervened. "Bree, I don't think that's what Art meant." Bree subsided, but she still looked stormy.

"You going to tell Marcus?" Bree asked.

Art sighed. "I think I have to, but I don't have to tell him you told me, if that's what's worrying you."

"So we should expect a visit from our favorite detective?" Meg asked, not without bitterness.

"Probably just a formality, Meg. Like I said, you knew all three of them." Art checked his watch, then stood up. "I'll get out of your hair now. I'll let you know if I hear anything new."

Meg stood, too. "Thanks for the barbecue and the food. What do I owe you?"

Art stepped back in mock dismay. "For shame, Meg — can't you accept a simple gift? Didn't cost much. And I'll make it back in cheesy jokes about 'grilling my suspects.' "

"Don't you dare! All right, thank you for the gift. It was very thoughtful of you, and I will think of you every time I grill something."

Meg said good-bye and watched Art pull out of the driveway, then rejoined Bree and Seth, who were talking about apples. She picked up a few pieces of discarded lettuce and wandered over to the goat pen to offer the snack to them. The goats accepted eagerly.

Seth joined her by the fence. "Nicky was really broken up by Sam's death. I can't see her killing anyone, unless someone criticized her cooking and she took a chef's knife to them."

Meg kept her eyes on the goats, who stared back. "But you don't think that about Brian?"

Seth sighed. "Meg, don't read something into everything anyone says. I didn't see Brian's first reaction, and when he showed up at the restaurant, he was mainly concerned with comforting Nicky. So I'm not going to judge one way or the other. I don't think either one of them is a killer, but I've been wrong before."

Meg turned to face him, leaning against a fencepost. "I can't see one of them killing Sam either, but we've *both* been wrong. Damn it! I like them. Think they'll cut and run now, if it really is murder?"

Seth watched the goats meander away, once the lettuce was gone. "I don't know. I hope not, on behalf of the town. Heck, even for myself — I can use the work, and I kind of wanted some good food, too. I won't push them, but if they want to open in September, they've got a lot to do between now and then. They can't afford to waffle about it."

"Don't they get any time to grieve?"

Seth was quick to reply. "Of course. They can push the date back. Or they can throw in the towel. It's up to them."

"And if they do decide to stay, now they have to find a new sous chef. You have any ideas about that?"

Seth's eyes grew distant. "Maybe. There used to be a decent diner at the east end of town — closed a few years ago when the last owner died. They had a cook working for them who was pretty good, name of Edna Blakely. She would have bought the place, but she couldn't round up the money.

She's been kicking around, working here and there, ever since. Maybe she'd be interested."

"If Brian and Nicky go forward, you could mention her. You know, Seth, it never ceases to amaze me how you know everybody in town, and their entire life histories. What would this town do without you?"

"Muddle along, just like they have for the past two or three hundred years. Still, I like to help out."

"I know. And I'm grateful. I don't know what *I* would have done without you."

"You would have muddled through, too — you're not a quitter." Seth moved closer. "But I'm glad you stuck it out, and I'm glad I could help."

"Mmmm." Meg closed the gap between them. The goats watched them with interest.

8

Meg spent the next few days worrying, even as she kept busy with orchard-related tasks. She hadn't heard from Detective Marcus, for which she was grateful. Nor had she heard from Nicky, but Meg hesitated to intrude on her grieving.

Finally Nicky called. Without preamble she said, "Meg, would you and Seth meet us here at the house this afternoon?"

"Sure, I can be there. Although I don't know where Seth is."

"That's okay, I'll call him. How about two o'clock?"

"That's fine. See you then." Nicky hung up before Meg could ask anything further.

Meg looked down at her cat, Lolly, who was taking a leisurely bath in the middle of the kitchen floor. "Well, cat, what do you think? Is she going to tell me that they've had enough of Granford and they're running back to Boston?"

Lolly gave Meg a brief glance and resumed washing.

"Gee, thanks. You're a big help." With or without the cat's input, Meg really wasn't sure which way Nicky and Brian would decide. She didn't know them well, not enough to guess, so she'd have to wait to find out.

Meg went back to her chores, which kept growing week to week. Feed cat, feed goats. The painting of the ground-floor windows was nearly done, but apparently she should repoint the foundation before winter, whatever that meant. During the few trips she had made to the basement to check on the furnace, she had noticed plenty of air whistling through the gaps in the fieldstone. Of course, once she had an income from the orchard, she could probably take out a home equity loan for the improvements, but she didn't want to saddle herself with payments, and she'd probably be depressed by how little the house was worth, particularly in the current economic climate. Cash would be better. *Don't I sound like an old Yankee?* Meg chided herself. At least the apple storage compartments were paid for out of her severance pay — although she suspected that Seth had undercharged her. Still, it was a fair trade-off for the space he occupied in the barn. She reflected again on how convenient it was to have a plumber and handyman around. For repairs, of course . . . and for other things.

Meg left the house in good time for her two o'clock date at the restaurant, but as she drove past the green, she caught sight of Caroline Goldthwaite struggling to remove something from the trunk of her car, which was parked next to the store. On an impulse Meg pulled in next to her car.

"Can I help you with that?" she asked, getting out of the car.

Mrs. Goldthwaite straightened up, not without difficulty, and faced her. "Meg Corey, isn't it?"

"Yes. Let me get those for you."

Mrs. Goldthwaite moved to block Meg's path. "I'm perfectly capable of handling a few potted plants, thank you."

Meg stopped, surprised at the hint of rudeness in Mrs. Goldthwaite's tone. Maybe she didn't like to be reminded of her age? "I'm sorry. I only meant to help."

Mrs. Goldthwaite shut her eyes for a moment. "Perhaps I overreacted. And I would appreciate your assistance. I prefer to use well-established plants, rather than wait for seedlings to grow. They seem to take so long, and they look rather sparse until they

110

leaf out. But the larger pots are a bit heavy."

"I can understand that." Meg reached into the trunk and pulled out a pair of red geraniums in six-inch plastic pots. "Where do you want these?" she asked.

Mrs. Goldthwaite waved imperiously at the pair of dirt-filled planters flanking the door of the store. "Over there, if you will."

Meg deposited them as directed. "Is this a town beautification project?" She went back to the car and reached in for another pair.

Caroline Goldthwaite sniffed. "Hardly. The town can't afford such things. I had hoped to persuade the shopkeeper to volunteer to do this, but apparently he isn't interested. The church has managed to find the time. I also contributed the flowers in front of the Historical Society."

Meg pulled out a flat of lush purple petunias and carried it over to the steps. "This will look lovely — and it's a great idea, since so many people pass through here, particularly in summer."

"I do want Granford to put its best foot forward, so to speak," Mrs. Goldthwaite said primly. "I suppose there's no point in asking *those* people to participate," she added, nodding toward the restaurant building at the top of the hill.

"Why? Have they told you they're not

staying?" Meg felt a spurt of concern — wouldn't Nicky and Brian have shared that with her and Seth first? Or maybe it was wishful thinking on Mrs. Goldthwaite's part? At the meeting Meg had attended she had seemed to disapprove of the whole idea of the restaurant, sight unseen.

"No, nor have I had a conversation with them about their plans. I believe Seth Chapin has spent considerable time with them. But what with the trouble they've had lately . . ." Mrs. Goldthwaite appeared reluctant to be more specific.

Meg bristled at defining Sam's death in Granford as mere "trouble." "You mean what happened to Sam Anderson. Well, I for one hope that they'll be staying. I like Nicky and Brian, and I think Granford can use the business."

Mrs. Goldthwaite stiffened. "You are entitled to your opinion, just as I am entitled to disagree with you. Thank you for your help, but I think I can manage from here." Mrs. Goldthwaite turned her back on Meg and rummaged in her trunk for her gardening tools.

I've been dismissed, Meg thought incredulously. But there was no point in prolonging the conversation, so she got back in her car and headed up the hill.

Still fuming from her uncomfortable encounter with Caroline Goldthwaite, Meg pulled into the restaurant parking lot. The presence of the Chapin van indicated that Seth had already arrived. She knocked at the front door and was greeted by a distant "Come on in, it's open!"

She found Brian, Nicky, and Seth in the kitchen. It looked almost finished, all the new appliances in place, gleaming softly. Now there was a long worktable in the middle of the room, and some chairs, their seats still wrapped in plastic. Meg and Seth looked briefly at each other as they settled around the table. Meg wasn't sure what was coming, but she was surprised by how much the outcome mattered to her — and that she really wanted them to stay.

Nicky had lost some of her sparkle; even her dark curls seemed limper. She greeted Meg in a subdued tone. "Thanks for coming on short notice. I wanted to talk to you both, since you've been part of this from the beginning. Sit, please." Nicky took a deep breath. "Brian and I have decided we want to stay in Granford. Sam was part of our plans from the beginning, and we're really going to miss him, but I think he would have wanted us to go ahead, rather than just shut down and mourn for him.

113

Besides, we've already sunk most of our money into this, and if we pull out, we won't be able to start over. Right, Brian?"

Brian nodded. "It sounds kind of crass to put it that way, but it's true. Sam wanted this to work, and we've got to try."

Meg smiled with relief. "I'm glad. I think this town needs you. And you know Seth and I will do whatever we can to help."

That finally brought an answering smile from Nicky. "Thank you, Meg. Don't think we won't call on you. And Seth — I don't know what we would have done without you. Look, there are some things we need to work out. Would you like some coffee? I made brownies."

They all waited silently while Nicky filled and distributed sturdy white mugs, and laid a platter of brownies on the table. Nicky sat down and waited a moment before speaking, and Meg wondered if she saw a gleam of tears. Then she looked up and plastered on a brave smile. "Eat and drink, please. We can talk while you do. Here's the deal: most of the structural stuff is done, right, Seth?"

Seth nodded, his mouth full of chocolate.

"I think we're going to have to hold off on the decorating a bit. We can always revisit that later, but for now we're going to keep it simple."

114

Seth swallowed, then said, "I don't think that's a problem. It's a great building — let it speak for itself."

"Thanks, Seth. Okay, second problem: we need to find a sous chef to replace Sam, because we need to start working together, make sure our cooking styles are in synch. I was thinking about contacting the cooking school in Providence — I'm sure there are plenty of people who'd like a shot at getting in on the ground floor."

Seth helped himself to another brownie. "Have you thought about looking locally?"

Nicky looked blank. "We don't know anybody around here, and we don't have a lot of time to interview. Do you mean at the university? Or did you have any ideas?"

"One. There's an older woman I know, with plenty of experience. Want me to get in touch with her?"

Nicky still looked uncertain. "I guess so. But is it going to be a problem, what with Sam's death and all? I mean, maybe people would feel funny about working where . . ." She trailed off.

"I don't think so," Seth said firmly. He hesitated a moment before asking, "I don't mean to pry, but are you okay financially? Did Sam have money in the business?"

"No. Most of it's coming from me," Nicky

replied. When Brian started to protest, Nicky went on, "Wedding present — to both of us. I want to be able to pay Daddy back eventually, and we're both willing to work hard to make that happen. I know you probably think we're a pair of starry-eyed dilettantes who'll bail out at the first sign of trouble, but we've been thinking about this, planning it, for years, and I — we — don't want to give up now."

"Good for you!" Meg said.

Nicky rewarded her with a smile. "Thank you, Meg. Seth, I'll be happy to talk to your friend, but no promises. Okay, next problem: staffing."

"I don't think you'll have a problem there," Seth said. "Plenty of people looking for jobs around here. You planning on lunch and dinner?" Nicky and Brian nodded. "If you can offer flexible shifts, you'll have a broader pool — you know, students, mothers with kids in school during the day."

"Bree said she might know some people," Meg volunteered.

Nicky nodded. "Great. And we'll offer what benefits we can, which may not be much, at least in the beginning. Okay, last problem, and it's a big one: food. Sam was looking into local suppliers, but he wasn't the greatest record keeper, and I'm not sure

116

who he talked to, or what terms he might have suggested. So we're kind of restarting from scratch. I know he got in touch with the local farmers' collective, so maybe that's a good place to start."

"I don't know what I've got coming along, but I told Sam I'd be happy to sell you whatever apples you need — at a reasonable rate."

"Can I make a suggestion?" Seth said. "Why don't you talk to the selectmen, formally? I mean, it's just the three of us, but it could be important that the town know what you're doing, and that you make them part of the process. Come to one of the open meetings, which the public attends. We can get the word out. And the meetings are broadcast on local cable, so even more people would see you."

"Well, sure, I guess," Nicky said. "What would they — you? — want to know?"

"Just what you've told us so far — that you're here to stay, that you'll need ongoing help with staffing and supplies. We can help, and we will."

Nicky looked at Brian and grabbed his hand. "See, Brian? I knew we were right. We can make this work. Seth, when do you meet?"

"Tuesday nights. How about coming to

next week's meeting?"

Nicky and Brian agreed enthusiastically, and then Brian and Seth wandered off to look at construction details, leaving Nicky and Meg at the table with the depleted tray of brownies. Meg nodded toward it. "Those are terrific. Is that the kind of thing you plan to serve?"

Nicky looked shocked. "Oh, no — that's just comfort food. I want something more elegant for the restaurant. Not fancy — but more refined, you know? Subtle. We're still working on the menu. We want to keep it simple, with a limited number of dishes, based on what's available locally. Would you eat in a place like that?"

"Of course," Meg said promptly. She couldn't speak for the rest of the town, but she'd be waiting at the door on opening night. "Listen, Nicky . . ." She hesitated, unsure how to broach the subject. "So I, um, heard that Sam was . . . gay?"

"Yeah," Nicky said, her brow wrinkling. "So? Is that a problem?"

"Not for me, no. But have you considered that it might be a motive in his death?"

Nicky stared at her, uncomprehending, and Meg realized that the thought hadn't even occurred to her. "Nicky," she began, choosing her words carefully, "have the state police told you that Sam was murdered?"

Nicky nodded, looking miserable. "Yeah, and they asked who might have wanted him dead. I told them I didn't have the slightest idea. Sam was the sweetest, happiest person I know. Why would anyone want to hurt him?"

"I assume Brian knew. He was okay with it?"

"With what? That Sam was gay? Sure, he knew, but we didn't talk about it much. He was cool with it."

"Do the state police know he was gay?" Meg asked. If they did any investigation at all of Sam's background, no doubt they would find out about Sam's orientation.

Nicky looked blank. "I don't think it came up. I know I didn't mention it — I didn't think it mattered. Maybe if they check with his friends in Boston, they'll find out, but they haven't asked us anything."

"He was new around here. Maybe he stumbled into something he didn't expect."

Nicky bristled. "He wasn't stupid, Meg. And he wasn't sleazy either. He didn't just pick up random guys, if that's what you're asking. Are you telling me that there are a bunch of bigots around here?"

"No offense intended, Nicky. And no — as far as I've seen, people in Granford are

119

pretty much 'live and let live.' But the police have to consider it. There's an active gay scene in Northampton, and Sam might have misread it."

"No way I would believe that. I mean, Sam had an ex-boyfriend back in Boston. They'd broken up, but they parted on good terms, and he was going to come visit once things were more settled. I think Sam was still getting over him. Besides, we were pretty busy — when would he have found time?"

"Well, let's hope that it's not an issue," Meg said firmly. She thought it was definitely time to change the subject. "So tell me, what kind of menus are you planning?"

Nicky perked up immediately at the thought of talking about food. "You've heard of the locavore movement?"

"Sam mentioned it to me once, but I haven't had much time to look into it. What's your take on it?"

Nicky all but bounced in her seat with enthusiasm. "It sounds surprisingly simple when you describe it, but in this country we've put so much distance between the food we eat and where it comes from. You ever look at the labels at the supermarket? I mean, really — blueberries from Mexico, lamb from New Zealand? Maybe that's the way economics works, although I can't believe that it's really cheaper to grow something that far away and ship it halfway around the world. But worse, you lose flavor, freshness. And the local farmers suffer, because they can't compete with the big international firms. So they give up farming and do something else."

Meg laughed. "I told Sam he should talk to Christopher Ramsdell — he's a professor at UMass, and he's kept my orchard going for years now. He feels much the same way about apples. And you're saying it applies to a lot of other crops?"

Nicky nodded vigorously. "And meat, too. We've all been sucked into this corporate mentality about food production — bigger is better, more efficient. And don't think that consumers aren't guilty, too. People expect to find fresh fruits and vegetables in stores year-round now, like it's a right. They're completely disconnected to what's in season."

Meg held up her hands in surrender. "Hey, you don't have to convince me. But how do you translate that into a menu? Don't people expect to find their favorite dishes at a restaurant every time they come? How do you tell them, sorry, that's not in season right now?"

"You have to educate your patrons, too. I don't think it's hard; just give them some fresh food — I mean, *really* fresh — and they should see the difference. And if they don't, then we don't want them."

Meg wondered how long they'd stay in business if they blew off patrons who wanted a simple and predictable meal, but she had to admire Nicky's eagerness. She certainly hoped Nicky was right, that their guests would recognize and appreciate the difference.

"Sam told me he was handling the suppliers?"

"Yes. You know how a restaurant works?"

"Not really. At least, not the behind-the-scenes stuff."

"You have to have some basic division of labor — you can't have everyone flying off and doing whatever they feel like. Me, I cook. That's what I want to do, and that's what I do best. Sam was a good cook, but he didn't have as much experience as I do. The sous chef does a lot of the prep work — you know, making stocks, chopping stuff. And in his case, shopping. Brian will handle the front — talking to people, bookings — and he does the budgeting and planning. We made a good team, because we each have our strengths." Nicky's face fell again.

"It's not going to be easy, fitting someone new in. But we have to. Brian and I can't handle it all ourselves."

"Let's wait and see if Seth's friend works out, before you panic," Meg said.

"He sure knows a lot of people around here, doesn't he?" Nicky said wistfully.

"Sure, but he's lived here all his life. It takes time, and people have to get to know you."

"You seem pretty settled, too, Meg."

Meg laughed. "I've only been here a few months, and I've been kind of busy, learning new things, so I haven't met nearly as many people as I should have."

"That's all? I thought you'd been here longer."

"Nope, I moved here from Boston in January. Someday, if we both have a lot more time, I'll have to tell you about it. But that's how I know Lauren."

"Lauren?" Nicky looked blank.

"Lauren Converse? She's the one who told me you were looking for space in this area?"

"Oh, right — that Lauren. I don't actually know her. She's a friend of the owner of the restaurant where I was working before we moved here. So you worked in Boston, too?"

"I did, until my job disappeared and I

ended up here. Like I said, long story. Seth lives next door, and he's moved his office into my barn . . ." Meg trailed off. It certainly was a complicated story, and the bare outline didn't do justice to it. "Anyway, Seth's a good friend to have around here."

Seth and Brian emerged from the kitchen. "I'll set up the wiring inspection for the dining areas for next week. Looks like we're still on track."

"Thanks for coming. We really feel you two are a part of this, and we wanted you to know what we were planning."

After Nicky and Brian had ushered them out the door, Meg and Seth dawdled in the parking lot. "I have to say I'm relieved," Meg said. "Do you think they'll like your friend?"

"They'll like her food, I'm pretty sure," Seth replied. "As a person? I'm not going to guess. Edna can be kind of prickly, but she knows what she's doing. You headed home now?"

"Yes. I don't seem to make any headway at all on my to-do list, and then Bree keeps adding things to it. You?"

"Welcome to the world of the small farmer. I've got to pick up a load of supplies in Springfield. See you later!"

9

When Meg arrived home, she found Bree sitting at the kitchen table with stacks of papers in front of her and her laptop open next to her. "Anything I need to know about?" Meg asked.

"Not yet. I want to get this straight in my head first, and then I'll explain it to you," Bree said, tapping out a few lines on the laptop. "Your phone's been ringing."

"You didn't answer it?"

"Didn't think it was for me," Bree said unapologetically.

At least Bree hadn't made some snotty remark about how she wasn't a secretary, Meg thought as she carried the handset into the front room to check her messages. Only one, or rather only one person multiple times: Lauren. Meg punched in the number from memory. It was close to five, but she knew her friend would be at her desk for at least an hour longer.

Lauren picked up on the second ring. "Lauren Converse," she said crisply.

"Hi, Lauren. Why the batch of calls?"

"Oh, hi, Meg. Word is that you've gotten yourself in a mess out there."

"With your help. How did you find out?"

"This guy from the state police called me and asked all sorts of questions. Markham, Markey, something or other . . . ?"

"Detective Marcus. *Not* a friend. So he must be checking out the Boston end of things. What did he tell you?"

"Not much. He was all 'I'll ask the questions, ma'am.' What's the story?"

Meg sighed. "You know those kids you sent my way? They bought an old house here to use as a restaurant, along with one of their friends, a guy they brought along to be their sous chef. And now the friend, Sam Anderson, has died in rather mysterious circumstances. Did you know him?"

"Heck, I didn't even know the baby chefs; I was just doing a favor for a friend. You remember Zora's?"

"Is that a place?"

"Yes, dummy — the hot restaurant of the moment."

Meg tried to dredge up any memories of eating out in Boston, which seemed a lifetime ago. "Newbury Street?"

"Just off it, on Clarendon. Anyway, I met one of the investors, and he said that one of the staff had her heart set on her own restaurant and asked me if I had any ideas, and the rest is history. Listen, Meg," Lauren hesitated, uncharacteristically. "You said you wouldn't mind having me come out there for a visit?"

"Of course I wouldn't mind. When were you thinking?"

"Maybe like this weekend?"

Meg tried to read between the lines. *What's the hurry?* But if Lauren was still in the office, maybe she didn't feel comfortable talking about her reasons on the phone right now. "Sure, no problem. If I can find the bed in the spare room — I think I saw one there."

"Look, if it's too much trouble, I can find a hotel."

"Lauren, I'm kidding. I'd love to see you, and I can show off the house and my orchard. Come ahead. Late dinner Friday?"

"Oh, you don't have to cook. We can eat out."

"Not in Granford we can't — at least, not until the restaurant opens. Don't worry, I've got a working kitchen. It'll be great to see you."

"Thanks, Meg. See you then."

Bree looked up when Meg came back into the kitchen. "Problems?"

"I don't know," Meg said slowly. "A friend of mine from Boston — she's going to come out this weekend. She hasn't seen the place. Do we have anything important going on, that I need to be on hand for?"

"Not this weekend. But can we sit down and go over the forward calendar? That's what I've been working on."

"Sure." Meg sat down beside her and tried to concentrate on Bree's numbers, while a small part of her brain chewed over what Lauren might want.

Lauren pulled into the driveway in a rental car late Friday afternoon. Meg had managed to declutter the so-called guest room, which had a bed, an old dresser, a rickety chair, and not much else. The sheets were clean, and Meg had made sure the windows opened. She'd also aired the room out, since it hadn't been used for a while. Meg went out and stood on the granite stoop outside her kitchen while Lauren extricated herself from the car. As she approached the car, Meg studied her friend. Slender, as always, her sleek dark hair stylishly cut, and dressed more for a lunch at a beach club than a day at the farm. But though Meg hadn't seen Lauren for a few months, she thought her friend looked a little frayed at the edges.

"Thank God for GPS," Lauren called out. "Where the heck am I?"

"Scenic Granford, Massachusetts, population 1,364 on a good day. The center of town is over that way." Meg waved vaguely to the north. "Everything you see on this side of the road is mine — or at least twenty-five acres' worth, fifteen of it orchard. Damn, it's good to see you!"

"Likewise."

They met halfway between the door and the car and exchanged hugs. Meg thought Lauren felt unusually thin — and tense. "So what's the big rush to get out of Boston?"

"Oh, you know — summer weekends, the heat, stuff. Listen, I wasn't sure what you had to eat, so I stocked up at Whole Foods on my way down. I've got some yummy cheeses. You have anything to drink, perchance?"

"You mean anything alcoholic? Yes. Listen, you want to bring your stuff in and freshen up? You know, I've never understood what that means. Wash your face? Take a nap? Sounds so Victorian. Here, give me your bag." Meg knew she was babbling, but this was the first time Lauren had seen her new home, and it mattered to her that Lauren liked it.

Lauren handed her a tote bag from the trunk, and then retrieved a couple of bags that must be food — a pair of baguettes protruded from the top of one. In the kitchen, Lauren stopped dead at the sight of Bree, who was washing dishes. "You have help?"

Meg could see Bree stiffen. "Oh, heavens — I never told you, did I? Bree's actually my orchard manager, and she lives here in the house. We share cleanup duties. Bree, this is my friend Lauren Converse. Lauren, Briona Stewart."

Bree took her time drying her hands before she answered. "Hello," she said in a neutral tone.

"Hello, Bree. Sorry, I didn't mean to insult you." Lauren offered a hand, and Bree took it.

"No offense taken. Meg, I'm meeting Michael in Amherst, so I'll get out of your hair. Nice to meet you, Lauren." Bree disappeared up the back stairs that led to her room.

Lauren turned to Meg. "I'm sorry — I was rude, wasn't I?"

Meg looked at her friend with concern. "I should have warned you. But actually, you were, and that's not like you. What's up?"

Lauren sighed. "Can I change into something comfortable, and can you dig up that wine, before we get into it?"

"Sure. Follow me." Meg decided the tour of the house could wait until morning. Lauren obviously had something on her mind. Meg led the way up the stairs and directed Lauren to the front bedroom opposite hers. "Bathroom's back that way — oh, and we only have the one for all three of us, until I can afford to add another one downstairs. But there's plenty of hot water. Come on down when you're ready."

"Thanks, Meg."

While waiting for Lauren to reappear — and worrying about what might be troubling her, what would lead her to leave work early and drive all the way to the western end of the state — Meg unpacked Lauren's trove of food goodies, fed Lolly, hunted down a pair of matching glasses, located her corkscrew, and put an additional bottle of wine in the refrigerator. This might be a long session. She was searching for a tray large enough to transport all of this outside when Lauren came back, looking unfamiliar in a simple tank top and well-worn jeans.

"Can I help?" she asked.

"Grab the bottle and the glasses, if you

131

will. I thought it would be nice to sit outside."

"Sure." Lauren held the door for Meg and followed her out to the broad open space beside the barn, where Meg had recently installed a clutter of secondhand Adirondack chairs and a small wooden table that she had sanded and repainted, to take advantage of the view of the Great Meadow. Lauren looked around before throwing herself into the chair and helping herself to a glass of wine. "Nice. You want some?"

"Sure." Meg sat and accepted the glass that Lauren held out.

"You know, I had trouble picturing you here. I mean, a house, a barn, an orchard? Who would have guessed? And what the heck are those?" Lauren nodded toward the pen where the goats were watching them intently.

"Those are goats. My goats. It's a long story."

"Sounds like you've got a lot of stories to tell. You look good, Meg — this must suit you."

"I haven't had my hair cut in six months, I do laundry about twice a month because I'm scared of my basement, and now I have an orchard to keep running, or bearing, or fruiting, or whatever orchards do. If you think I look good after all that, maybe I really do. I wish I could say the same for you. Lauren, what's wrong?"

Lauren sat back in her chair and sighed. "What isn't?"

"Job? Love life? The fate of the world?"

"All of the above. Sorry, Meg — I probably shouldn't inflict myself on you, but I just had to get out of there, get some perspective. The bank's got some serious cash problems, and nobody knows what's going to happen. You're lucky you got out when you did."

"It didn't feel like it at the time, but I have to say I don't miss the place much. You should be able to find something else." Wasn't that what she was supposed to say? Meg realized she didn't know what was going on in the Boston banking community anymore — and didn't really care.

"Maybe. Probably. The thing is, I'm not sure I want to keep doing what I've been doing. It's becoming kind of repetitive. And you asked about my love life? That's nonexistent. Do you know, I'm barely thirty-five, and every guy I meet seems to be a newbie with a bright shiny MBA, out to take over the bank and make his first million before he's thirty? That's how I knew about the baby chefs — I was so desperate to talk about anything that wasn't related to the financial world that I was chatting with the bartender at Zora's. Even *he* turned out to be one of the investors, filling in for the regular guy. And no, he didn't ask me out, but we did talk a lot about the restaurant business. Which, by the way, I have no desire to get involved with — it sounds pretty uncertain. What's going on with the place here, by the way?" Lauren reached for the bottle to refill her glass.

"Things looked good, before Sam died. They've got a nice building in town, and the build-out has been going well. I haven't had a chance to try their food, apart from the occasional pastry, but they talk a good line. Now, I don't know."

"So what happened?"

"The sous chef, a really nice guy named Sam Anderson, was found dead in a pig wallow."

Lauren tried and failed to suppress a snort. "Well, you're not going to hear *that* in Boston. A pig wallow?"

"He was found facedown in the mud. The police would have called it an accident, but there was a nice fat shoeprint in the middle of his back. Apparently somebody held him down until he suffocated." Meg felt a sudden pang of guilt. "But don't tell anyone

134

you know that — I'm not sure it's public information."

Lauren wasn't smiling anymore. "I hear you — but I kind of guessed it wasn't a natural death when I got that call. I mean, if it had been, why would they have bothered to call me? But that's awful! Have they figured out who did it?"

"Not yet. You said Detective Marcus called you? What did he ask?"

"Mostly if I knew the deceased, personally or by reputation. If I knew anything about his lifestyle or his friends in Boston. I really couldn't tell him much, since I never met the man. Do the police think the killer was from Boston?"

"Believe me, the state police don't tell me anything. And they haven't even announced officially that it was murder. I have the feeling they'd like to think the killer came from Boston, because they don't seem to have any strong candidates here. Sam hadn't been around long enough to make either friends or enemies in town. I'm glad Marcus is following up with Sam's Boston connections. And about the lifestyle thing — he was gay."

"So? Oh, you mean people around here have a problem with that?"

"Not that I know about — and before you

jump to conclusions, most of the people around here are pretty decent, and probably as liberal as you or me."

Lauren held up her hands in mock surrender. "Sorry, sorry — I really don't mean to keep insulting you and your friends. You want me to set this Statie straight?"

"What?"

"Tell him what the Boston scene is like, if this Sam was really a part of it?"

"Lauren, people around here are definitely aware of alternative lifestyles. Why? Are you even familiar with that scene anyway?"

"You're right, not really. I'm just trying to help. But I'd kind of like to see how a real investigation works."

"No, you wouldn't. I've seen plenty in the last few months, and you're not missing a thing. Maybe you should eat something," Meg added dubiously as Lauren drained her second glass and reached for the bottle again.

"Yes, Mother, I *am* planning to get mildly drunk, and I'm hungry. You don't mind if I dump on you, do you? I really need to vent, and you're the only person I could think of who would listen to me."

"That's what friends are for." Meg shoved the platter with cheese and sliced bread and cold cuts toward her.

Lauren took a piece of baguette and slathered it with Brie. She took a huge bite. "Ah, bliss. Damn the calories, full speed ahead."

Something was definitely not right with Lauren. She was usually very much in control, and upbeat. Now she had fled Boston and was depressed and getting drunk? Meg wondered if she should push Lauren to spill her guts, or just let the slower pace and the peace and quiet of Granford do its work. Somehow Meg doubted that a single weekend would be enough to unwind Lauren.

"You okay?"

Lauren sighed. "I will be. So, what do you do for fun around here?"

"What's fun? I work on the house — I refinished the kitchen floor a couple of months ago, I'm learning about the orchard and how to run it — all sorts of stuff, like storage facilities, and pesticide spraying, and hiring pickers, and selling the crop. There's not a lot of time left over. Oh, and I work on cataloging old records for the Historical Society in town."

Meg looked to see Lauren shaking her head. "Who would have believed it? Farmer Meg, with goats and a barn." Lauren took another long swallow of wine, and looked out over the meadow, where the treetops were gilded with light, while the grass below was in shadow. "I envy you."

"Me?" Meg said, startled. "Why? I have no money, and no idea what I'm doing."

"But you care about it. You're involved, and excited, and you're learning new stuff. Maybe you can't see that, but I can. It suits you."

"Thank you — I think. I am enjoying it, I guess. Apart from the uncertainty."

"That's everywhere these days. Ain't no sure thing, in Boston or here." Lauren waved a hand in the air. "Who's that?"

Meg followed her gaze to see Seth walking across the meadow. "That's, uh, Seth." She scrabbled to remember what she had told Lauren about Seth so far.

"So that's the plumber guy you haven't been talking about? Nice." Seth was wearing faded jeans and a long-sleeved shirt with the sleeves rolled up.

"Well, yeah, I guess." Meg felt like a teenager fumbling for words. "But he's a lot more than a plumber. He's a neighbor — he lives over the hill, on the next property. He's running a home renovation service out of the barn here, when he finishes setting it up. And he's a town selectman," Meg finished lamely.

"Ah. You people out here are into multitasking, I see. Hello, neighbor Seth," she said when he drew into earshot. "I'm Lauren Converse, Meg's friend from Boston." She didn't get up — Meg wondered if she could, after three glasses of wine on a virtually empty stomach — but she did stick her hand out.

Seth took it and shook. "Hi, Lauren. I think Meg's mentioned you. Are you visiting?" He pulled a third chair forward.

Lauren refilled her glass and waved it airily, sloshing a bit of wine over the rim. "I have fled the big bad city to seek the wisdom of my one true friend, out here in the bucolic reaches of the far west of Massachusetts. Oh, and that detective person called me, so I figured, why not kill two birds with one stone? Find a sympathetic ear for my problems *and* explain the ways of the city to your rural constabulary."

Meg looked helplessly at Seth. Lauren was doing everything in her power to give a bad impression — and doing it well. "Did you need something, Seth?"

Seth looked briefly at Lauren, who seemed lost in her own miserable thoughts. "Not really. I talked to Art today, but he didn't have anything new."

Lauren perked up. "Ooh, are you a sleuth, too, Seth? Hey, that's not easy to say. Sleuth

139

Seth, Seth the Sleuth . . ."

"Lauren, stop it," Meg said sharply. "You're drunk."

"Yes I am." She looked at Meg, and her face fell. "I think maybe I shall retire to my room before I make a real mess of things. Seth, it was nice to meet you." Lauren stood up unsteadily and aimed herself toward the kitchen door. Meg was relieved that she left the wine bottle behind, even if it was nearly empty anyway.

When Lauren had made it to the kitchen without falling down, Meg turned to Seth. "I'm sorry. She's not usually like that. She's upset, but I haven't had time to find out why."

"Don't worry about it. Did Marcus really call her?"

"He did. I guess he's checking out Sam's Boston connections, but I don't know if that's good or bad. Maybe it shifts the focus from Granford, at least."

"Maybe."

"You want what's left of the wine? There's another bottle."

"No, thanks. I should get going anyway — just wanted to say hi. Lauren staying for the weekend?"

"I gather. And she says she wants to talk to Marcus, although I can't imagine why.

Maybe she's trying to distract herself from her own woes."

"Interesting. Maybe she can wangle his secrets out of him. If there are any."

10

In the morning Meg and Bree were conferring about the roster of pickers, due to arrive any day, when Lauren stumbled down the stairs and made a beeline for the coffeepot.

Bree cast a quick glance at her, then returned to her lists. "I want them here by the end of the month. Your first apples will be ripe in August, if the weather cooperates, but I want to get to know the pickers, let them get to know me and you, and make sure everything is working right. And they can mow the grass in the orchard, check out the equipment, that kind of thing."

"Where are they staying?"

"Not our problem," Bree replied. "Some of the bigger orchards provide housing, but we can't do that. Most of them have been coming here for years anyway, and they know people, know where they want to stay."

"Okay, if you say so."

Bree nodded vigorously. "How you doing on selling the crop?"

Meg felt a pang of guilt. "I'm working on it. I did offer some to the restaurant, but I have no idea how many that would be, or how much to charge them."

"The rate they're going, they won't be able to pay you anyway."

Lauren had swallowed half a cup of coffee while staring out the window over the sink. She topped off her cup from the pot and sat down at the table. "Am I interrupting?"

"Nope, we're about done." Bree stood up. "I've got stuff to do. I probably won't be around for dinner, so you two can hang out."

"Michael?"

Bree shrugged without answering, then clattered up the back stairs. Meg turned to Lauren. The morning light wasn't exactly flattering to her. "Sleep well?"

"Like a log. Maybe a rotting log. Sure is quiet around here."

"It is." Meg sipped her cooling coffee and waited for Lauren to volunteer something more.

Lauren sat back and ran her fingers through her hair. "Just how many people did I manage to tick off last night?"

"Bree. Seth. That's two."

"Not you?" Lauren scraped together a smile.

"No. You aren't acting normal, and it's not just the fresh air and pretty views. If you want to talk about it, fine, I'm listening. If not, I can drag you off to do something touristy. Or just leave you alone with the goats."

"While I pickle myself? Not a good idea. I gave you the bare bones last night, if I recall correctly — before I started making nasty comments about your colleagues here. I told you the bank's in trouble? I'm sure you get that much news even out here. The merger last year didn't go as well as they had hoped, and now the general economy has gone to hell, and nobody knows what to do."

"Is your job secure?"

Lauren shrugged. "As much as anyone's. But I don't even know if I want it anymore. I mean, I've always worked hard, been the whiz kid, sucked up to the right people, and I've got it made, by most standards. But like I said, suddenly I'm not the 'kid' anymore. There's a whole new generation nipping at my heels, and I'm tempted just to let them have the whole mess. Let *them* figure it out."

"You have any ideas about what you'd like

144

to do instead?"

"Nope. That's the problem. I've been so focused that I haven't had time to look around and smell the roses. No relationship, no kids, no house — and no clue. Not that I want to go quite as far as you did, with this place!"

"It wasn't really my decision, if you recall, and it certainly didn't start off well. But the longer I hang around here, the better I like it. It grows on you. Of course, I like learning new things. And I guess I'm less afraid of failing than I used to be."

"Good for you. I mean that. But I don't know what I want to be when I grow up. So anyway, what's with you and this Seth guy?"

"What do you mean?"

"Oh, come on, Meg — you kind of lit up when he arrived."

Meg could feel herself blushing. "I don't know. I've got too much going on to even think about it."

"Uh-huh. Meg's got a boyfriend, Meg's got a boyfriend," Lauren chanted.

"Shut up!" Meg laughed.

"I will — but let me say one thing first. After your last jerk boyfriend, you deserve a nice guy in your life, so don't ignore him too long, okay?" Lauren sat up straighter in her chair. "Well, the caffeine seems to be doing its work. What's on the agenda for today?"

Between twelve hours of sleep and a jolt of coffee, Lauren seemed to be in a much more positive mood this morning, Meg noted. "What're you up for? Shopping? Eating? You should meet the chefs, since they're here because of you."

"What about the murder investigation?"

"What about it?"

"Come on, Meg — you can't think that this restaurant is going to succeed with something like a murder hanging over it? The sooner that mystery's cleared up, the better. How far away is this place?"

"The restaurant is about two miles away, as the crow flies, or a five-minute drive. I can show you the rest of the town, while we're at it, but that shouldn't take more than another five minutes, unless you want to meet all my ancestors in the local cemetery."

"I'll pass on that last part, but the rest sounds good. I can look over the place, and then maybe we can check out one of their competitors for lunch. Can I grab a shower first?"

"It's all yours."

While Lauren showered, Meg cleaned up the kitchen and inventoried the contents of

146

her refrigerator. Much as she'd love to check out the lovely array of restaurants in Northampton and Amherst, she didn't think her budget would be happy about it. And she definitely needed to stock up on wine, even if Lauren had stopped trying to drown her sorrows. Last night's bottle was history, which left only one more.

Lauren emerged clean and dressed, and not even overdressed. "Let's do it!"

"My, you bounce back fast. Okay, I'll grab my bag and we'll go to town."

Meg offered brief comments as they drove toward town. "That's the Chapin property, over there — it runs to the highway, except they've lost a chunk to the new shopping center. We're coming up on the town now: library on your left, the church is obvious, Town Hall up the hill on the right."

"Wow! You weren't kidding when you said it was small. Is this all there is?"

"A couple of feed stores and gas stations along the highway, but yes, what you see is what you get."

"And the restaurant?"

"That white brick building at the end of the green." Meg drove slowly along the two-lane highway toward it.

Lauren looked at it critically. "Nice. Good site. Good parking, too. That'll make a difference." Her tone was sincere. "They aren't going to tart it up with neon signs or anything?"

"I don't think so." Meg laughed.

"What's the capacity?" Lauren asked.

"I don't know. You can ask. They'll be doing lunch and dinner, I think. They had to rebuild the kitchen entirely — that's the wing off to the left. It was a residence until pretty recently."

"I can see the potential. Do they know what the local market can handle?"

Meg pulled into the parking lot. "I think they're still working out details about the menu and stuff like pricing. They live upstairs here, so they should be around."

The inner door was open behind the outer screen when Meg and Lauren walked onto the porch. Meg called out, "Anybody home?"

Nicky came down the stairs, still toweling dry her hair. "Oh, hi, Meg — you're out and about early today. What's up?"

"I didn't mean to bother you, but I thought you'd like to meet Lauren Converse. She's visiting this weekend, and she wanted to see what you've done so for."

"Lauren, Lauren . . . oh, you're *that* Lauren!" Nicky's face lit up. "You know Jeremy! In fact, you're the reason we're here. Please,

148

come in. Brian?" she yelled up the stairs.

"Yo!" Brian answered from somewhere.

"We've got company!" Nicky yelled back. Then she turned back to Meg and Lauren. "I was just going to make some breakfast. You hungry?"

"You have coffee?" Lauren said.

"Sure do. Come on back." She led the way to the kitchen.

Once there, while Nicky bustled around starting coffee, whisking eggs, slicing bread, Lauren looked around at the kitchen. "Nice. Efficient. How many are you planning to serve?"

"We figure we can accommodate maybe forty diners max in the big rooms up front, maybe another twenty in the smaller ones. Two seatings, at night. We've got three rooms, and we want to use the parlors with the fireplaces, but we can shut off one or two if things are slow, or use them for private functions."

Lauren nodded. "Sounds good. I like the place. What are you doing about decorating?"

"Arguing, mostly," Nicky said with a grin. "It's the last thing we're going to worry about, after we get all the structural stuff done, and get the permits — and see how much money we have left. We had some ideas when we arrived, but we're kind of letting the place speak to us."

"Simple works here. You going to have a liquor license?"

"We hope so. We've put in the applications, but I gather we need some approvals from the town. We're talking to them next week." Nicky set plates of French toast in front of Meg and Lauren, then went to the kitchen door. "Brian? Food's up."

Lauren dug into her food. "Oh, Nicky, this is great. Or maybe it's just all this fresh country air." She sneaked a glance at Meg, who swatted her. "What style of food are you planning?"

"Local American. Good quality, simple preparation. We're trying to line up vendors, but we're still trying to figure out who to talk to. Seth's been a big help, but he's pretty busy."

"Ah, Seth again. He does get around, doesn't he?"

"He's doing the construction here," Meg said mildly. "That's his job, you know."

"Right." Lauren turned her attention back to her food, which was disappearing rapidly.

Meg looked at Nicky. "How are you doing with vendors?"

"Working on it. We've got a couple of people lined up, but we've been so busy

150

here we haven't done as much as we should."

"I wouldn't wait too long. I'd guess that farmers contract for their stuff as soon as they can." Meg reminded herself that she should practice what she preached: she hadn't found buyers for her own crop.

Brian appeared in the kitchen, and Nicky introduced him to Lauren. "And Meg says we should talk to the farmers sooner rather than later."

Brian looked pained. "I know, I know. I'd kind of hoped the sous chef could handle that, but we haven't got one yet."

"Are you going to talk to the woman Seth mentioned?" Meg asked.

"She's coming by later today. I hate to make a quick decision, but we don't have a lot of time, so I hope she works out."

"Seth handles personnel placement, too?" Lauren said, eyebrow arched.

"Lauren, I keep telling you, it's a small town. Seth knows a cook who can use the job, okay?"

"Mmm-hmm," Lauren replied skeptically, swabbing up the last of the maple syrup with her final bite of French toast. "Hey, is the syrup local?"

Nicky beamed. "Of course, from about a mile away. We snagged the last of this spring's crop."

"Keep it up," Lauren said. She swallowed the last of her coffee. "Meg, what's next?"

"I thought I'd take you over to Northampton. It's a fun town, and then we can have lunch over there somewhere."

"Food again? If the whole weekend is like this, I won't fit in any of my clothes." She stood up. "Nicky, Brian, I like your place. I can't wait to see what you do with it."

"We'll invite you to the opening."

"Great — I'll be here. Meg?"

"Thanks for breakfast, guys." Meg followed Lauren out the door. Once back in the car, she asked, "What did you really think?"

Lauren buckled her seat belt. "Good location, not a lot of competition — or from what you tell me, none, really. They're awfully young, but high energy, and Nicky can cook, based on that breakfast. I hope their money holds out — these things always end up costing more than you expect. Is Seth cutting them a good deal on the construction?"

"I think so. I think as a selectman he wants to see this succeed. And he'll be able to help with the local permitting."

"And Nicky seems to know what she's doing in the kitchen. Sometimes you can cook up a storm but not efficiently. She seems to have that covered. Too bad about her sous chef. You think this local person might have whacked him to take his job?"

"Lauren! That's an awful thought."

"You have to consider every angle. If there aren't many jobs around here, people might get desperate. Maybe I'll suggest that to the detective."

"What, you're still thinking of talking to him?"

"Why not? I like to see who I'm dealing with. He's the one who called me, and here I am, in his backyard."

"Just don't expect me to come with you," Meg muttered.

"You have issues with him?"

"I didn't particularly like being considered a suspect. He didn't even know me."

"He got it right in the end, didn't he?"

"With my help. I just don't want to talk to him any more than I have to."

"Okay, I'll go in alone, no problem."

"Lauren, it's Saturday!"

"So? This is a murder case. Don't cops work around the clock for important cases?"

"Just don't be surprised if he isn't there. You can leave a statement or something."

Lauren swiveled in her seat to confront Meg. "What is your problem with this guy?

You're scared of cops? You're hiding something? What?"

Meg sighed. Maybe she was acting irrational. "Detective Marcus and I have had some run-ins in the past. I'm not his favorite person."

Lauren's face fell. "Oh. You don't have to come if you don't want to, but I'm going to talk to the guy."

Meg considered. In Lauren's current state of mind, she wasn't sure if Lauren might do more harm than good, and Meg certainly didn't want her to make any more trouble for Nicky and Brian. Better to keep an eye on her — or maybe she meant a muzzle — than risk Lauren making a mess of things. "I'll come. Just let me find a parking space — it's not easy in Northampton on a Saturday."

Meg made a few cursory circles around the block, then gave up and headed for the municipal lot behind the main street. She was lucky to snag a space from someone leaving, and purchased a parking voucher from the vending machine, while Lauren watched with an air of amusement. Once Meg had deposited the slip in plain view on her dashboard, she said to Lauren, "Follow me."

Lauren dutifully followed as Meg wove

154

her way through the back of a commercial building and up a set of stairs. "Where are we going?" Lauren asked.

When they reached the sidewalk in front of the building, Meg pointed toward the ornate brownstone building in the center of town. "Town Hall, or more specifically, the annex behind it."

"Gotcha. Cute little town here. Nice boutiques. Are we going to have time to shop, or are those apples calling you?"

"I said we'd have lunch, didn't I? After that, we'll see. Let's get this over with."

They entered the building through the side door and stopped at the guard desk. "We're here to see Detective Marcus."

The young, buff, and buzz-cut uniformed officer asked, "Is he expecting you?"

"No. Tell him it's about the Anderson death in Granford."

The officer picked up the phone and turned away to talk while Meg studied the floor. Lauren, as she could see from the corner of her eye, seemed all too eager, her foot tapping, her eyes bright. The officer hung up and said, "He'll be right down."

No escape now. How was she going to explain her presence here? Meg wondered. She was sure that she was the last person Marcus wanted to see today. Damn Lauren.

Meg needn't have worried. As soon as Marcus appeared, Lauren took one look at him, assessed his evident seniority and authority, and extended her hand. "Detective Marcus? I'm Lauren Converse, from Boston. We spoke on the phone about Sam Anderson's death?"

Meg was secretly pleased that Marcus appeared nonplussed by Lauren's frontal assault, and actually took her hand. "Ms. Converse, there was no need for you to come all this way to talk with me." Then he spied Meg, lurking behind Lauren, and his expression hardened. "Ms. Corey."

"Detective Marcus," Meg replied as neutrally as she could.

Lauren slid adroitly between them. "That's right, you know each other. I'm here visiting Meg, and I thought I'd come in and see if I could tell you anything more about Sam."

"Ms. Converse, you told me on the phone that you had never met the man. What could you have to add?"

"Lauren, please. And you won't know until we talk about it, will you? I can give you a better sense of the Boston community where Sam and his friends worked. After all, I feel responsible, since I was the one who sent them all out here. What

156

do you say?"

Marcus wavered, then answered, "All right. Officer, can you give me two visitor badges, please?"

Formalities completed, Meg followed the suddenly chummy pair up a flight of stairs and to Marcus's cluttered office. It looked as though he worked hard and didn't worry about filing. Marcus pointed toward two wooden armchairs in front of his desk. "Have a seat."

They sat, and then Lauren leaned forward. "Detective, I know you're a busy man, and I'm not here to chitchat and waste your time. But I do know something about the restaurant scene in Boston, and I want to be sure that you see Nicky and Brian and Sam in the correct context, before you make any assumptions."

Marcus's eyes flickered toward silent Meg. "What have you told her?"

Meg sat up straighter. "No more than she already guessed. You called her, and she figured you wouldn't have done that unless it was a suspicious death. I don't know any more than that, so I can't exactly spill the beans."

Marcus looked pained, but said nothing, only nodding once. "Ms. Converse," he began.

157

"Lauren," Lauren reminded him sweetly.

"Lauren, Sam Anderson was killed by person or persons unknown, who held him down in a pigsty until he suffocated in the mud. And if either of you says anything about what I am telling you to anyone else, I'll have you arrested for obstruction of justice. Understood?"

Meg nodded her agreement. Lauren said, "Of course. And I do understand about discretion, Detective. But if there's any way I can help, I'd feel terrible if I didn't come forward. What can I tell you?"

There followed fifteen minutes of an exchange that Meg had never thought to see. Marcus recited the bare bones of the case — and Meg was surprised at how little information there was, not because Marcus and his staff hadn't looked, but because it simply wasn't there to find. Sam had led a completely bland life: no criminal history, no debt, no complaints against him. He had gone through college and cooking school with a solid record, and had worked steadily since. Apparently nobody had a bad word to say about him. His parents were devastated by his death, as were his many friends in Boston. None of the information pointed toward either a motive for murder or a suspect. The only crumb they gleaned was that Marcus was still looking for Sam's most recent boyfriend, who was said to be out of the country.

Lauren corroborated what he had learned about the Boston scene and added a few details. More often she nodded sympathetically and made appropriate sounds of agreement, and Meg watched incredulously as Marcus softened bit by bit, until he appeared almost human. She kept her mouth shut, afraid to break the spell that Lauren had cast over him.

"So that ex is the only loose end to tie up, isn't it?" Lauren said.

"Just about." Marcus glanced at his watch, then stood up. "Sorry, but I've got a briefing to attend. Thank you for coming in, Lauren. Meg. I'll see you out of the building."

Since silence had worked so well this far, Meg stuck to it as Marcus led them back down the stairs. It wasn't until they were out on the street that she felt free to speak. "I can't believe it — the man may be human after all."

Lauren flashed her a grin. "Why, whatever do you mean? He seemed perfectly nice to me. Overworked, and frustrated because he doesn't have a lot to go on, but not the ogre you made him out to be. Do you know if he's single?"

"Lauren! You would actually go out with him?"

"Why not? Well, is he?"

"I have no information about his personal life. You're on your own."

"Fine friend you are. So, what's next on the agenda? Lunch, I hope? I'm starving."

"I saw you eat breakfast barely an hour ago! You can't be."

"The combination of fresh air, sunshine, and the performance of my civic duty always makes me hungry. What are our choices?"

"In Northampton, anything you want. What are you in the mood for?"

Lauren studied the bustling street. "I feel like something plebian, like burgers and fries. Can this town handle that?"

"Of course — there's a good brewpub near the parking lot."

"Lead on!" Lauren said grandly. At least she seemed to be enjoying herself, Meg thought wryly.

11

It was too early for lunch, and the pub was half-empty. Meg was still trying to figure out the rhythms of the town: the college kids had gone home for the summer, and though there were plenty of local young people around, they didn't usually eat in restaurants like this, preferring the cheaper and funkier places along the main street. She and Lauren could probably enjoy some privacy — if Lauren had anything private to say.

They took their seats and accepted menus. Then Lauren looked around the room. "This is nice. Reasonable prices, comfortable. Is this typical of the area?"

Meg laughed. "There is nothing typical about Northampton. You can find French, Italian, Mexican, Indian, Japanese, Chinese, Thai, Argentinean, Tibetan — you name it, all within walking distance. But this is probably the closest to what Nicky and Brian have in mind, only they're going for more emphasis on local foods, and less fried stuff."

"Okay. I'm having a beer. What's good?"

She and Meg conferred over the menu, ordered a couple of beers and sandwiches. When the waitress had taken their orders, Meg asked, "Okay, you've had your foray into investigation. What did you think?"

Lauren sat back in her chair and contemplated Meg. "You know, you had me expecting a monster. He's a nice guy, actually."

"Easy for you to say."

"Meg, he's just doing his job, and doing it by the book. He works for the DA, you know, and he wants his cases to be airtight."

"Why do you know who works for whom?"

"I checked online. You don't think I go walking into things like this without doing some homework, do you? Actually I was surprised he was willing to tell us anything at all. He must be desperate."

Lauren's cell phone rang in the depths of her bag. She fished it out and opened it. "Hello? Oh, hi. Tonight? I think so." She glanced at Meg and listened for a few moments. "All right, I'll meet you then." She closed the phone with a snap. "You know, I don't think he ever really suspected you of anything, but you were an unknown quantity, at least in the beginning."

"Lauren!"

"Joke! You are so not a criminal. He knows that. You know, Meg, you don't have to be paranoid. You two *are* on the same side, and he wants to see this murder solved as much as you or anyone else does."

"I don't think we learned anything that we didn't already know," Meg said, trying to keep the petulance out of her voice. Okay, he hadn't been hostile, but she didn't like being chided by her friend.

"Maybe I can worm a bit more out of him over dinner," Lauren added casually.

"You're having dinner with him?" Meg said, incredulous.

"That was him on the phone just now. Am I supposed to say no? I'm sorry — did you want to spend more time together?"

Meg considered her conflicted emotions. On some level she still considered Marcus an adversary, and he'd been downright rude to her on more than one occasion. And she wanted her time with Lauren to try to ferret out whatever was troubling her friend. On the other hand, Lauren was a grown woman and could see whomever she wanted; and maybe she could learn something about the investigation by having dinner with the detective. "I guess we'll have to

163

assume he's not married, won't we?"

"Apparently. Are you okay with this?"

"Sure. Just as long as you loosen him up a bit. What do we know?"

Lauren sat back and ticked off points on her fingers. "He's talked to Nicky and Brian, of course, and checked into the finances of this deal. Sam's death didn't benefit them, or anybody else for that matter, financially. None of them has a lot of money, except what Nicky's dad chipped in. He talked to the guy who owns the place where the body was found, who knows exactly nothing."

"Jake Kellogg," Meg said.

"Right. Anyway, this farmer guy was busy up at his barn, which is out of sight of the pig field, or whatever you call it. When he checked the pigs in the afternoon, he found the body, and the guy had been dead for a couple of hours by then. There are no neighbors with a clear view of that field — that's one of the reasons he picked it, because nobody would be bothered by the sight or the stink. I gather pigs can really stink."

"So I've heard. Not much, is it? Where are you meeting him tonight?"

"He suggested a place in Amherst. You can tell me how to find it, right?"

"Sure. We ain't got many roads out here in the hinterlands."

Lauren impulsively laid her hand on Meg's. "I'm sorry — I know I came to visit you, and here I am running out on you. But he seems like a nice guy, and I don't meet many of those. I promise I'll fill you in on everything at breakfast. And I don't have to be back in Boston until late, so we can go gather flowers or talk to the goats or whatever it is you do for fun."

"It's fine, Lauren. I guess I'm just annoyed that he likes you better than he likes me."

"Oh, come on. You've got Seth."

"I don't mean it that way. By the way, Marcus and Seth have a history, so I wouldn't bring up Seth's name."

"Curiouser and curiouser. I'll try to be tactful as I pump the man for information. I guess it's kind of early to seduce him?"

"Lauren!" Meg wasn't sure whether or not Lauren was kidding.

"Okay, I'll save that for later. Now I'm hungry."

Their sandwiches appeared, and they spent the rest of the meal talking about unrelated things.

After lunch Meg took some small pride in showing Lauren the town of Northampton, and Lauren bought some shoes and a silver necklace. They retraced their steps to Granford and arrived back about three o'clock to find Bree and Michael in the kitchen.

"Hi, Michael," Meg said cheerfully. "This is my friend Lauren Converse, from Boston. Lauren, Michael's a local expert on organic agriculture."

Lauren sent Meg a look that said "Why do I care?" and Meg smiled pleasantly.

"Hi, Michael — good to meet you," Lauren said. "What do I need to know about organic food?"

"How long have you got?" Michael said.

Lauren leaned against the counter. "I'll settle for the short version."

"I deal mainly with local growers around here, help them with what they can use on their crops, and also how to market them. And I try to educate local consumers, and that includes chefs."

"Really. Is Meg's orchard organic?"

Michael shook his head. "No, even though I tried to convert her."

"Lauren," Meg protested, "apples are notoriously hard to manage, if you want unblemished fruit, which is what most buyers are looking for. I use what's known as an integrated pest management approach, which limits the use of chemicals, but doesn't eliminate them entirely. But that doesn't stop Michael and me from arguing about it."

"Listen to you!" Lauren smiled to soften her comment. "Michael, are you helping Nicky and Brian find organic foods?"

"Bree asked me about it, and I talked to Sam before . . . you know. To qualify as a true organic restaurant, you have to comply with a lot of rules, and I don't think they're interested in going that route. But I'm happy to put them in touch with local growers and producers."

"What grows well around here? Don't you have pretty hard winters?" Lauren took a seat at the table; she looked honestly interested.

Michael took a seat opposite Lauren, and Meg watched the two of them with almost maternal pride. "What doesn't?" Michael said. "Apart from the local orchards like Meg's, we've got a full range of vegetables around here. Heck, Hadley, one of the towns nearby, is well known for its asparagus crop. There's even a farm over toward Amherst that's growing ginger. Then you've got livestock — did you know that Hampshire College has a buffalo herd?"

"Wow! No, I had no idea. I come from Boston, and I shop in supermarkets. I guess I've seen some signs there recently for local

167

produce, but I don't spend a lot of time thinking about where it all comes from. I apologize for my ignorance, though I do shop at Whole Foods, if that helps."

"Some. They still fall on the commercial end of the organic spectrum, but they're trying." Michael paused and checked Lauren's expression to see if she was mocking him, but in the end he smiled. "I'm kind of enthusiastic about the whole thing. But organically grown food is better for you, and it tastes better, too. So think about it next time you go shopping, okay?"

"I will."

"Michael, we should get going," Bree broke in. She turned to Meg. "We're going to catch an early movie, then get something to eat. We figured you'd be busy anyway."

"That's fine. You two go have fun."

"Bye, Lauren. Nice to meet you."

When they'd left, Lauren said to Meg, "Ah, young love. Were we ever that young?"

Meg laughed. "They've had their ups and downs. But I like Michael — he's a good guy, and Bree likes him, which is what matters. And he does keep me on my toes about organic farming."

"Ah, Meg, Meg . . . Like I said, you seem to be thriving on all of this."

"I like learning, and I like challenges. The

fact that I'm supposed to make a living doing it makes it interesting — when I'm not panicking about it."

"I wish I could see myself making a one-eighty change like you, but I kind of like my creature comforts, not to mention an income."

"Coming out here was my mother's bright idea, although she had no idea what she was getting me into."

"Has your mother seen the place since you moved here?"

"No, not yet. I'm dreading the day I pick up the phone and she announces she's arriving the next day. No doubt it'll be right in the middle of the busiest part of harvest season."

"I don't suppose she'd pitch in and help?"

"My mother? No way. Although she might take it upon herself to instruct the workers on how to get the job done more neatly and efficiently."

"Maybe you should be proactive and invite her out at a time that works for *you.*"

"I'll think about it. When are you supposed to be in Amherst?"

"Changing the subject, eh? Not until seven. I'd be happy just to take some time and smell the roses. Why don't you show me the orchard?"

169

Meg was surprised by Lauren's request. "Sure. I didn't think you'd be interested."

"I don't know if I am, but I won't know unless I look at it, right?"

"Okay, orchard it is."

Meg led the way up the hill to the orchard and stopped, silent, to let Lauren take it in.

Lauren didn't speak for a few moments. "So this is all yours?" she said finally.

"Fifteen acres of trees. There's more land that goes with the house, but it's too wet to plant."

Lauren took a few tentative steps forward, stopping in the first row of trees. "What's it like, owning a whole bunch of living things like this?"

Meg considered. "Scary. Reassuring. That sounds contradictory, doesn't it? Scary because I know so many things that can go wrong before I can get a crop out of them — insects, diseases, natural disasters. But at the same time, there have been apple trees here since the seventeen hundreds, and here they are still. So they'll hang on, no matter what I do. Maybe this year's crop will be lousy, but there's always next year. I told you my ancestors built this place? Well, it gives me a kind of connection with them, makes me feel more a part of the place."

Lauren reached out to lift a branch.

"Look, baby apples. What kind are they?"

"I have no idea yet. Bree might know, and Christopher certainly would. We've got a lot of different ones here, some heirloom. I'll know better after they ripen."

Lauren was quiet for several moments, and Meg let her be. Finally she said, without turning around, "I think I've figured out something. All this" — Lauren waved her hand across the orchard — "it seems a lot more real than what I do. I mean, you put in work — and I mean hands-on, messy work — and in the end you have a product you can touch, hold, eat. It's real. Me, I get a piece of paper with numbers on it."

"Is that what's bothering you? You don't believe in what you're doing anymore?"

Lauren turned around then. "I don't know if I ever did, really. I mean, it was a challenge, and it was interesting — but it was all on paper, playing with numbers. And playing politics with the competition, in-house and at other banks. A big game. You know that; you were part of it."

"I suppose. I never liked the competitive side. I was a lot happier running numbers in the back office."

"Well, for a long time I liked being in the game. Now, I'm not so sure. I mean, it didn't take much to make the whole house of cards fall down in the financial sector, did it? All that work we did, erased in a few months. Now nobody even trusts us, and nobody inside knows what to do about it. It sucks."

"It does. But I can't see you as a farmer. What else do you think you'd like to do?"

"I really don't know. But thanks for letting me vent, and for letting me visit you here. It gives me something more to think about."

"Any time. You can come pick apples later, if you want."

Lauren smiled. "Maybe. But right now I have to go get pretty for my date with the scary policeman. You sure you don't mind being left on your own tonight?"

"Anything resembling free time is always a treat. Don't worry about me."

12

Meg had been in bed, although awake and reading, when Lauren returned that night, but since she hadn't tapped at her door, Meg had decided not to bother her. The next morning the weather held — Lauren was lucky. She might not wax so poetic about the rural life if she was cooped up in the house while the lawn turned into a sea of mud.

Meg had spent a quiet but productive evening going through yet another box of documents from the Historical Society. She had taken on the task of cataloging what she could, at the urging of Gail Selden, the Society's overworked director, and had found she enjoyed it. It made a pleasant change from the manual work in the orchard and around the house, and she never knew what she was going to find among the old and brittle documents. It was also nice that there was no urgency to the project: the documents had been waiting patiently in their boxes for decades, so anything Meg could get done was a big step forward.

Last night's find was an 1873 printed map of Granford, on which all the then-residents' names were printed. She traced the road in front of her house: it was labeled "Warren," and there was also another Warren next door — she'd have to look into that sometime. There was the brook that trickled through the Great Meadow, and kept it boggy. There was the Chapin place, over the hill. The town green, and the Stebbins house at the north end. And there was the Kellogg property, where Sam's body had been found, over toward the north end of town, where there had been few houses in the nineteenth century. To the best of her recollection, there weren't a lot more now. What *had* Sam been doing out there? If he had wanted to talk to Jake Kellogg, they had never connected — or so Jake had said. Did he have a reason to lie?

In the morning, Lauren stumbled down as Meg was scrambling eggs. "There's coffee." Meg nodded toward the stove.

"You are a goddess."

Meg handed her a mug. "I heard you come in last night," she said tentatively.

"We had a nice time. He's a reasonably

intelligent guy, he actually has some interests outside of law enforcement, and no, I didn't sleep with him." Lauren took her coffee mug and sat down at the table.

Meg set a plate with eggs and toast on it in front of her. "Well, that about covers it, doesn't it?"

Lauren gave Meg a hard look and burst out laughing. "No, I mean it. He's pretty knowledgeable about food — he picked a great restaurant, and knew what to order. He's kind of a history buff — the American Revolution. No kids, no pets, no alimony. And he actually likes his job."

"You going to see him again?" Meg asked.

"I don't know. I mean, it's not like we're in love, or even in lust, and we live a hundred miles apart. But I think we both enjoyed ourselves, so it's a possibility."

"Well, I'm *so* relieved!" Meg sat down with her own breakfast.

"So, what's on the calendar for today?" Lauren asked, ignoring Meg's sarcasm. "You have to go till something, or chop something, or spray something?"

"I think my schedule's clear. What are you up for, city girl?"

"How about taking a run up toward the Kellogg farm?"

"Where Sam was found? Why on earth

would you want to do that?"

"Oh, come on, Meg — you know you're curious. Sure, Bill interviewed the guy, but you probably know better what questions to ask."

"So it's 'Bill' now?"

"That *is* Detective Marcus's name, after all." Lauren retorted. "Anyway, you'd be helping Nicky and Brian, right? Clear up this murder mess *and* find them some nice pigs, all at once."

Meg didn't know what to say. "Lauren, let me get this straight. You're volunteering to go with me to talk to a pig farmer?"

"Maybe I have ulterior motives. And it'll make a great story when I go back to Boston. 'Guess what I did over the weekend? Worked on a murder investigation, at a pig farm!' That'll get attention."

"Did your pal Bill put you up to this? Suggest it? Hint at it?"

"Not really. But from the way he talked, he doesn't have access to a lot of local information, and I gather he's not very welcome in Granford."

"Huh." Had the natives of Granford really taken her side over Detective Marcus's? That merited thinking about. "Okay, I can go introduce myself to Jake Kellogg, tell him I'm a local farmer, and find out if he wants to sell pigs — or pork — to the restaurant. And it's certainly likely that Sam will come up in the course of this conversation. So your role would be . . . ?"

"Faithful sidekick. Everybody needs one of those, right? I can ask lots of stupid questions. Hey, it'll be fun."

"Right, Tonto." Meg wasn't convinced, but neither could she see any harm in it. And she did want to get to know more people in Granford. "It may be muddy, you know. I've got some boots you can borrow — I'll stick them in the trunk."

"Great. Now, what does one wear to call upon a pig farmer? Can we just drop in?"

"I'd wait until church lets out, just in case. Other than that, people around here do a lot of 'just dropping in,' and in case you haven't figured it out, farmers don't get a lot of downtime. The pigs have to eat every day, so he should be around there somewhere."

An hour later they were driving toward the Kellogg farm at the north end of town.

"What's that hill?" Lauren asked. She looked surprisingly interested in her surroundings.

"It's actually a ridge that runs east-west. That's where the town ends — Amherst is on the other side. And the Connecticut

177

River is over that way. I think we're getting close . . . yes, here we are." Meg pointed to a large mailbox with the name "Kellogg" written on it in faded letters. Next to it was a long unpaved drive, leading to a trim and well-maintained farmhouse, with a large barn behind. Meg pulled into the driveway and stopped next to the barn. A man in his fifties, wearing well-worn jeans and a shirt with its sleeves rolled up, came out from the barn and stood waiting. He was followed by a dog, who sat next to his feet. Both looked reasonably friendly, or at least non-threatening.

Meg got out of the car. "Hi. Are you Jake Kellogg?"

"Sure am. And you'd be?"

"Meg Corey. I've got an orchard south of town."

"The old Warren place. You here about the body?"

At least Jake had been the one to bring it up. "In part. I'm also interested in your pigs."

"Okay. And your friend?"

Lauren had climbed out of the car and advanced on Kellogg, her hand outstretched. "Hi, I'm Lauren Converse, Meg's friend from Boston. I just came along for the ride — I've never seen a pig farm."

Jake gave her a long look, and finally smiled. "I'll bet. The pigs are maybe half a mile down that way." He gestured toward the rutted dirt road that led past the barn and beyond. "Think you can walk it? We can talk along the way."

"No problem," Meg said, relieved. "And thanks for being willing to talk to us. I'm sure you've already given your story to the police. And the press?"

"Yes to the first, no to the second. I thought that might be who you ladies were. But I guess I'm not photogenic enough for our local paper." He smiled, deepening the crow's feet by his eyes. "Let's go, then."

As Lauren picked her way among the ruts, she asked, "It wasn't the pigs . . . ?"

"That killed him? No way." Jake set a brisk pace, and Meg had to hurry to keep up. "That's a myth. Pigs might've nosed around a little, to find out what a dead guy was doing in their wallow, but that's about it."

"Is farming your main occupation?" Meg asked.

"Heck, no — I couldn't make a living at it even if I tried. I'm a construction engineer for a company over in Springfield."

"Then why the pigs?"

"Sentiment, mostly. I've got generations of farmers behind me who worked this land,

179

and I kind of hate to see it end. Besides, I like pigs. They're smart, they're cleaner than you'd think, and they're not hard to manage."

"Do you sell them?"

Jake sighed. "Enough to keep my numbers down. There are a couple of restaurants in Amherst that buy the meat. I let somebody else do the killing and dressing."

Meg felt obscurely relieved. It would be hard, she thought, to kill an animal you'd raised. Apples didn't inspire the same feelings, even when you bit into one. "Have you heard about the new restaurant opening in town?" She hoped "opening" was still true.

"Sure. Hard not to, what with their chef being found dead here and all. You saying they might want pigs?"

"I'd like to talk about it. You didn't see Sam?"

"Nope, not when he was alive. Of course, I'm not around all day. But it does seem kind of wrong to wander around a person's property without permission."

And to die on it, Meg added silently. "We think he was looking for providers for the restaurant. Didn't the police mention that?"

"Might've, but since I never met the man, it didn't make much difference. Here we are."

Meg looked out over a gently sloping field dotted with what looked like little tents. The field was bordered on two sides by sparse forest, on the third by the lane where they stood, which continued on past the pig field. The whole was enclosed with a sturdy wire fence, at least three feet high, and in good repair. She looked around but couldn't see any houses, not even Jake's farmhouse. She noted that there was a muddy patch at the lowest corner, and she thought she detected a pungent whiff of pig manure. There were perhaps fifteen pigs wandering through the field; maybe half had turned to look at the human intruders, and a few of those were ambling toward the fence for a closer look.

"Tell me about the pigs," Meg opened.

"What do you want to know?"

"Assume I don't know anything about them, which is pretty much true. For a start, I didn't know you could raise them in an open field. What are all those little buildings?"

"Pigs need shelter. They can sunburn, you know. Those shelters are called pig arks, and they've got bedding inside. You move them around now and then, to let the ground recover. Pigs keep their dung away from their living areas, as you can see."

"What do they eat?"

"Mostly grass. It's a good deal — they keep the grass down, and they churn it up with their feet. Their dung helps fertilize it. I supplement their diet with some feed, but I don't have to do it every day. Heck, sometimes I come out just to talk to them. They're good company." He looked at Meg and Lauren, trying to gauge their interest. "And if you're thinking about them as food, a pig raised like this tastes better. They grow slower, which lets the fat develop. You know, sometimes I feed 'em apples. If you end up with a bunch of windfalls you can't sell, I'll be happy to take them."

Meg smiled. "I might. This will be my first crop, so I don't know what I'm going to have, but I'd love to let you have some. Would you be willing to sell pigs to the restaurant?"

"If they can pay. I have to cover my costs, but maybe we could work something out. Tell 'em to call me."

Meg felt a surge of warmth — she'd actually done something to help Nicky and Brian. It was quickly squashed by Lauren's next question. "Where'd they find the body?"

Jake grimaced, but answered, "Over in the corner there, in the muck."

Lauren strode over to the corner. "The

182

guy was found inside the fence? He would have had to get over it, right? Why would he do that, do you think?"

"No idea. He was a city guy, right? Most city folk keep as far away as possible from livestock. Heck, a lot of the restaurant people, they don't even know how to break down an animal. They like to buy their meat all neatly packaged. Maybe your restaurant guy wanted to get up close and personal with the pigs he planned to cook. Or maybe we'll never know."

"I met him a couple of times," Meg said. "He seemed very enthusiastic, so I could see him wanting to know the whole history behind the pigs he bought."

"Did they find his car?" Lauren said.

"Police asked about that," Jake replied. "Wanted to know if it was in my driveway, or down this lane. I told 'em I hadn't seen it — I think they found it down the road a ways. Looks like he came in on foot."

"What do *you* think happened to him?" Lauren asked.

"Don't know. Best I can figure, he might've been leaning on the fence and had some kind of fit and pitched over it, then passed out. He was a big guy, wasn't he?"

"He was," Meg agreed. And a strong one.

183

But apparently Jake hadn't noticed, and the police hadn't shared, the information about the muddy footprint on Sam's back. She wasn't about to fill him in. Privileged information — isn't that what they called it? Which meant mainly that Meg was privileged to form the mental image of an incapacitated Sam being held down in this otherwise peaceful meadow until he died. *Too bad pigs couldn't testify.*

Another thought occurred to her. "Did you touch him at all, make sure he wasn't still alive?"

"I could tell it was too late — the guy's face was smack in the mud. I didn't need to get too close. I just called Art Preston and waited for him to show up."

So he hadn't seen the footprint? Meg wondered. "What would the pigs have done? You said they were curious."

"They probably wandered over and checked him out. He would have been kind of hard to ignore, even if you were a pig. When I got here, they were kind of milling around, upset."

Seeing the site of Sam's death for the first time, Meg realized that if someone *had* held Sam down inside the fenced field, then that someone had to be familiar with pigs, or at least not afraid of them. Did that narrow

184

down the list of possible suspects? Didn't that eliminate Nicky and Brian? They were unfamiliar with farm life. Or, Meg amended, she knew that Nicky was. What about Brian? He'd never said much about where he came from. Were there any other suspects? She refused to believe the farmer standing in front of her could have had anything to do with it. But who did that leave? Half of Granford and beyond, but no one with a known motive. But apparently with some knowledge about pigs — she'd have to think about that.

"Seen enough yet?" Jake asked.

"I'm good," Lauren said promptly. "You ready to go, Meg?"

"I guess. What else do you raise here, Jake, besides pigs?"

"Not much anymore. Enough vegetables for the family . . ." Small talk took them back to the house. Jake stopped in front of it. "You want some coffee, something to eat? My wife makes a mean cobbler."

Lauren seemed ready to decline, so Meg stepped in quickly. "That would be lovely, if it's no trouble."

"Nope. Besides, she'd be pissed if she missed a chance to meet you, Meg. You're kind of a local celebrity."

Meg flinched inwardly, but smiled outwardly. "I'd be happy to meet her."

An hour later, full of coffee and a cobbler that had lived up to Jake's billing, Meg and Lauren managed to extricate themselves and head back to Meg's house.

"And what did we learn from that exercise?" Lauren asked.

Meg checked her tone for sarcasm, and decided that Lauren was serious. "We learned that Jake Kellogg is a nice guy who raises clean and healthy pigs, and that he might be able to supply some for the restaurant. We learned that my reputation precedes me even in the wilder reaches of Granford. And he doesn't seem to know that Sam was murdered or, at least, not how. You have anything to add?"

"Sure. We know that just about anyone who was ambulatory could have followed Sam and offed him, and there was nobody to see it. And we learned that whoever it was must know something about pigs. I can't see *me* climbing into a field full of pigs, no matter how mad I was at the guy I was chasing. I'd find some way to do the deed outside the fence, maybe dump him in after."

"You noticed that, too? So that suggests that the killer was familiar with the layout of Jake's farm, and knew something about pigs. Which almost has to mean that he's local. Damn."

"Exactly."

13

"I really hate to go," Lauren said, leaning against her car, her keys dangling in her hand.

"So don't," Meg countered.

Lauren sighed. "I'd better hang on to my job, as long as I have one. But I'm jealous, Meg."

"Over this? A drafty old house, a barn that would love to fall down, and a batch of trees that I know all too little about?"

"At least you have a place here, people who know you. In Boston, if I died in my apartment, it might be a week until somebody missed me, and the neighbors wouldn't notice until my corpse started to stink."

Meg felt a spurt of guilt. How often had she called Lauren, now that they didn't see each other regularly? Once a month? What kind of friend was she? "I know what you mean, although this place does take some

188

getting used to; everybody knows who you are and what you're doing from day to day. I'm not going to say it's better than what you've got. I mean, you've got so much going on in Boston — movies, plays, music, lectures, restaurants."

"Yeah, none of which I ever have time to enjoy because I'm working all the time. Besides, you're going to have a real restaurant soon. And Northampton was terrific. Don't sell it short, Meg, at least not on my account. You've given me a lot to think about."

"You can come back whenever you want, as long as you're willing to pick apples."

"Fair enough. Okay, I'm leaving now. Really. Thanks, Meg." In a move that surprised Meg, Lauren grabbed her in a quick hard hug before getting into her car.

Meg watched as Lauren turned her car around and headed out of the driveway, back toward the highway, back toward the big city. It was clear that Lauren wasn't happy, but Meg wasn't sure what she could do about it. Was she happy herself? Maybe she was. As she had told Lauren, she was enjoying the challenges that the house and the orchard presented. She was getting used to forming different kinds of relationships with people, and far faster than she would have in the city. Maybe she was too close to see the changes in herself, but Lauren had certainly noticed them.

"She take off?" Bree's voice startled Meg. She turned to see her leaning on the door-jamb. "I wanted to give you and your friend some space," Bree continued. "You don't see her often."

"No, I don't. It's hard to keep in touch, since we're going in such different directions. It was good to see her, though."

"She looked kind of frazzled to me," Bree commented.

"She did. The usual stuff — job worries, man worries. I think she had a good chance to unwind here." If you didn't include tagging along on an ad hoc murder inquiry, but then, Lauren had initiated that, hadn't she? "So what's up?"

Bree straightened up. "We need to go over how you can tell when your apples are ripe."

"Already?"

"Yup. It's been pretty warm lately, and you've got some varieties that could be ready to pick within the month, so you should know what you're looking for."

"You want to do it now?"

"Why not? The weather's good. And since other things keep popping up, we'd better cover it when we have the time."

190

Meg followed Bree inside, and supplied with iced tea, they sat at the kitchen table. "What do I need to know?" Meg asked.

"We've got to inventory your equipment. You know, crates, picking buckets."

"I thought you said the pickers usually had their own buckets."

"Sometimes, but it never hurts to have extra. Have I explained how you estimate your crop yield?"

Meg sighed inwardly: yet more things she didn't know. "Not lately."

"Okay. You've got to factor in the age of your trees, what variety they are, how many you've got per acre. Your orchard is low-density, so you should get maybe fifteen to twenty bushels per tree, which comes out to anywhere up to one thousand boxes per acre. Christopher did a rough estimate right after crop set, but we need to do another one, now that we're past 'June drop.' "

"What's June drop?"

"Trees always shed some fruit early on, in June. It's normal, so you don't try to make any estimates until that's over."

"Thanks. You said a thousand boxes per acre? And I've got fifteen acres?"

Bree smiled. "Relax. That doesn't mean you need fifteen thousand boxes. Your picking season runs from August to November, and different trees ripen at different times. And they don't always bear evenly. You've got some biannuals out there, which produce every other year. So you can get by with less than that — you sell one batch of your apples and that frees up boxes for the next batch. You'll need orchard boxes for the field — ones with handholds so you can pick them up — and you need some bulk bins. If you're selling to a major producer, they'll probably want you to use their bins, for uniformity."

"So why am I building storage units, if I'm selling them as fast as I pick them?"

"It's a balancing act. There's almost always a lag time between picking and sale, and you've got to figure out when to pick if you know you're going to hold them for a bit. Too early, the apples can end up sour, tough, starchy; too late and they're overripe and mealy. Some apples hold better than others, or even improve with storage. When you're picking, you've got a window to work in, from maybe a week to up to three weeks."

"You're going to tell me when to pick what, right?"

Bree nodded impatiently. "Of course, but you should know how to tell when your apples are ready." Bree proceeded to outline several processes for testing ripeness, until Meg's head started to spin. There were so many individual decisions that required expertise she didn't have. After a while she reached information overload and held up a hand. "Look, Bree, I admit I know nothing, and I'll do what you tell me. And this means as much to you as it does to me: if you want to have a job next year, we have to sell a decent crop this year."

"That's the plan. I don't mean to dump all this on you at once, Meg, but you've got to be thinking about it, and about who's buying the apples, because that affects when we pick. Sooner rather than later."

"I hear you. I need to talk to Christopher again. And if you have any ideas, or hear of anything, let me know. Would it be easiest to just go with a bigger local market chain?"

Bree shrugged. "Probably not an option — your crop's not big enough to interest them, and your harvest is going to be too spread out, timewise. I'd go after the specialty markets, farmers' markets, maybe restaurants. If all else fails, you can make the whole mess into cider."

"I can?"

"Well, no, not you personally, but you can go to one of the local cider houses and they'll do it."

Meg laughed. "Let's just get one harvest in and see how that goes before we pulp it all, okay?"

"Right. Just wanted you to know what was going on."

"And I appreciate it, and I agree with you — I *should* know all this. Just not all at once. So, on to easier decisions. Any ideas for dinner?"

Meg and Bree were chopping vegetables side by side when the phone rang. Meg dried her hands and answered.

"Meg?" Nicky said in a breathless voice. "You know that Seth wants Brian and me to talk to the selectmen on Tuesday night, sort of semiformally, right? Kind of, meet them and chat, but also give them some details about what we're planning, the permits that we want for the restaurant, so we look like we know what we're doing. Could you go over the presentation with us, maybe? I don't know the people around here, or how'll they'll react . . ."

"Sure, I'll be happy to help."

"Great! Thank you, Meg. I know you've got to be busy, and I really appreciate it. Can you come by tomorrow morning, maybe around ten?"

"I guess so." And she could tell Nicky

about her conversation with Jake Kellogg while she was there.

"Great! See you then!"

When Meg hung up the phone, Bree said, "Let me guess — Nicky?"

"Yes. She wants me to help her review the restaurant plan they're presenting to the Select Board. You don't approve?"

Bree snorted. "Those two are so helpless! It's like, 'Let's take Daddy's money and open a restaurant! We like to cook, right? It should be easy.' And then they ask everybody else to do the work. They're setting themselves up for disappointment."

"You think it won't work?" Meg sat down again and faced Bree.

"Hey, I think it's a great idea. I just think they're naive, is all. They're asking you to help out, and Seth, and how many other people? They just aren't prepared for what they're doing. Look, I took a food services course at UMass, just to see what the markets were like, where crops actually went. A restaurant is a business, you know? It's not just, 'Gee, I love to cook, let's open our own place.' "

"I see what you're saying, and I agree, up to a point. But what's wrong with asking for help? This is a small town, and we need to work together. And it's a good way to build relationships with future customers, isn't it?" Meg wondered briefly if Bree herself was too concerned about being independent and self-sufficient, but she wasn't about to mention that now.

"Maybe. I don't know. But you've got plenty of your own stuff to do, without babysitting Nicky and Brian."

"And I'm relying on you to keep me on track there. The orchard comes first, no question — and if you need me here, tell me and I'll be here. Look, I appreciate your bringing this up, and maybe I'll have a better sense of where they really are, how ready they are, after I talk to them tomorrow. I promise I won't let myself get sucked into their problems. Okay?"

"Okay."

They had almost finished eating when the phone rang again: Seth this time.

"Hi, Seth — what's up? I hear Nicky's getting ready for the Select Board meeting this week," Meg said. "She wants me to go over their presentation with them. This isn't a big formal thing, is it?"

"No, not at all. Of course, in this town a high turnout is maybe ten people. It's good that Nicky and Brian want to be prepared, but nobody's going to pick apart whatever they have to say. It'll be fine."

"I'm sure it will."

"Anyway, I just called to let you know that Edna's coming in tomorrow to talk to them."

"Oh, good. That's one less thing they'll have to worry about, if it works out. Thanks again, Seth."

When Meg hung up, Bree said, "You all sure do live in each other's pockets. Everybody's got their nose in everybody else's business."

"It's called neighbors helping neighbors. Try it — you might like it."

"Maybe."

14

Meg arrived at the restaurant a few minutes before ten to find the place bustling. The interior framing was done, and Sheetrock was going up. She peeked around behind the stairs — yes, even the small washrooms now had walls and fixtures. Every time she stopped by, she could see more tangible progress, and she thought everything looked great so far. Maybe the September deadline wasn't so unrealistic after all.

Nicky emerged from the kitchen to greet her, talking a mile a minute. "Hi, Meg. Can I get you some coffee? Thanks so much for coming. I really appreciate it, and so does Brian. He can put together the numbers, but you know these people. Better than we do, at least! And now Seth's friend Edna is coming over, and I don't really know how to interview people — and jeez, I've got to get some wait-staff lined up soon — but I feel so scattered because there's so much going on, and there's a shipment of furniture due today and Brian said he had errands to do, and —"

Meg held up a hand. "Nicky! Take a breath. The place looks good, and I'm sure this woman is perfectly nice, if Seth recommends her."

"I know, I know. But I'm not sure what questions to ask her, and I don't know what kind of pay she'll expect, and —"

"How about that coffee?" Meg wondered just how many cups Nicky had already had, but she could use some herself, if only to keep up. She followed Nicky into the kitchen. "You know, I really love this space. Have you had a chance to test-drive it?"

"Some, mostly to make sure everything works. Which is does, so far." Nicky handed Meg a cup. "I hope it's big enough. We had to balance the space we had against the number of customers we expect, and then there was the budget. So it's not exactly what I wanted, but pretty close. Of course, so far here I've only been cooking for two or three at a time, and I could do that with a hotplate. The real test will be a full house, but that's still a ways off."

"Sooner than you think," Meg replied. "Bree keeps telling me my harvest is starting any minute, which scares me. I haven't got buyers lined up yet, and I'm not even sure where to start. Tell me, how do you, as a restaurateur, decide what to order?"

"That's easy: what's local, what's fresh, what's good."

"Sounds simple. But how do you plan menus when you don't know what you'll have on hand?"

"You do have to be flexible, and know your foods. But that's half the fun of being a chef — improvising. I wouldn't want to run a big place and have to turn out the same boring stuff day after day. I saw enough of that in Boston. And no way do I want to use prepackaged stuff. You'd be amazed at what some of the big restaurants get away with, because people don't know any better."

"The chefs, or the patrons?"

"Both. The chefs settle for what's easy, like canned sauces, and the patrons accept it because that's what they expect. You have to educate both sides."

Meg hesitated a moment before saying, "I've got one piece of good news for you: Jake Kellogg said he'd be willing to talk to you about supplying pork."

"Isn't that the place . . ." Nicky's voice trailed off.

"Yes, but Seth says he's the best supplier

around. If it bothers you, you don't have to use him."

Nicky squared her shoulders. "It's okay. I can handle it. And thanks, Meg." Talking about food, which she clearly loved, seemed to have calmed Nicky down, and she didn't flinch when Seth's voice called out from the front, "Anybody home?"

Nicky gave Meg a quick smile. "Here we go!"

Meg followed her to the front room, where Seth waited with Edna Blakely, the potential sous chef. She was an older black woman, with close-cropped hair, mainly silver. She was nearly as tall as Seth, and taller than Nicky. Her eyes were wary.

"Hi, Nicky, Meg. This is Edna Blakely. Edna, Nicky Czarnecki. Is Brian here, Nicky?"

Nicky strode forward and extended her hand. "It's good to meet you, Edna. No, Brian had something to do in Springfield, but he might get here before we're done. Why don't we sit in the kitchen? As you can see, Edna, we're still just setting up out here — I thought we should get the kitchen right first."

"Pleased to meet you, Nicky. And you got that right — the kitchen's the heart of the place. Nice space you've got here. How many covers?"

"We're thinking two dinner seatings, at least forty each." Nicky led the way back to the kitchen and doled out coffee to the newcomers. They all found seats, with Nicky and Edna across from each other at one end, Meg and Seth at the other end.

"Okay, Edna, tell me your background," Nicky began.

Edna's expression gave little away, but Meg noticed that she kept twisting her hands in front of her, maybe unconsciously. How badly did she want this job?

"I didn't grow up around here," Edna began. "Came with my husband, Luther. He was a restless sort, never could figure out what he wanted to do. We lived in Ohio before here, and Tennessee before that. He's gone now. I always worked, some factory work, back a good few years. Then the Millers opened up that diner on the highway — you remember, right, Seth?"

"I do. We used to go there Sundays after church, for breakfast."

"I'd always cooked, but whatever training I got, I got at Millers' diner. Open eighteen hours a day, breakfast, lunch, and dinner."

"Did the Millers do most of the cooking?"

"Early on, yeah. When they got older, I took over more and more of it."

"What was the menu like?"

" 'Bout like what you'd expect for a diner — sandwiches, hamburgers, big breakfasts, served all day. We did a couple of daily specials — I was pretty much responsible for the idea, and then for cooking 'em. Got to be pretty popular, too."

"What happened to the diner? It's closed?"

"Five years now. Mrs. Miller died, and Mr. Miller kind of lost interest. He tried to sell it, but nobody wanted it — he'd let it get pretty run down, over the years. I tried to put together enough cash to buy him out, but Luther didn't leave me much, and the bank wasn't about to help, so in the end it closed. It was out where that gas station is now."

"And what have you been doing since, Edna?"

Meg suppressed a smile: Nicky was trying so hard to be professional and dignified as she interviewed a woman old enough to be her mother. She sneaked a glance at Seth, who had been quiet, allowing Nicky to handle things.

"This and that," Edna said. "Mostly prep cook for a couple of places around here. I can give you names, if you want. But I'm tired of chopping up stuff for other people's dishes. I can do more. What you looking for, Nicky?" Edna gave Nicky a direct, almost challenging, look.

Nicky gave a small sigh. "I don't know how much Seth has told you, but here's the story. My husband, Brian, and I moved here with a friend of ours, Sam Anderson. I'm the head chef, and Brian's the manager, front of house, and the numbers guy. Sam was going to be my sous chef and forager. You've probably heard that Sam . . . died."

"Found dead in Kellogg's pigpen. Somebody kill him?"

Nicky looked startled by the direct question. "Maybe. Is that a problem, Edna?"

"Nope. I didn't know your man. I do know the Kelloggs, though — good people. Good pigs."

"How do you know that?"

"Used to be he'd smoke some bacon, now and then. When he did, I grabbed it up for the diner."

"Ah." Nicky looked speculatively at Edna, but it wasn't an unfriendly look. "Tell me, how would you see working with me in this kitchen?"

Edna took her time looking around. "Good layout, plenty of room. Your husband's gonna cover the front of the house?

Because that's not what I'm good at."

"Yes, Brian's going to do that. Can you handle suppliers?"

"Sure can, no problem. But listen, I'd want to do more than chop up your onions. I want to cook." Edna's chin came up.

Nicky studied Edna's face. Finally she said, "Show me."

"Now?"

"Why not?"

"With what you got on hand?"

Nicky nodded. "Exactly. Show me what you can do."

Edna thought for a moment, then nodded in response. "Okay. But can you all clear out for a bit, let me get a feel for the place without everybody watching?"

"Fair enough. Edna, the kitchen's all yours."

When they'd left the room, Edna closed the door behind them.

"This is an interesting approach, Nicky," Meg said. "What are you looking for? And what the heck does she have in there to work with?"

"What I really want to know is what her approach to food is. I've been stocking up on basics — we've been eating here for a few weeks, so she's got more than a can of beans and some bread to work with. I hope

205

I didn't insult her, Seth, but if she's a real cook, she'll understand."

"She seemed to take it well. Look, Nicky, she needs the job, but you aren't under any obligation to give it to her if she's not a good fit."

"Thanks, Seth. I'd hate to hurt her feelings, but I need to know what she can do."

Seth nodded. "Now, what do you want to know about the selectmen's meeting?"

"Oh, goodness, I don't know. What do I need to know? Who's going to be there, what they need to hear. Are we going to run into any problems? Who's in charge of permits? Is there an inspector? What questions are we supposed to ask?"

"Slow down!" Seth laughed. "Look, there are three selectmen — me, Tom Moody, and Caroline Goldthwaite. We're all elected. The town secretary may be there, to take the minutes, even though we videotape the meetings these days. At some point you'll have to talk to the town assessor, but that can wait. There should be some outsiders — local citizens — there, mostly those who are curious about what you're doing with the place. And the handful who believe in attending every public meeting on principle."

"Are they going to ask about . . . Sam's

death? Are people really saying it was murder?"

Seth shrugged. "Maybe, although it would surprise me. Mostly they'll want to know about what kind of food you're planning to serve, and whether they can afford it. As for your other question, I'd guess the cat's pretty much out of the bag, no matter what Detective Marcus may think."

"Huh. Well, what *can* people in Granford afford?" Nicky asked.

"Hard to say. Are you aiming for a casual, local kind of place, or a special occasion place?"

"Somewhere in the middle, I think. I mean, I want people to feel welcome, and I don't want them to think they have to dress up to walk through the door, but I want the food to be special. Something that might attract people from Northampton and Amherst, and maybe tourists, but I don't want to price my neighbors out of the place. Is that going to be impossible?"

"Nicky, I honestly don't know. But I think you've got the right idea. If it helps any, we're thinking of including a nonchain lunch place in Granford Grange — that's the new shopping strip south of town — so you wouldn't have to cover that part of things."

"Okay." Nicky chewed her lower lip. "I'm sorry if this sounds kind of vague. I mean, before we got here, I didn't want to get too wedded to any one idea before I actually knew what kind of place we'd have, and even now that we've got this place, I'm still thinking about a lot of things. That's why I can't give a lot of details yet. Can your selectmen help with finding providers?"

"Maybe. You might want to talk to the Agricultural Commission."

"Will they be there?"

"Not this time, but I can put you together with the head of the commission."

The kitchen door opened. "You all ready?" Edna asked.

"That was fast!" Nicky whispered. It hadn't been more than ten minutes since they'd left the kitchen.

Meg didn't know whether Edna's speed was good or bad, but she promised herself to keep an open mind. After all, she liked diner food, but she wasn't sure if that was what Nicky was aiming for.

In the kitchen, Edna had arrayed plates around the table, each with a colorful salad, carefully arranged. They took their seats, and Nicky said, "Tell us what you're serving us, Edna."

Edna stood at the head of the table, her

arms crossed. "Fresh tomatoes, goat cheese — is that from Kibbee's? — and fresh basil, with a mustard vinaigrette."

Meg looked down at her plate, reluctant to spoil the pretty ensemble. It certainly matched anything she'd had back in Boston restaurants. She picked up her fork and took a bite. Lovely balance of flavors: the tomatoes were at the peak of ripeness, the basil was bright and green, the goat cheese was tangy and crumbled into pieces that neither overwhelmed nor disappeared into the other ingredients. She took a second bite, and a third, then looked up to see Nicky's reaction. After all, it was Nicky's opinion that counted.

Nicky was beaming. "Edna, this is terrific. This is exactly what I want. How did you know?"

Edna shrugged, but permitted herself a small smile. "Get good local products, and don't mess 'em up. That's what I do. Glad you like it."

Meg noted that everyone's plate was clean in moments.

Nicky said firmly, "Edna, we can't pay a whole lot, but if we can agree on a salary, I want you to work for me, for us. Are you interested?"

"We can work it out."

"How soon can you start? Because I'd love to have your input on our menus, and where we can get more stuff like this. And you're right — it is Kibbee's cheese. Sam found it, and I think he'd be happy you used it."

"I oughta give notice where I am now, but maybe a week or two? When you thinking on opening?"

"September, we hope."

"Whoa. You don't mess around. But that'll give us a couple of weeks to work things out between us. And I can give you a list of the people I used to buy from. Some of them, they're out of the business now, but most are still around, maybe only to please themselves these days."

"Wonderful. Could we do that now? And then you can meet Brian when he gets back."

Edna agreed, and Seth stood up. "Edna, this was great. I've missed your cooking since the diner closed. Nicky, I've got to run — I'm picking up some lumber in Chicopee. But I'm glad it looks like things will work out with you two."

"Thank you so much, Seth! I'll see you tomorrow night at seven, right? At Town Hall? Oh, Meg, we haven't even had a minute to go over the numbers. Can you stay a bit longer?"

"Sure," Meg said. "Just let me see Seth out and I'll be back."

Meg followed Seth out to the parking lot. "That looks like a match made in heaven, Seth. What a great thought, putting them together."

"I've known Edna for years — she's been wasted on the places she's working now."

"Even I can see that. What really happened to the diner? Wasn't there enough business to make it viable?"

"No, there was. It was a local hangout, and not just for high school kids. But the Millers let it go too far, and Edna couldn't scrape together enough money to buy it and fix it up. I'll have to admit the town wasn't much help — they figured the gas station and the convenience store would bring in more money than the diner, which is probably true. But people still miss the diner."

"Too bad 'quality of life' doesn't come with a dollar value attached."

"Exactly."

"So I'll see you at the meeting?"

"Of course. Now I'd better get back in there and help Nicky polish up their pitch."

15

When Meg arrived at Town Hall for the meeting of the Granford selectmen, she was surprised to see that most of the adjacent parking lot was filled. She wondered if it was because Nicky and Brian were unveiling their plans for the restaurant, and if so, how the word had gotten out. There was no local press, although Granford meetings were listed in the Springfield paper. E-mail blast? Phone tree? Or good old-fashioned word of mouth?

Once inside, Meg followed the buzz of voices to the meeting room on the first floor. The selectmen sat at a table at the head of the room, their name plates in front of them. About thirty folding chairs had been arrayed in rows facing them, taking up most of the available space. Two-thirds of the chairs were already filled, ten minutes before the meeting was scheduled to begin. Meg scanned the group for familiar faces and was happy to see Gail Selden from the Historical Society, who waved and pointed to an empty seat next to her.

Meg slid along the row and sat. "Quite a turnout, isn't it?" she said.

Gail grinned. "Obviously we don't get a lot of excitement around here. And people are certainly curious about what's going on. You've been inside the building after they started renovations, right? What's it like?"

"Nice. They've kept it simple. I for one think it's going to be a real asset. You have any idea what the rest of the town thinks?"

"I haven't heard anything negative. Too bad about the murder, though."

"So people are saying it's murder now?" Meg asked, troubled. *When had it become public knowledge?*

"What else could it be?" Gail replied. "Young guy just keels over of natural causes in a pigsty? Nobody's buying that. What did the cops say? Do they have any idea who did it?"

Meg shook her head. "Not that I know of, although they're not likely to tell me." Would Marcus be more willing to share now that he'd gotten so friendly with Lauren? "I'm happy it hasn't discouraged Nicky and Brian."

"They're really a cute couple, but do they

213

know what they're doing?" Gail asked in a low voice.

"As far as food goes, I'd say yes. On the business side, I don't know, although I understand that Brian has at least taken business courses. And I don't know how deep their pockets are. The kitchen's finished anyway, and they're working on the front of the house. And they've hired Edna Blakely to help with the cooking."

"Oh, good. She deserves a break."

"You know her, too?"

"Meg, I've lived here forever. I know everybody, living and dead. Speaking of dead, how's the cataloging coming?"

"Slowly, but I really enjoy it. It's a nice change from working in the orchard and on the house. The problem is, I keep getting sidetracked by interesting documents, so I'm probably not getting as much done as quickly as I could. And I have to take advantage of the good weather when I can, for both the stuff that needs doing in the orchard, and the outside of the house. I can't afford to paint the whole thing yet, so I'm kind of slapping paint on the worst parts, like the window frames."

"I hear you, and I'm not in any hurry on the cataloging. Consider whatever gems you find one of the perks. Anything interest-

214

ing lately?"

"A nice old map of the town. Don't you love it when they draw in not only the houses but the trees? And it's so kind of those old mapmakers to label who lived where."

"Yeah, they took that seriously in the old days. Of course, there were fewer people then, and they pretty much stayed put for generations. Nowadays the map would be out of date by the time it was printed." Gail looked toward the front of the room. "Well, looks like things are about to start."

Tom Moody had stood up in the front of the room, and glared at the group in front of him until they quieted. He nodded toward the high school kid at the back of the room, who flipped a switch on the video recording system. "The meeting of the Select Board of Granford is now in session. All three board members are present, as is the chair of our finance committee, Eli Nash."

He and the others dealt with some ordinary business items and fielded a few questions from the floor. Seth's comments were generally short and upbeat; Caroline Goldthwaite was well informed but seemed to radiate an air of constant disapproval. After about half an hour, Seth said, "We have an

215

unusual item on tonight's agenda. Let me introduce Nicky and Brian Czarnecki, who have bought the Stebbins place across the street, and who are planning to open a restaurant there in a couple of months. Brian, Nicky, why don't you come up and tell us about it?"

Brian and Nicky had been seated in the front row; now they moved to a pair of chairs at the end of the selectmen's table. Meg wondered how they were going to handle their presentation, and crossed her fingers. Nicky looked nervous — she was clearly more at home in front of a stove than in front of a group. Meg sneaked a quick look at her neighbors in the audience, who all appeared interested. At least they weren't hostile. She settled back in her chair to listen to Brian, who had begun to speak.

"Thank you for inviting us to speak at your meeting. We haven't had the opportunity to meet most of you — we've been busy working on the building — but we're looking forward to getting to know our neighbors soon. I'm Brian Czarnecki, and this is my wife, Nicky." Nicky waved and smiled nervously. "We're from Boston most recently, but we wanted to get away from the competition among restaurants there, so we looked around for an area where we'd like to live and work, and found this town. There's not a lot of competition here."

Some members of the audience laughed.

Brian went on, "Nicky's the cook in the family, and I'll be handling the business side and the front of the restaurant. This is our first venture on our own, although between us we've worked in something like seven different restaurants. Right, Nicky?" She nodded. "So we're kind of learning as we go. I know we need approvals from the town, permits and that kind of thing, so we wanted to give you a chance to get to know us and to ask any questions you might have."

"What kind of food you going to cook?" a voice behind Meg asked.

"Nicky, you want to take that?" Brian said.

Nicky stood up, somewhat reluctantly. "First and foremost, food that people here will want to eat, and can afford." Another laugh rippled through the crowd. "What we want to do is to use the freshest local produce, and make simple healthy food at reasonable prices. Nothing too fancy — we'll leave that to Amherst and Northampton. But we hope we can attract people from all over." She swallowed, then resumed. "What's more, we're hoping that you all can help us with supplies. I know there are

217

farmers' cooperatives around here, but I'd love to know what grows right here in Granford. And that includes what moos and swims and anything else. Ideally we'd like to see you harvest it in the morning and deliver it to our door the same day. Or we'll even pick it up."

"You gonna have a liquor license?" said a female voice Meg didn't recognize.

Brian answered that. "We've applied for one. But don't worry that we're going to have a roadhouse with a lot of drunken patrons staggering out onto the town green in the middle of the night. Our place is going to be about the food, not about drinking."

"What about the dead guy?" a male voice from the rear asked.

There was a moment of awkward silence until Brian swallowed, then spoke. "Sam Anderson was a good friend of ours, and we'd hoped he would be part of this restaurant. We were deeply saddened by his death, but we believe he would have wanted us to go forward."

"I heard he was a fag," the same voice said.

Seth stood up quickly. "Jim, that statement is both insulting and inappropriate in this meeting."

Meg looked over her shoulder to see who

was talking — a short and clearly angry man at the back of the room, already on his feet, his arms crossed. "Why? You think I want to eat in a place with people like that doing the cooking?"

Nicky and Brian exchanged glances. Seth stared at the speaker, his expression carefully neutral. "Jim, I'm going to have to ask you to leave. You have a right to your opinion, but it has no place here."

Meg turned back toward the front and stared at her hands. Who was Jim, and why did he have an axe to grind? Why was anyone's sexual preference relevant to their cooking? And did Jim represent a real — and bigoted — faction of Granford's population?

Jim glared at Seth, then turned and stormed out, all but knocking over his flimsy chair. Seth waited until he heard the front door slam before he addressed the small crowd. "I'm sorry about that. If Jim has issues about any one individual, he can stay away from the restaurant. But I hope the rest of you don't share his opinion."

Nicky, her cheeks flushed, spoke unexpectedly. "Sam was one of the nicest people I've ever known. He was warm and funny, and he was a good friend. So if any of you have a problem with us working with a person who isn't just like you, you'd better let us know now."

Meg was surprised when Gail spoke up, "Nicky, as far as I'm concerned, the only important thing here is the quality of your food. We really need a restaurant in this town, and what you're planning sounds great."

"Thank you. I'm sorry, I don't know your name?" Nicky responded.

"I'm Gail Selden. I'm head of the Historical Society, among other things. If you want to know anything about the history of your building or the town, just ask."

"Thank you, Gail. I'd like that. We do want to keep the place pretty authentic — not that we can afford to make a lot of changes anyway. Does anyone else have any questions?"

"What do the police think about the death?" another male voice from the rear threw in.

When Seth made another move to divert attention, Brian stopped him. "I want to answer that. We don't know anything more than you do, I'm sorry to say. We've told the state police everything we know. Listen, this isn't the way we wanted to start out with the restaurant, but it happened. I hope you all won't hold it against us. And if you have

220

any other questions, or ideas, or whatever, you know where to find us — right across the street. Please, feel free to drop in and talk to us. We're there all the time. We're looking forward to getting to know you all."

Seth took charge again. "Thank you, Brian, Nicky. I know there will be some issues about permits and the like that will come before this board again, so it's good that you've had a chance to let people learn something about you. Is there any new business?" Seth looked at the other board members. Tom Moody shook his head "no"; Caroline Goldthwaite stared straight ahead, her face blank. She had expressed reservations about the restaurant earlier, and had sat in stony silence since Brian had begun to talk. What was she thinking now? Meg wondered. She didn't look happy. But at least she wasn't actively speaking out against it.

After a few more details, Tom Moody declared the meeting adjourned. People stood, stretched, then drifted out, except for Gail, who made her way to the front to greet Nicky and Brian. "Welcome to Granford. I meant to come by and introduce myself sooner, but it's summer, and my kids are out of school. You two don't have kids, do you?"

Nicky smiled. "Not yet. I think we're going to be a little busy for the next few years anyway. But thank you for introducing yourself. I would love to know more about the building and the town. Maybe we could put together some historic dishes?"

"That's a nice idea, although it may be a challenge to find anything like recipes. Most of the women around here were farm wives, and they didn't write down a lot, just kept all of their recipes in their heads. Meg, would you keep your eye out for anything like that in the archives?" Meg nodded.

"Wasn't there a cookbook published recently about old family recipes?" Nicky asked. "By a couple of sisters in Boston? That's exactly what they did — tracked down a lot of scribbled notes and file cards and put them together with some history. It would be nice to know for sure how people cooked in the days before preservatives — heck, even before refrigerators. Would people around here like that kind of food, Gail?"

"If it tastes good, sure. Just don't poison anybody." She immediately looked contrite. "Oops, that was a stupid thing to say. I was thinking of salmonella or something like that. Look, I've got to go — my husband's home with the kids. But it was good to meet you, and I'll look forward to talking with you again." Gail beat a hasty retreat, just as Seth disengaged himself from a conversation with Tom Moody and walked over to where Meg, Nicky, and Brian were standing.

"I apologize for Jim — he has a brother who's gay, and he's not too happy about it," Seth said.

"I hope you're not going to tell me you've got a whole bunch of homophobes in Granford," Nicky said dubiously.

"No, of course not. Jim's the exception, and that's personal. Aside from him, I think the meeting went pretty well, overall. Although" — Seth dropped his voice and looked around — "Mrs. Goldthwaite doesn't seem to have warmed to the idea much. If she had her way, nothing around here would ever change."

"Is that going to be a problem?" Brian asked.

"I don't think so. Tom's definitely on board, so you have a majority. But it would be easier for all of us if Mrs. Goldthwaite accepted the whole idea. She has loyal supporters in town."

They left together, Nicky and Brian crossing the now-empty road toward the restaurant, hand in hand. Meg and Seth turned toward the parking lot alongside the Town Hall.

"You don't see any problems, do you?" Meg asked.

Seth shook his head. "Not really. They sell themselves well."

"I thought so, too. Sam's death isn't too much of an obstacle?"

"I don't think so. He wasn't around long enough for anyone to get to know him. Now, if someone had dumped his body in the middle of the town green, it might be different. But since he died under muddled circumstances on the edge of town, most people haven't paid much attention. Don't hold it against them — he just wasn't on their radar."

"I can understand that. Well, I'd better get back and —"

Meg was interrupted by the sound of raised voices coming from the direction of the restaurant. Seth set off in that direction immediately, and Meg followed. As they came nearer, it was clear that the noise was coming from one person — a drunken one, whom both Nicky and Brian were trying to hush.

"No!" howled the man, "I will not shut up. It's you and this backwater town that killed him! And everybody just says, oh, it's some queer from the big city, and forgets about him. It's not right!" The man appeared close to tears. Despite his slight build, he seemed to have a wiry strength that Brian was having trouble controlling.

"Derek, you're drunk," Brian said flatly. "Come inside before you wake up the whole neighborhood."

"Why should I care about these hicks?" Derek said, volume undiminished. "They killed him, one way or another."

"Problem?" Seth asked quietly when they were in earshot.

Nicky answered, "Derek is Sam's ex-boyfriend from Boston. He's upset."

"I can see that. Brian, let me give you a hand." Seth took hold of one of Derek's arms, Brian the other, and with surprisingly little fuss they steered Derek into the restaurant, leaving Nicky and Meg alone on the porch.

"I feel terrible about Derek," Nicky began.

"Don't worry about it," Meg said quickly. "Did you invite him here?"

"No! I tried to reach him when Sam died, but I couldn't. Apparently he just heard about it. He was really pissed that it was the police who told him, not us."

"Were they still together?"

Nicky shook her head. "No, it was over

225

before Sam came out here, and I think Derek was on a beach somewhere with his new guy, which is why he didn't hear for so long. But now I think he's wallowing in guilt or something — and decided to take it out on us."

"Don't worry. I'm sure once he's sobered up, he'll settle down." Meg wasn't sure if she believed her own words.

Nicky smiled ruefully. "Seems like all I do these days is worry — what to buy, what to order, who to hire, will the money hold out until we open? Taking care of Derek is the last thing I need right now."

Seth came out of the front door, shutting it quietly behind him. "Brian's got him calmed down and is pouring coffee down his throat. Can you two handle him?"

"Sure, Seth. He's not a bad guy usually — he's just upset now. Thanks for stepping in. We'll make sure he doesn't do this again. 'Night." Nicky slipped into the building.

Meg smiled at Seth. "You have to admit that the entertainment around here has stepped up since the restaurant came to town. Let's hope Jim doesn't hear about this."

"Right on both counts."

16

Meg was surprised to find Bree sitting at the kitchen table leafing through a stack of documents when she let herself in after the meeting. "Hi. You're up late," Meg said.

"Just going over the forms for the pickers," Bree responded.

"Ah. I assume I'm supposed to sign something? Have you got everyone lined up?"

"More or less. I started with the crew Christopher's been using for years. A few of 'em dropped out — some are getting too old, others got a better offer somewhere else. We've recruited some new ones. The younger ones, though — they don't want to work as hard."

Meg suppressed a smile. Bree was no more than twenty-two. "It's not personal, right? I mean, it's not that they don't want to work for women?" Meg poured herself a glass of iced tea, then sat down at the table across from Bree. Lolly strolled in from somewhere, rubbed her head once against Meg's ankle, then wandered off again.

Bree shook her head. "Nah, nothing like that. These days, any job's a good job. When do you want to get together with them?"

"Do I need to see them all at once? Is there a foreman I should talk to?"

"Raynard Lawrence — he's the foreman. I'd talk to him first."

"And he's worked in this orchard before?"

"He has. And he's willing to come back, maybe because he's my aunt's husband's cousin and she'd give him hell if he didn't." Bree grinned.

"Well, I won't complain. You go ahead and set up the meeting, then. You'll be there, won't you?"

"Of course. It's part of my job." She sighed, looking down at the cluster of papers on the table. "I'm trying to hold the salaries steady from last year. They deserve a raise, but they know we're just starting out and can't afford it right now."

"I'm sure you'll be fair." Meg drained her glass and stood up. "Well, I'm going to bed. See you in the morning."

Meg made her way toward the front of the house, turning off lights. She checked the lock on the front door, then trudged up the stairs to her room. She'd left the windows open an inch or two, and evening air riffled the curtains. It was still surprisingly cool at night, out here in the country. She climbed into bed and pulled the light blanket up to her chin.

It was hard to believe that in a month she'd be picking the first of her apple crop, all things willing. She had to check with Bree about whether they needed any more apple crates, how to order additional picking bags. And she really had to line up purchasers for her apples, something she'd been putting off. *Why?* she wondered. Because somewhere deep inside she harbored the fear that they would all laugh at her and say no, and she would fail even before she began? She'd done her homework: better to go after the smaller and more appreciative stores. She needed to talk to Christopher again . . . She drifted off to sleep.

The next morning she had barely started her coffee brewing when Seth's sister, Rachel Dickinson, knocked on the frame of the screen door, carrying the inevitable basket issuing good smells. Rachel and her husband, Noah, ran a B&B in Amherst, which Rachel kept supplied with delectable pastries. It always startled Meg to see a smaller, rounder female version of Seth.

"Hi, stranger. I haven't seen you in weeks!" Meg exclaimed as she let Rachel in. "Are you swamped with guests? And you don't have to bribe me with food every time you come by."

"It was crazy for a month or so, what with all the local graduations and weddings. But now it's calmed down again, and since it's midweek, I've only got one guest, who's already out hunting through graveyards — another manic genealogist. The kids are at day camp. Noah's pounding on something. I've been working out a new recipe with strawberries. They're hard to bake with because they go mushy so fast, so I keep experimenting. This time I tried a layer in the middle, instead of mixing them in with the batter. You're my guinea pig. I'll trade you a muffin for a cup of coffee."

"It's a deal. They smell great. So, sit down and tell me what you've been up to."

Rachel grimaced. "Just the usual. Sounds like you've been busy in Granford, though."

Meg brought coffee mugs over, along with plates and butter. "Do you mean the restaurant?" she said innocently.

"No, dummy, the death. But that's connected with the restaurant, isn't it? What's the story? All I heard was that he was found in Jake Kellogg's pigsty. What a lousy way

230

to go! Did you know the guy?"

Meg sighed. "I met him a couple of times before he died. His name was Sam, and I gather he'd been friends with the owners, Brian and Nicky, back in Boston, and with Nicky even before that. By the way, they've hired Edna Blakely to replace Sam as sous chef."

"Oh, good. I like Edna, and she's a great cook. Plus she's really calm and steady, and knows the business. She should be an asset."

"That's good to hear." Meg reached for her second muffin. "These are great, by the way — I think you've got the balance of fruit to batter just right. But I need to test a few more, to be sure."

"Help yourself. So, what else have you heard about the death?"

"As far as I know, Sam died where they found him. He suffocated in the mud."

"How on earth did that happen?" Rachel asked.

"Someone held him down until he died," Meg said. "But don't spread that around. The state police have been shying away from saying 'murder,' although that's what everyone thinks anyway."

They were both silent for a moment.

"Poor guy," Rachel said softly. "Why

would anyone want to kill him? He didn't know anyone around here, did he?"

"Just Nicky and Brian. He had a boyfriend back in Boston, but Nicky said that was over before Sam arrived."

"Did any of them want Sam dead?" Rachel asked.

"I can't see why," Meg replied. "Nicky and Brian are really torn up about it, and Sam was important for their restaurant plans. I don't know about Derek — that's the ex-boyfriend — he showed up last night, loud and drunk. I gather the police told him about Sam's death and he took it hard."

"So who could've done it, then?"

"Nobody seems to know. And the Staties aren't sharing, if they know anything more. Oh, though this should amuse you: You remember me mentioning my friend Lauren, from Boston? She came out for a weekend — and she hit it off with Detective Marcus. They even went to dinner."

"Ooh, how funny. You mean he's actually not a zombie?"

"Apparently not, according to Lauren. If I'm really lucky, maybe she'll soften him up a little bit toward me."

"Don't hold your breath. Is she going to see him again?"

"I don't know. I told her she's welcome to

come back and visit."

Rachel raised an eyebrow and grinned, then changed the subject. "Hey, how're the apples coming along?"

"Either too fast or too slow, depending on when you ask me. Bree says she's got pickers lined up. I'm supposed to meet with their foreman and finalize things."

"Sounds good. How's Seth doing? He's been so busy I haven't seen him in weeks, even at Mom's. Is he working hard?"

"He's handling the restaurant build-out, and I gather he has plenty of other jobs. And all those selectmen's meetings. He finished up my apple chambers in the barn, but he really hasn't had time to work on his office and storage space."

"He always did take on too much — he can't bear to disappoint anyone. Are the selectmen happy with this restaurant plan?"

"Seth says Tom Moody's behind it. I'm not so sure about Caroline Goldthwaite."

Rachel snorted. "That woman always had a stick up her you-know-what. Hates change, hates anybody whose family hasn't lived in Granford for at least two hundred years. And thinks everyone in town should bow to her wishes."

"She did get elected. More than once, I hear."

"Yes, she did. But I think most of her supporters in town are as old as she is, so I don't know how long she'll hold on."

"She must be close to eighty."

"Yup, she is. She's been old since I was a kid. But we Yankees are tough. Hey, can we go talk to the goats?"

"Sure. I haven't managed to name them yet. You have any ideas? Maybe your kids can help."

"I'm not sure you want to go there. You might end up with a goat named Miley. How're they settling in?"

"Fine, as far as I can tell, but what do I know? I feed them, I talk to them occasionally. They haven't complained."

Rachel stood up and began clearing off the table. "Well, I still want to say hi to them. I always think goats look intelligent. More so than sheep anyway."

After stacking their dishes in the sink, Meg led the way out to the goat pen across the driveway. The two does approached eagerly, their eyes, with the disconcerting horizontal irises, curious. Meg felt a pang of guilt: maybe they did want more attention. But they had each other, didn't they?

Rachel was making crooning animal talk. "Hi, babies, how're you doing? You like it here? Your food looks good." The larger goat

234

cocked her head at Rachel, looking for all the world like she was listening. The smaller one tried to butt her head against Rachel's leg through the wire fence. "Yes, you're good girls, aren't you? Of course you are." She scratched between their ears, and the goats looked blissful.

"You could take them home with you," Meg said hopefully. "They really seem to like you."

"You're not going to foist them off on me, Meg Corey. They're your goats. They're very nice goats. You just have to get to know them."

"Right." Meg heard the screen door bang shut and turned to see Bree approaching, a mug of coffee in her hand. She looked sleep-rumpled.

"Morning, Meg, Rachel. Those your muffins on the table?"

"They are. Help yourself." Rachel gave the goats one last rub. "Well, I should get going. I think I'll treat myself to a little shopping — it's so rare that I get any time to myself. Keep the muffin basket — I'll pick it up the next time I come by."

"Thanks for dropping in, and for the muffins. I'll try to get over your way before too long."

"Those Chapins have enough energy for a

235

power plant, don't they?" Bree said after Rachel pulled out of the driveway.

Meg laughed. "You're right, they do. I get tired just watching them sometimes."

"Well, I'm gonna get a muffin or three — and Raynard, the foreman, said he'd stop by this morning."

A half hour later, Meg had finished cleaning up the kitchen when a battered pickup pulled into her driveway, and a lanky man in well-worn clothes climbed out. He appeared to be about fifty, with toffee-colored skin, and dark hair skimmed with silver. He saw Meg watching him from the kitchen window and dipped his head, pulling on the brim of his faded baseball cap, in a curiously courtly gesture. This had to be Raynard Lawrence. "Bree?" she called up the backstairs. "I think Raynard's here."

"I see him," Bree yelled from somewhere on the second floor. "Be right down."

Meg felt awkward leaving the man to wait in the driveway, so she went out the back door. She extended her hand. "I'm Meg Corey, the owner. And you'd be Raynard Lawrence?"

"That I am, ma'am." He took her hand and shook it carefully, as though holding back his full strength.

Meg swallowed a laugh. "Please don't call

236

me 'ma'am'! It makes me feel old. It's Meg."

The man nodded once again, without speaking. His gaze shifted to the kitchen door, where Bree came tumbling down the steps. "Briona! You're looking fine."

"Raynard, don't try to sweet-talk me. I'm the boss here now, remember?" Bree tempered her statement with a smile.

"You won't let me forget that, will you? But I'm happy to help out two such lovely ladies."

"Can the charm, will you?" Bree snapped with a small smile. "Let's go over the orchard, and the changes in the barn, and then we can talk details about the crew. That work for you?"

"All business? Fine, fine. Where you want to start?"

"The orchard — that's what matters most, right? No crop, we don't need pickers."

"I know the way." The man led the way up the hill, followed by Bree, hard on his heels, then Meg, trailing behind. For all that he must be twenty years older than Meg, Raynard was spry and moved quickly. At the top of the hill he paused while Meg caught up.

"How many years have you been working this orchard?" Meg asked, only slightly breathless.

"Thirty years, easy. I know every tree." He took a leisurely moment to scan the orchard before turning back to her. "Looking good. You and the professor, you've done good work so far, with the help of our girl there. Now we need a bit of rain and a bit of sun, and we'll have us a harvest."

"Sounds good to me," Meg said. "Can you tell how soon?"

"Have to take a look at the early harvest varieties."

Meg nodded. "Mr. Lawrence, you have to know right now that I have no idea what kind of apples I've got here. I'm willing to learn, but right now you'll have to forgive me if I sound like an idiot."

"I go by Raynard. Long as you trust me to tell you what's right, we'll be grand. Now, your orchard here, you've got mostly newer crosses — like Spencers, which is a McIntosh and Red Delicious cross, and the Empires. Some Baldwins, but there aren't many folks as like them these days. A few of what they call now the heirloom apples — been here who knows how long, but somebody cared enough to keep them going. You'll get to know 'em soon enough."

"I'm also still deciding how I'll be marketing them. Is it safe to say that I don't have a whole lot of any one kind?"

"Not enough to make the big stores sit up and take notice, no. Local farmers' markets, more like. Or sell 'em for cider. Couple of cider mills nearby, if you want to go that route."

"I'll keep that in mind. How big's your crew?"

"Eight, ten maybe. We move around a bit, and it depends on what's ripe."

"And they're all here and ready?"

"Not all, no. Some come early — we can help you clean up the orchard, make sure your equipment can get around. Briona says you have new holding chambers?"

"I do. Why don't we take a look now, and then we can finish up the paperwork? I think Bree's got all the papers ready for you." Meg looked at Bree, who nodded.

Raynard waited for Meg to lead the way to the barn. Out of the corner of her eye she thought she saw him give a nod to the goats.

Half an hour later, tour completed and forms signed, Raynard rose from the kitchen table. "I will see you in a few days, Meg. Briona, please give my good wishes to your aunt. I can find my way out."

After he had left, Meg stayed at the table with Bree. "Do you know, I feel better about the whole thing. I was afraid he would treat

239

me like an idiot child, or just run right over me like a steamroller. I think I'm going to learn a lot from him. Are you comfortable with all this?"

"He's a good man, knows his stuff. And he's family, so he can't screw us over."

"He wouldn't do that, would he?"

Bree shook her head. "No, not Raynard. There are some guys who'd try to take advantage, but he'll do right by you."

"Thank you, Bree. I don't know what I would have done without you."

"Just doing my job." Despite her words, Bree appeared pleased by Meg's comment. "And better rest up now, because we're going to get real busy real soon."

17

Making her way toward town for her usual round of errands, on a whim Meg pulled into the construction site that soon would be the Granford Grange shopping center. The name was grander than the place itself, which consisted of a row of single-story stores, still unoccupied. But it was new business for Granford, which Seth had fought long and hard for. He had told her he'd convinced the vet, Andrea Bedortha, to leave her group practice and strike out on her own with a space here, so that was one more slot that would be filled. Meg was hoping for a bookstore, too, but nothing had been finalized.

Seth's van was parked in the newly paved parking lot, and she could see him talking with a number of the workers. Meg looked around: her orchard wasn't quite visible from here, but she knew that Seth's family house lay just behind the ridge, no more than half a mile away. Finally he disentangled himself from a couple of carpenters dangling circular saws and came over to where Meg leaned against her car. "Hi. What're you doing here? We didn't have anything lined up, did we?"

"No, nothing like that. I was passing by and I wanted to see how things are coming along. When's opening day?"

"We're aiming for sometime in August. I thought we could have some sort of picnic in the parking lot here, maybe a cookout, games for kids, that kind of thing."

"That sounds good. You can count me in, if I'm not too busy in the orchard. Once harvest starts, my life may not be my own."

"How's that going?"

"Good, I think. I met with the pickers' foreman, who seems like a good guy. Bree's pleased. And it looks like we're getting pretty close to picking some of the early bearers."

"That sounds about right. I know when I was a kid, we were always bored by August, and sometimes we made some change by helping out with the early harvest. You need help?"

Meg laughed. "You don't have enough to do? Anyway, you'd have to ask Bree. She's handling all the staffing. I don't know if you'd measure up."

"You cut me to the quick, madam. But you're right; I'm pretty much fully booked. Kind of surprising, given the current economy, but it looks like more people are fixing what they've got rather than building new."

"Then that should be right up your alley — lots of renovation. Is the restaurant about ready?"

"More or less. There's still a lot of finish work to be done. And Nicky and Brian are experimenting with recipes daily, along with Edna. I'm beginning to wonder if I should ask to be paid in food."

"Is it that good?"

"It is. Now and then I have to remind them to keep it simple, at least for local folk, but most of the time they get it right."

"Has the liquor license come through?"

"Soon. We've cleared the rest, as far as permits go — electrical, plumbing. As I said, from here on out it's mainly prettying up the place."

Seth's attention was diverted by the arrival of a police car. Art Preston climbed out, and Meg found herself hoping it wasn't bad news — things had been going so well for the past few days. At least Art didn't look grim.

"Hi, Art," Seth greeted him. "What brings you this way?"

"Just checking out my little kingdom. Looks good. Any word on the sandwich shop?"

"We're still talking."

"That won't conflict with Nicky's restaurant, will it?" Meg asked anxiously.

"Apples and oranges," Seth said. "This will be breakfast and lunch only. I don't think they need to worry."

"Those kids attract trouble like magnets," Art said.

"What? Something new?" Seth asked.

Art slouched against Meg's car. "Last night. That friend of theirs from Boston, Derek Woodfield, got into it with Jim Burnett."

"Damn," Seth said. "I thought we'd headed that off. What happened?"

"Remember what you told me about the meeting Tuesday?"

"You mean when Jim made an ass of himself about Sam being gay? I told him to take it outside."

"Yup. Apparently he kept stewing about it after he left. And then this Derek character showed up, right?"

"Yes, after the meeting was over. Derek was drunk, but I thought Brian had him under control. So how did he and Jim get into it?"

"Let's say Derek was being rather vocal in his grief yesterday. There might have been more strong drink involved. Jim had business at Town Hall, and then he spotted Derek, sitting on the porch of the restaurant. Since you've met him, you know Derek looks like, well, an out-of-towner, and Jim took offense. He said something to the effect that 'we don't want your kind here,' and Derek told him he didn't like his tone — or much else about him."

"Oh, dear," Meg said. "Did they get into a fight?"

"More or less. Jim claims that Derek provoked him, Derek says Jim started it. They met up in the middle of the green and blows were exchanged, but luckily most of them didn't land anywhere important."

"Then what?"

"I showed up a few minutes later, broke it up, and put both of 'em in a cell until they dried out or cooled off. Then I sent them home without charging either one of them. Derek told me he didn't plan to stay here any longer than it took to comfort Nicky."

"Just Nicky? Not Brian?"

"Apparently Sam and Nicky were tight,

and Brian was the third wheel. If you believe Derek. He would have been happy to give me the whole history, but I cut him off."

"What about Jim?" Seth interrupted. "Is he going to be a problem?"

"Hell, I don't know. He's never been in trouble before, but I hear he's lost his job, and could be he's just looking for any reason to take his frustrations out on somebody. At least it's not his wife and kids, not yet anyway."

"Art," Meg said slowly, afraid to put her thoughts into words, "do you think Jim could have had something to do with Sam's death?"

"I thought about that, but I don't see it. I mean, Sam was a pretty husky guy, in good shape, and you've seen how skinny Jim is. You think Jim could have taken him?"

Meg shook her head. "I guess not, but I'm not a good judge. Still, I can't see him wrestling Sam down and holding him in the mud for any length of time."

"Does Jim have an alibi?" Seth asked.

"Checking it out now, on the quiet."

"Nothing new on cause of death?"

"Nope. Still asphyxiation. But even if the crowd in Northampton turned up something, they wouldn't necessarily share it with me. You know I'm not Marcus's best

246

buddy — he might tell me if he was about to make an arrest, if it was local, but that's about it."

"Are you going to tell him about Jim?" Meg asked.

Art didn't answer immediately. "I don't think so, not unless I turn up something. I have no reason to believe that Jim and Sam ever met. Jim doesn't have a history of violence. He's just a bigot in a bad mood, but that doesn't make him a killer."

"No, of course not. But I'd be very glad if someone would solve this thing, so we can get on with our lives. Particularly Nicky and Brian."

"Amen," Art said. "Well, I'd better finish my rounds. It was too nice a day to waste it all sitting at my desk, but there's plenty waiting for me there."

After Art had pulled away, headed toward the center of town, Meg looked at Seth. "Poor Nicky and Brian. Art's right — they seem to attract trouble. I hope Derek isn't going to be a problem."

"I'll see if I can keep Jim out of the mix," Seth said. One of the carpenters approached and stood waiting expectantly to talk to Seth. "Well, duty calls." He gave her a quick salute, and they parted ways.

Now what? Meg wondered. She was

nearby; she might as well touch base with Nicky.

It took Meg no more than three minutes to reach town and pull into the restaurant's parking lot. There were a couple of vans and cars there already: it looked like the painters were at work. As she climbed the steps, Meg noted that several attractive wicker chairs had appeared on the porch, their cushions still covered in plastic. When she rapped on the screen door, one of the painters nodded toward the kitchen. "They're in back," he said.

"Thanks." Meg let herself in and threaded a path through the paint buckets and drop cloths to the kitchen door. She could hear raised voices before she reached the doorway. Nicky and Derek were facing off across the large prep table in the middle of the room, and neither one looked happy. Brian was nowhere to be seen.

"I can come back later if you're busy, Nicky," Meg said from the doorway.

Nicky tore her gaze away from Derek and took in Meg's presence. She straightened and pulled her apron down. "Oh, hi, Meg. Did you want something?"

Meg hesitated, looking at Derek. "I, uh, just wanted to see how things were going."

Derek's lip curled. "You mean, you heard

about the little brouhaha on the green yesterday? My, news does travel fast in Hicksville. I'm Derek Woodfield."

"Hi, Derek, I'm Meg Corey. We actually met Tuesday night, although I guess you don't remember."

"Ah, that's right. You were with that guy who strong-armed me. I don't think we had time to observe the social niceties. I was a bit under the weather."

Nicky interrupted. "You were roaring drunk, Derek. And you were yesterday, too. I will not accept this. I know you're hurting, but you can't just show up here and make trouble — I've got to live with these people, and I want them as customers."

Derek recoiled in mock dismay. "Well, excuse me for caring."

"Derek, please . . ." Nicky said helplessly.

Derek slumped against the counter, his expression contrite. "I'm sorry, Nick. I know how much this place means to you — and what it meant to Sam. I don't want to screw it up for you. But don't you get the feeling that nobody cares that he's dead? That nobody's doing anything?"

"That's not true, you know," Meg said mildly. "It's just that people around here didn't know Sam well enough to miss him. And the case is being handled by the state police, out of Northampton. They are investigating."

"Sure they are," Derek snarled.

Meg stiffened. She understood his anger, but he wasn't being fair to Granford. "Derek, you're wrong. The police are doing their jobs. These things take time."

Derek sighed. "Okay, okay. It's just hard to accept. I mean, Sam was so alive, so excited about what he was doing. So interested in everything. He was really looking forward to learning about country living, and finding all sorts of good natural food. And I hate it that somebody squashed that — squashed *him,* like a bug." Derek turned and stalked out of the kitchen, and Meg heard the screen door slam.

"I'm sorry," Nicky said. "Damn, there I go again, apologizing. I'm not responsible for Derek. I wondered if maybe one reason Sam was so happy to leave Boston was to get away from all of Derek's drama."

"I thought you said Derek had moved on?"

"He had, but as you can see, he likes to make scenes. I just wish he wouldn't do it here, now."

"Nicky, I'm sure the police have asked you this, but do you think there's anyone from Sam's life in Boston that could have wanted him dead?"

"You mean, like Derek, or one of Sam's earlier boyfriends?" Nicky shook her head vigorously. "No, no, nothing like that. Sam was monogamous, strictly one guy at a time. He and Derek had been together for a year or so, and then it ended, a few months ago. We were talking about moving out of Boston and Derek didn't want to, so that was that. Sam wasn't involved with anyone else, and when he knew he'd be moving out here, he didn't push it. He figured he'd have time . . ." Nicky swallowed a sob. "I miss him," she said softly.

Meg was torn. She wanted to comfort Nicky, and she wanted to know more about Sam, and what his life had been like before he moved to Granford. But she also wanted to keep an eye on Derek, who had gone storming out of the building. Who knew where he would go, what kind of trouble would he get into? Maybe he wasn't a suspect in Sam's death, but he was still capable of making trouble for Nicky and Brian. She settled for a compromise. "Listen, why don't we go sit on the porch and talk? You need to get out of the kitchen now and then."

Nicky saw through her ruse. "And we can make sure Derek doesn't stir anything else up? Sure, good idea. You want something cold to drink? I've got iced tea with mint."

"Sounds good to me." Meg waited while Nicky filled a couple of glasses, then followed her out to the porch. "I like the new chairs. They suit the place."

Nicky threw herself into one, without removing the plastic. "I want people to be able to sit out here and sip wine and eat little yummy things, you know? I want the whole dining experience to be seamless — relaxed, comfortable. Like you're in your own home, only the food's a whole lot better and you didn't have to cook it or clean up."

"It sounds like exactly the kind of place where I'd like to eat." As Meg sipped her tea, she realized that this was the first time that she and Nicky had been alone together, without something else demanding their attention. "So, how long did you know Sam?"

"Years. I met him the first week in cooking school, before I met Brian, even," Nicky replied. "Sam was so much fun! And it rubbed off on other people when we were all working in Boston, sometimes a bunch of us would get together in our free time and cook; Sam was usually the one who suggested it, and he'd come up with wacky themes — like go to Haymarket and bring back one item you'd never seen before, much less cooked. Or go stand on a dock when the boats came in and find out what the fishermen had caught, and try something new. And then we'd make something out of the ingredients and share. We had some disasters, but we all had a really good time."

"Did Brian participate?"

"After a while. I think it was more to do something with me, than about the food. Brian used to be sort of shy, kind of the opposite of Sam. And he was always more into the management side. Once he suggested that we set a dollar limit on what we brought, like maybe two dollars, and see how many people we could feed well on next to no money."

"What made you first realize that you wanted to be a chef?" Meg asked.

Nicky relaxed into her chair. "I told you I grew up in New York, right? It was just my father and me, and we ate out a lot, at wonderful restaurants. And I learned to cook young — because I wanted to, not because he was helpless. We cooked together for years, and gradually I took over. So he wasn't exactly surprised when I told him I wanted to go to cooking school, though he wasn't too pleased about it at first."

"So why'd you start working in Boston, then, instead of back in New York?"

"The competition in New York is wicked. Boston used to be kind of stodgy, but in the past decade or so they've really turned around the food scene, so I thought I'd catch that wave, get in on the ground floor rather than butting heads at all the New York restaurants. And the cooking school had better connections with the Boston restaurants. So then we all — me and Brian and Sam — moved to Boston together after."

"Did you always know Sam was gay?"

Nicky glanced at her. "Of course. He didn't hide it. It was just part of who he was. Nobody cared."

"Did you ever wish he wasn't?"

Nicky turned in her chair to face Meg. "You mean, then the two of us might've . . . ? No! He was a friend, but, not to speak ill of the dead, I couldn't imagine living with the guy. He was *so* high energy! I am, too, and the two of us together would have been a disaster. Brian — he's the opposite. He grounds me. He calms me down when I start bouncing off walls. He's good for me."

"You two sound like a good fit." Meg wondered briefly if an outsider would say the same about her and Seth. Seth was outgoing, relaxed but energetic at the same time. He liked people, and people liked him. She was more shy, more reserved; it was harder for her to make friends. She gained a lot from his companionship, but what did she have to offer him?

Apparently Nicky was on the same wavelength. "How about you and Seth?"

Meg sighed. "I've only known him a few months, and I'm not the kind of person to rush into things. And I guess I worry that I'm taking advantage of him — I mean, he's introduced me to half the town already, and he's a great builder and plumber, and he really cares about Granford. Sometimes I feel like a leech."

"He cares about you," Nicky stated bluntly.

Meg wrestled with conflicting emotions. Some silly girlish part of her wanted to ask why Nicky thought that. A more mature and responsible part declared that she really didn't want to look too closely at whatever their relationship was and where it might be going. She dragged her attention back to Nicky's plight. "Do you know how long Derek's staying?"

Nicky shrugged. "I don't think long. He really hates the country, so I suspect that his whole trip out here was mostly for show, so that we'd all know how much he's hurting. But now he's had his little adventure — I'm sure he'll regale anyone who will listen with the story of being tossed into jail by the yokel police officer. And I do think he loved Sam, in his way. But I'll be glad to see the last of him!"

"Just can't wait to get rid of me, eh?" Derek said, sauntering around the corner of the building.

Nicky stood up abruptly. "Eavesdroppers deserve what they hear, Derek. Meg, I've got some more dishes to test out." She stormed into the building.

Derek settled himself on the porch stairs. "I feel *so* welcome here," he drawled.

Meg didn't see any good reason to mollycoddle him. "What did you expect? Nicky and Brian are upset about Sam's death, but on top of that they've moved to a new place and are trying to get a new business started, all at once. The last thing they need is to hold your hand."

Derek stared at her as he slouched against the stair rail, then shrugged. "Point taken. But Sam deserved better." He studied Meg critically. "What's your game here?"

"I don't have a game. I'm pretty new in town myself, and I know how hard it can be. I like Nicky and Brian, and I want to see them succeed. You wouldn't know anything useful about Sam's death, would you?"

"Fancy yourself a small-town sleuth?"

"Not at all!" Meg wondered what he'd heard about her. "I'm just trying to help. Brian and Nicky have got enough on their plates without worrying about a police investigation."

"Well, I don't know anything, and I have a cast-iron alibi: I was on a beach about a thousand miles from here, with plenty of witnesses. And my meager budget doesn't extend to hiring hit men. Besides, I bore Sam no ill will. My, that sounds Victorian, doesn't it? What Sam and I had had run its course, end of story. We parted friends, more or less. I had no reason to want him dead, and I don't know of anyone who did. Satisfied?"

"I don't think you were involved in his death, if that's your question."

Derek sprawled back in his chair, looking out over the tranquil green. "So which of the fair citizens of this backwater *do* you suspect?"

Meg was startled into silence. It was a question she had avoided asking herself. But Derek had a point: if he and Sam's other friends from Boston were ruled out, Sam's killer had to be someone local. But who?

Derek looked at her with a wicked gleam in his eye. "Makes you uncomfortable to think that one of your precious neighbors might have had anything to do with it, doesn't it?"

"What makes you think *anyone* had a hand in it?"

Derek gave a short, derisive laugh. "Oh, come on — you know, and I know, that Sam didn't die from natural causes. Those ham-fisted state police of yours wouldn't have bothered tracking me down if poor Sam had just keeled over one day. So it's murder. Somebody here helped him die." He cocked his head at her. "Who's your candidate for killer?"

"I don't have one. You're right — I don't want to believe it's anyone from here, but it almost has to be." Meg recalled what she had told Lauren: the killer had to be someone who knew the layout of Kellogg's farm, and knew pigs. "If I knew, I'd make sure something was done about it. I liked Sam, you know. And I want to see whoever did this caught."

Derek turned back toward the green, slumping back against the cushions. "Thank you. I believe you do. And Sam would be grateful to you," he said quietly.

They sat in silence for a few moments, then Derek jumped to his feet. "Well, given the warm welcome I've had here, I suppose I should take myself back to Boston. I'll just say good-bye to Nicky." He gave her one last look. "Thank you, Meg Corey, for our enlightening chat. And good luck."

He went back into the building. Meg felt a twinge of distress over his attitude but decided to let it slide. Instead, she focused on enjoying the last of her iced tea and the peaceful view. This really was an ideal setting for a restaurant, and right now the town laid out below her looked like every postcard she had ever seen for scenic New England. Once Sam's murder was solved, there was no reason why everything shouldn't go smoothly for Nicky and Brian. She hoped.

18

Meg's tranquil mood did not survive the trip home. She had enough problems of her own, with trying to keep her apples growing and healthy, trying to manage a crew of pickers, and trying to figure out how she was going to sell her apples. "Trying" was the key word here, and she wasn't sure how soon she was going to be able to move any of those tasks to the "Accomplished" column. She pulled into her driveway and turned off the engine. As always, the goats had trotted over to the fence, eager to see who was there.

Meg went over to the goat paddock to say hello. The larger goat cocked her head at Meg and gazed at her with her golden alien eyes. The smaller goat came over and bumped against her companion, demanding her fair share of attention. She really needed to name them; the goats deserved that much. She had come to recognize their distinct personalities: the larger goat was older and more dignified; the smaller goat was inquisitive and a real clown.

Did she know anyone she wanted to honor — or insult — by naming a goat after them? She racked her brain for any useful literary references to goats, and came up blank, although she could name any number of cats, dogs, pigs, rabbits, and mice who rambled through popular fiction. *Billy Goats Gruff* was not going to be much help — wrong gender.

Bree emerged from the house and joined Meg at the fence. "You were gone awhile."

"I stopped to see how Granford Grange was coming, and ran into Seth and Art. Then I went to the restaurant and had a chat with Derek."

"Derek?"

"Oh, that's right, you haven't met him. He's the latest fly in the ointment — Sam's ex, here from Boston, loudly lamenting Sam's death to the world at large. Which annoyed our local homophobe, so there was a fight and Art had to toss them both in the pokey to cool off."

"And here I thought small-town living was peaceful," Bree said. "So you thought you'd talk to the goats instead?"

"That's about it. They don't talk back.

Got any ideas for names?"

Bree studied the goats, and they stared back solemnly. "You know that if you name them, you'll never be able to eat them."

Meg laughed. "I wasn't planning to eat them."

"Okay, then: Isabel and Dorcas."

"Why?" Meg asked.

"Well, Shakespeare had these two lady goatherds in one of his plays — *Winter's Tale,* I think. Dorcas was one of them, and I always kind of liked the name."

"What was the other goatherd named?" Meg asked cautiously.

Bree wrinkled her nose. "Mopsa. I wouldn't wish that on a goat, or anybody else. But Isabel's the name of my mother's older sister, and I always thought she sounded like a goat."

Meg laughed. "Works for me. So which is which?"

"Isabel's the larger one — she looks more serious."

Meg turned back to the goats. "Isabel?"

The larger goat put her front hooves on the wire fence; at that height she could nearly look Meg in the eye.

"Well, I guess that's a yes. How about you, Dorcas?"

The younger goat bleated, then wandered

off in search of a tasty clump of grass.

"Well, that's a weight off my mind. Now the goats have names and I don't feel like such a bad goat owner. Did you need me for something?"

"Actually, yes," Bree said. "I've asked the pickers to come over tomorrow afternoon, so we can all take a look at what you've got and what you'll need."

"Okay, let's go over what we need to talk about with them . . ."

The next afternoon Meg watched as a motley crew of mostly men, and a couple of women, assembled in the driveway outside her barn. Bree went outside to greet them, as Meg paced nervously around the kitchen and Lolly retreated to the safety of the dining room. How quickly would the pickers see through her? Bree possessed more technical knowledge, but would her youth stand in the way of getting them to listen to her? Bree said something to Raynard, then let herself in through the kitchen door.

"Listen, this is just an introduction, okay? They know you're new at this," Bree tried to reassure her.

"Do we have enough people? Too many?"

"Meg, we've been over this. A good picker can pick maybe ten bins a day — that's like four tons of apples. And they know how to pick the ripe ones, and the ones that are the right size, and how to handle them so they don't bruise. They know how to take care of themselves — position their ladders, stay out of woodchuck holes. These guys are good, and they've been doing it for years. You've gotta trust them."

"I do," Meg sighed. "It's me I don't trust. Well, let's do it." She squared her shoulders and led the way out to the driveway in front of the barn.

Raynard stepped forward, then turned to the group. "This is Meg Corey, who owns this orchard. Briona Stewart here is the orchard manager. Meg is new to picking, but that does not mean that you can slack off, not while I'm in charge. She's going to show you the improvements she has made this year, and then maybe we can walk through the trees, so we all know how close to picking we are." He turned to Meg expectantly.

She stepped forward and swallowed. "Thank you, Raynard. And thank you all for coming. You've heard I'm new at this, but I want to do things right, and I need this harvest. I appreciate your signing on, and I'll take all the help I can get. And I promise I'll listen to you, because you're a whole lot more experienced than I am. Is everyone comfortable with that?"

A man at the back of the crowd spoke up. "Who we take orders from? You or young missy?"

"Bree is my employee and my representative. You do what she says. I'll try to stay out of everybody's way, but I want to learn about all aspects of harvesting, so I'll be there watching. And tell me if there's something wrong with the equipment, or something else I need to get. Let's start by taking a look at the new holding chambers in the barn."

Bree had opened the barn doors earlier, and the pickers turned and headed in that direction. Meg and Bree brought up the rear. Meg asked in a low voice, "Okay so far?"

Bree gave her a thumbs-up. "Thanks for backing me up. And Raynard's a good guy. They all want to see a good harvest. They've got their pride — and they're paid based on how much they pick. You want me to run them through the details of the chambers?"

"Please." Reassured, Meg watched as Bree threaded her way through the small crowd and positioned herself by the control panel of the nearer chamber. "What we've got here is . . ."

The pickers departed before four, in a couple of rattletrap pickups and a few cars. They had walked through the orchard, where it was quickly obvious that they knew the trees well. Some commented tree by tree, and Raynard usually nodded his agreement. He made a few notes in a tattered notebook he kept in his shirt pocket. Bree, less confident, trailed behind him, listening intently. Raynard was the last to leave.

"Looks like the Gravensteins will be ready maybe second week of August. You have a buyer lined up?" he asked Meg.

Meg felt another, now-familiar wave of guilt. "Not yet. Do you know who's buying?"

"Talk to the big farmers' co-op — introduce yourself. Bree, that boyfriend of yours, he have any ideas?"

Bree blushed. "Yes," she said curtly.

Raynard turned back to Meg. "Best get that set up soon. Harvest will be here before you know it, weather willing."

"I will, I promise. Thanks for all your help, Raynard. I'm looking forward to working with you."

Meg raised a hand in salute as Raynard pulled away. "That went well. Didn't it? Everybody's on board?"

Bree shrugged. "Seems so."

266

"How's it look, overall? I have nothing to compare this season with."

"Apples are funny. Some bear alternate years — that's one of the problems with the Baldwins. With others, sometimes all the conditions come together just right and you get a lot of apples, other years not so much. You've had good fruit-set, and the weather's been warm. Nothing to worry about yet."

Yet? Meg didn't like the sound of that, but she had to have faith — in Bree, in the pickers, even in Mother Nature. And she had no control over that last one. At least she was glad that her inexperienced eye hadn't missed any obvious problems. The trees looked pretty to her, but that was a silly criterion. Leaves were lush and shiny, and there were lots of small green apples clustered among them, some beginning to redden where they caught the sun. All good. The orchard itself looked tidy — she had managed to learn to use the mower attachment to her tractor, and found she enjoyed driving up and down the rows. The barn looked pretty good, too. Much of the decades' — centuries'? — worth of defunct farm equipment and miscellaneous junk had been hauled out and disposed of, so now there was room for her apple bins, ladders, and other equipment. Even Meg had

267

to admit she'd come a long way since she had first arrived in January.

Seth's van pulled into the driveway. He parked, then came over to where she stood, in the barn door. "Admiring your domain?"

"Actually, yes. I think it looks great, especially considering what it looked like a month or two ago. This whole thing may actually work. The pickers were here, and we went through the orchard with them. It got a clean bill of health."

"That's good to hear."

Bree came out of the back door. "I'm headed over to meet Michael in Amherst. Don't wait up," she said, not breaking stride.

"Have a good time!" Meg called out to her retreating back. She turned back to the barn. "I guess I should close up — I wouldn't want to lose my tractor. Did you stop by for a reason?"

"What, the pleasure of your company isn't enough of an excuse? Actually, I wondered if you had any plans for dinner."

"Not that I can remember. Did you have any ideas?"

"My mother wondered if you wanted to come to supper."

"Oh." Meg was panic-stricken for a moment. On one hand, it was about time she met Mrs. Chapin, one of her closest neighbors; she had been here for six months already. On another hand, this was Seth's mother — was she ready to "meet the relatives"? On a third hand, Meg wondered whether Seth's mother had already formed an opinion about her, and whether it was a good or a bad one. "Um, I guess so?"

Seth had been watching her with a half smile, as though he could read her tumbling thoughts. "You don't have to if it would make you uncomfortable, but I know she's been wondering when she'd finally meet you."

Meg shook herself. "I'd like that. Do I have time for a quick shower?"

"Sure. I've got some paperwork to catch up on. Let me know when you're ready to go."

Meg fled to the house, and went upstairs to the shower. *Meg, grow up. You're acting like a teenager.* Of course she would be delighted to meet Seth's mother. She knew that Seth's father had died some years ago, and that Seth and his sister, Rachel, had dinner at their mother's house regularly. They both seemed to talk about her fondly, so she couldn't be that bad . . . unless maybe she was one of those clingy, needy people? Only one way to find out.

Meg toweled her hair dry and rummaged through her closet to find something clean to wear, then slapped on a minimal amount of makeup. She fed Lolly and gathered up her bag with her keys, along with a light sweater to ward against evening chill. She pulled the kitchen door closed behind her and crossed the driveway to Seth's office.

"Office" was probably too dignified a term for the jumble of boxes, the stacks of papers, and the odd tool or fixture that cluttered Seth's working space. The only halfway clear area was the desktop; the desk itself looked like it had come from a yard sale.

"I love what you've done with the place," she drawled, leaning against the doorjamb.

Seth looked up from the invoices he had been sorting. "It's a work in progress, but at least it's weatherproof. Still not mouse-proof, but I can take care of than later. As long as they don't nest in the invoices."

"I do not want to think about mice. Are you ready?"

"Just about. You nervous?"

"Why? Should I be? Is there something I need to know about your mother?"

"Nope. She's a perfectly nice lady."

"I hope so. You might have given me a little more warning, though."

"What, so you could worry about it

longer? It's no big deal."

Easy for you to say, Meg thought.

19

It was a beautiful evening. The sun was still high in the sky, and fields and leaves were in the full flush of summer green. Birds dove after insects hovering above the grass, and the air thrummed with the sound of late bees weaving their way among the wildflowers.

"You want to walk?" Seth asked. "I can show you where our boundaries cross."

"It does seem silly to drive. Is there a path?" Meg asked.

"Sort of. Can you see anything?"

Meg studied the landscape in the direction of Seth's house. There seemed to be a faint indentation in the ground, meandering more or less in the right direction. But there were no markers as such. "I think I see something," she said dubiously.

Seth nodded. "You do. Since there weren't kids at the Warren place — your place — to play with, we didn't come this way too often when we were growing up. But if you go back further to the nineteenth century, this would have been the path from your house to town, if you were on foot. Ah, now you can see the houses."

They had stopped at the top of the rise. Off to their left lay Meg's orchard, the late sun filtering through the trees. Ahead of them Meg could see a pair of similar-looking white colonial houses nestled in the green meadows. One of them was Seth's house, which she had seen only once before, briefly and at night, under less-than-ideal circumstances; the other one must be his mother's. From this elevation she could make out the highway and the low roofline of Granford Grange a mile or so beyond, although the town center even farther away was obscured by stands of tall old trees.

"How old are the houses?" Meg asked as she followed Seth along the broad, indistinct path.

"Mom's is probably the same age as yours. Mine's a generation younger, built for one of the Chapin sons when he married, around eighteen hundred."

"No barns?"

"They shared the one, which used to lie between the houses — you can still see the stone foundation. But it's long gone. If it

273

had been in decent shape, Dad would have used it for the business, but he couldn't save it. Reused some of the lumber, though."

After another few minutes they reached the back door of Mrs. Chapin's house. "Mom doesn't stand on formality, and nobody ever uses the front door," Seth said. "You ready?"

"I guess." Meg smoothed her shirt down and took a deep breath. There was no reason to be nervous, right?

Seth called through the screen door, "Mom? Where are you?"

"Upstairs, sweetie. Be right down."

"No hurry," he yelled back. He held the door open for Meg. She stepped into a mud room, beyond which lay the kitchen. She inhaled, and smelled old wood and polish and cloves and roasting chicken. It all smelled wonderful — like a home. She followed Seth into the kitchen. It faced southeast, so it didn't get direct sunlight at this hour, but Meg saw a lot of old wood, worn smooth by generations of hands, and bright flashes of color. This was truly a lived-in kitchen: she inventoried a scattering of cooking implements, antique and modern; mementoes obviously made by children, or grandchildren. The refrigerator was layered with calendars, notes, and drawings, in no obvious order. In comparison, Meg's kitchen seemed bland and soulless.

Her contemplation of the room was interrupted by the arrival of Seth's mother, who looked very much like an older version of Seth's sister, Rachel. "Sorry to keep you waiting. So you're Meg!" said the woman. She approached quickly, and Meg quailed for a moment, bracing for a hug that never came, and was relieved when Seth's mother instead offered a hand. "I'm Lydia Chapin. Welcome! I hope you're hungry — I don't get to cook for other people very often these days, so I probably made way too much." She swatted her son on the arm affectionately.

"Hey, I'm over here at least once a week," he protested. "Give me a break!"

"I know, I know. But your sister's tied up all summer and every weekend. I never get to see my grandkids."

"Stop whining, Mom, or Rachel will dump them in your lap for the rest of the summer."

"Then we could put them to work in that orchard of yours. Right, Meg?"

Meg smiled, swept along by Lydia's warmth. "I'd have to check child labor laws, but it would probably be good for them."

"Hard work never hurt anybody, young or

old. And too many kids these days don't have a clue where real food comes from. How's your orchard doing, by the way?"

"Fine, or so I'm told. I'm sure you know it's all very new to me, but it's fascinating — there's so much that I never knew. And I'm just beginning to find out what I've got."

"I remember some good cooking apples — we usually borrowed a few, didn't we, Seth?"

"Who, me?" Seth tried to look innocent.

Lydia ignored him. "We've got a couple of trees out back, Meg, but with growing kids, sometimes our crop didn't last long. Chances are that we share some of the same varieties — people used to swap cuttings all the time in the old days." Lydia bustled around the kitchen, opening cupboards and getting out glasses. "I would have had you over sooner, but work's been busy," she said.

Meg glanced quickly at Seth — he'd never mentioned his mother's work. "What do you do?"

"I manage the books for a construction firm in Chicopee — I understand you and I have number crunching in common. I tried to retire after my husband died, but I got bored pretty fast. I don't do it for Seth, because his father and I raised him to know all sides of his business if he hopes to succeed, so he can darn well figure it out for himself. Right, Seth?"

"Yup. But you handled the books for Dad."

"In the beginning I had to, because we didn't have enough money to hire anyone else. But I enjoyed it, and of course, I knew the business better than anybody."

"You need any help with dinner, Mom?" Seth asked.

"Of course not. I could do this in my sleep. But you could set the table."

"Will do." Seth disappeared toward what Meg assumed was the dining room.

Lydia opened the oven door to check on the roasting chicken, then stirred a casserole of rice in the microwave. "You want something to drink? I've got wine."

"That sounds good," Meg said. "Your house reminds me of mine, only busier."

"That's a very polite way of saying it's a mess, but I'm happy." Lydia poured two glasses of wine and handed one to Meg. "Cheers. Nice to have you here. So, tell me something about yourself. What brought you to Granford?"

Meg fumbled for an answer. "You probably know most of it. My mother inherited the house from some relatives she hardly knew, and when I lost my job in Boston, she sent me out here to fix it up and sell it. I thought that would be quick and easy, but obviously I was wrong. And then I found out there was an orchard, except that it was about to be destroyed for commercial development, and I discovered I hated the idea. So now it looks like I'm staying, and I'm going to try to make the orchard viable. That's the short version."

"You've had a few bumps along the way." Lydia eyed her critically. "But you look like you're handling it. And I know you're probably nervous about the bumps you've caused me and mine, but I'm telling you now, I don't blame you. You were trying to do what you thought was right, and I don't hold it against you. It was his own fault, not yours, and that's all I'm going to say about that."

Seth came back before Meg could respond. "Table's ready. Where's the food?"

"Manners, Seth. Meg and I are engaged in polite conversation. We don't just rush to the table like hogs to a trough."

"When have I heard that before? Oh, right, here — several thousand times."

The next few minutes were devoted to transferring food from kitchen to table, and Meg had to admit that she was hungry, too. Farm work was hard, even if she wasn't hauling things around, and she had much more appetite than in the past. When everything was arrayed on the dining room table, Meg asked, "Do you grow your own vegetables?"

They settled themselves around the table before Lydia answered, "Mostly, especially this time of year. The lettuce is from my garden. The chicken came from up the road — I can't eat those mutants they try to sell us at the grocery store. I would have given you apple crisp, but last year's crop is gone, so you've got strawberry-rhubarb instead, both home-grown."

"I haven't even had time to think about growing something for myself to eat, although I can see where there was a vegetable bed out back. Maybe next year, when I have a better idea of what happens when."

"I do it because I like to garden, and the food's healthier. I don't know whether I save any money, but there are other factors that I give more weight to."

Seth interrupted, "Heck, when we were growing up, it was the equivalent of 'time out.' If we were acting up, Mom would send one or another of us out to weed the garden, which gave everyone a chance to cool off."

"Ah, Seth, you see right through me."

"Always did, Mom."

They all dug into the unquestionably excellent food. Conversation between mouthfuls drifted to local politics and town events. "What's going on with that restaurant in town? They have food yet, or just pretty menus?" Lydia asked.

"Construction's nearly finished," Seth volunteered, "and they're decorating. I know Nicky's been trying out dishes. Have you met her yet, Mom?"

"Nope. I wanted to get to the Select Board meeting, but I was running late that day. How'd it go?"

"Not bad. I think most people were happy with what they heard. Mrs. Goldthwaite's still in a snit, though."

"Caroline Goldthwaite's always in a snit. What is it this time?"

"I haven't wanted to ask. She knows Tom and I outnumber her on the Board, so she more or less held her tongue at the meeting. Mostly she sat there and radiated disapproval. If she had her way, she'd preserve the town in amber."

"At least if it was in amber, it wouldn't decay any further," Lydia said tartly. "Meg, what's your take on the restaurant? Didn't they hear about Granford from a friend of yours?"

Meg nodded. "Sort of, so I guess I feel

partly responsible for them. Nicky's a great cook, from what I've tasted so far. And she loves what she's doing. What troubles me is that I'm not sure they have enough capital to really get this up and running. Brian claims to have taken the right business courses, but reality is different from the classroom, and I don't know how much margin for error they have. Tell me, Lydia, do you think people in Granford will eat there?"

"If they pitch it the right way. I enjoy a good meal in a nice restaurant as much as anyone, but I only go once or twice a year, like when this one" — she nodded toward Seth — "takes me out to dinner on my birthday. If they want repeat business, I'd tell them to keep the menu simple and the prices reasonable."

"That sounds like their plan."

Dinner drifted to a close in a happy haze of wine and conversation. Finally Seth stood up and stretched. "That was great, Mom. You want me to do the dishes?"

"Seth, you always ask, because you know I'll say 'no.' Just carry this stuff into the kitchen, and I'll put it in that magnificent high-end dishwasher that you so kindly provided for me. Then you can see this lady home."

At the back door, Meg said to Lydia, "It was great to meet you, and I'm not just saying that. You'll have to come over sometime so I can return the favor."

"I'll hold you to that. Do you know, I can't remember that I've ever been inside the Warren house? I hear you've made some improvements."

"I'm trying, but it's an uphill battle. Thanks, Lydia."

On the back stoop, Seth looked up at the darkening sky. "I don't like the look of that. Maybe I should get my car and drive you back."

Meg followed his gaze. While they had been inside, massive storm clouds had gathered to the north. They were a peculiarly intense gray, and the remaining light of the setting sun looked greenish in comparison. Even to Meg's novice eye, the clouds looked menacing. "A storm? But I don't hear any thunder."

"Not yet. We can probably make it if we hurry."

"Then let's go, fast."

Perhaps it was the ozone levels in the air, or the weird quality of the light, but the approaching storm was making Meg very uncomfortable. They set off at a good pace, but they had barely arrived at the boundary of Meg's orchard when the wind picked up, tossing the branches.

"Maybe we misjudged," Seth said. "Let's hope we can get inside before it hits."

They dashed through the gathering gloom, dodging dry leaves spun by the wind, but they hadn't yet reached the back of the house before the clouds shut down the sun and loosed a torrent of water all at once. Meg could see the individual drops falling, looking like glass marbles that splashed as they hit the ground, which was soon covered with puddles. Seth tugged her into the open shed at the back of the house, but they were already drenched.

Meg looked at Seth and burst out laughing. "You look like . . . an otter, all sleek and wet."

"What do you think you look like?" Seth reached out a hand to push a soaked strand of hair behind Meg's ear. His hand stilled, then traveled around to the back of her head, and he pulled her toward him. He paused for a moment, looking into her eyes, and she met his gaze squarely.

As their lips met, lightning flashed, with a loud crack that made them both jump. "Wow — those romance novels got it right!" Meg murmured.

Seth grinned. "I wish I could take credit,

but I think some old tree near here just bit the dust . . . Meg, am I moving too fast?"

"No." She pulled him back. His shirt was cold with the rain, then warm as their bodies met. She found herself with her back against the rough boards of the shed, Seth pressed close. The rain continued to fall in torrents, drowning out all other sounds. "Seth," she breathed in his ear. "Bree's not coming back tonight. What say we move this inside?"

"I say yes."

20

Meg couldn't stop smiling at the eggs she was scrambling the next morning. Last night had been . . . unexpected. Surprising. In a way, she was glad she hadn't had time to think, only to react. Maybe she should trust herself more often, because it had been . . . wonderful.

When Bree let herself in the back door, she stopped in the doorway, surprised to see Seth at the kitchen table, sipping his coffee and reading the paper.

"Hi, Bree. Have you eaten?" Meg asked, without turning.

"Uh, yeah, thanks. Boy, you got lucky last night."

Seth started coughing, and Meg could feel herself turning bright red. She stared resolutely at the eggs, unable to think of anything to say.

Bree's gaze swiveled between Meg and Seth, and then the light dawned and she grinned. "What I *meant* was, I stopped at the orchard on the way in. Did you notice that storm last night, or were you too busy?"

Meg cleared her throat and managed to say, "Yes, I noticed that. In fact, we got drenched on the way home. Pretty spectacular, huh?"

"More than that. There was a lot of hail over toward Amherst, kind of a microburst. It did a number on the crops over that way, including apples. Flattened a lot of stuff in the fields. I was worried that it had hit here, but I didn't see any point in calling you last night. I mean, what could you do about it?"

Meg didn't know whether to feel guilty or relieved. While she and Seth had been . . . busy, other farms had been getting slammed by one of those unexpected events of nature. It was a cruel reminder about the uncertainty of being a farmer. "Good heavens, I never thought of that."

"Bet you didn't," Bree continued smiling at her. "You must have been distracted."

"Guess so," Meg retorted simply, eager to move on to a new subject. "I never realized I had to worry about hail. What effect does it have on the apples? Knocks them off the trees?"

"Some. More get dinged, which means they can't be sold as perfect. They end up going for cider, but the farmer gets less money for them. Lots less, like one third as much."

"I can't believe I came so close to losing a big chunk of the crop, and I didn't even know it."

"Weather's always a big worry. Like a freeze at the wrong time in the spring can kill off your blossoms, and that means no crop, but we got past that all right. Drought's a problem some years, although you've got the springhouse if you need to irrigate. That's a plus."

Meg distributed eggs and toast on two plates, set one in front of Seth, and sat down with her own. "If I were religious, I'd be sending up some thanks about now."

"You've got that right. So, what did you do last night?" Bree said, trying to look innocent and reaching for a piece of Meg's toast.

"We went over to Seth's mother's house for dinner. I'd never met her before, for all that I've lived here for six months. It's kind of hard to get to know your neighbors when the houses are so far apart. Of course, I didn't know my neighbors in Boston well either — I think there was some sort of unspoken rule about not intruding in each other's privacy."

"Huh. I never thought about that, but it's kind of the same in a dorm — you can hear everything that's going on, but you pretend you don't. Oh, by the way, Michael gave me a list of the small local grocery chains that should be interested in your apples. Some of the stores have a pretty good following of customers who like to support local products. Your yield should be about the right size for them. Do you want to call them, or should I?"

"Thanks, Bree. That's a big help. I think I need to do it, and anyway, I should probably introduce myself to them, face to face. Does that list include farmers' markets?"

"That's a different group, and you'd probably have to work harder to go that route, but it's still a possibility. Just don't tell me you want to set up a farm stand on the road here. No way I'm going to try to staff one of those."

"I agree. I can't see selling a couple of pounds at a time — too labor-intensive. And don't forget the restaurant, if we have the right varieties. You have a list of our varieties, when they ripen, and what they're good for, like cooking?"

"Yes to the first two, no for the last. You don't plan to *give* those apples to the restaurant, I hope?" Bree said.

"Maybe the first batch, but not after that. I'm running a business just like they are, and they'd better expect to pay us." Meg sighed. "Remind me again why I got into this?"

"You're preserving an agricultural heritage that stretches back centuries. You're supporting small farmers. You're producing clean, honest food. Besides, you needed a job. Is that enough, or should I keep going?"

Meg held up a hand. "That's fine, thank you. I suppose I should have thought this through more carefully when I started, but events kind of took over. But I like what you said, about traditions. It does mean something to me, that my own ancestors farmed this land, maybe even planted some of these apples. It makes me feel more connected somehow. You want to walk me through the orchard later and show me what happened?"

"Sure. What's your schedule look like?"

"I'm clear for today, I think. Seth, did you have any plans?"

Seth had been suspiciously quiet, watching Meg and Bree talk. "Nope. No jobs until Wednesday. Might hit some of the local flea markets and see if I can pick up any salvage."

"What, you don't have enough yet?"

"There's plenty of space left in the barn."

"But we just got it cleared out! I was kind of enjoying being able to see the floor. I guess it was too good to be true."

"I figured I'd better stake out my space before you started filling it up with apples." He drained the last of his coffee and stood up. "Thanks for breakfast. I'll give you a call later, okay? You want to see me out?"

"Hey, guys, I can look the other way if you want," Bree volunteered with a wicked smile.

"Nonsense, Bree." Almost defiantly, Meg went over to Seth, wrapped her arms around him, and gave him a serious kiss. He responded with enthusiasm. "There. Now you can go." She turned him toward the door and gave him a small push. "And if you see your mother, thank her again for me, will you?"

"Um, right. Bye." Seth, apparently tongue-tied, left. Once outside he started whistling as he headed for his office space.

Bree turned to Meg. "So?"

"What? We're both adults. I don't pry into what you and Michael do, do I?"

"Nope. Just checking. If it matters, I approve. He's a good guy."

"I think so, too."

"I'm just surprised you didn't jump him before this."

"Bree! That's not the way I do things. Besides, it just sort of happened. We got wet in the storm, and . . ."

"Uh-huh. Well, I know how to mind my own business. Just don't get too mushy on me — we've got work to do."

"Good. So let's go check the trees."

Meg pulled on her rubber boots, as did Bree, and together they made their way up the hill toward the orchard. It was another lovely day. The sun was burning off the last of the early mist, which still lingered over the Great Meadow below. The air was fresh, washed clean by the storm. Luckily, conversation was impossible while climbing the hill, so Meg could think about what had happened the night before. She had tried her best not to give any thought at all to the relationship she and Seth been dancing around for months now. Her track record with relationships was lousy, and she certainly had enough going on in her life at the moment without trying to fit in another person. And Seth had been careful not to press. Of course, he had been burned once before, too, so maybe he had reason to be cautious himself. Last night had just happened, without forethought, but it had

291

certainly been mutual, and Meg couldn't say she had any regrets. Nope, none. Where things went from here was anybody's guess, but she was going to take it one day at a time. Like the orchard: things could change really fast, and a lot of the factors she had absolutely no control over. Sometimes that was hard to accept, but she was learning.

"Yo, Meg?"

Meg focused with a start and realized they had reached the top of the hill. "Sorry, I was wool-gathering."

"We've got company." Bree nodded toward a bulky figure on the other side of the orchard, and it took Meg a moment to recognize beekeeper Carl Frederickson, decked out in his protective gear. He raised a hand and waved.

"Have you met Carl?" Meg asked Bree.

"Sure — he's been providing bees here for years. We should see how the hives are doing."

They crossed the wet grass to where Carl stood. He'd taken off his head covering by the time they arrived. "Morning, ladies. Your trees seem to have come through the storm pretty well."

"Hi, Carl. The hives okay?" Bree asked.

"Not bad — a couple of lids blew off in the storm. The new hives seem to be doing well. I hope that's the last we'll see of the colony collapse problem. Strange doings in town, eh?"

It took Meg a moment to figure out that he was talking about Sam's death. "You mean what happened to Sam Anderson? Did you ever run into him? You must cover a lot of farms around here."

"Might have. Big guy, youngish? I think so; he asked me about honey, was real curious about what I did. Shame, isn't it? Kellogg runs a nice pig operation."

How much ground had Sam covered in the short time he was here? Meg wondered. And how many people had he crossed paths with in his ramblings? Not many had come forward. Had the state police gone looking for them? "Where did you meet him?" Meg asked.

"Can't remember. Like you said, I cover a lot of ground. Kellogg keeps a hive for his vegetable garden — he's got maybe an acre planted, near the house. But a lot of other folks have hives, too."

Bree shot a glance at Meg. "I need to take Meg through the orchard so we can check for damage. Good to see you again, Carl."

"Likewise." Carl pulled on his headgear and went back to examining the nearest hive.

Bree turned to Meg. "Let's take it from the corner by the road."

As they walked toward the road, Meg scanned the scene. The ground under the trees was littered with small branches and leaves and, yes, a number of green apples. It tore at her heart to see them, even as she realized that they represented only a small portion of the crop. Surely there were far more still hanging on the trees? "What should I be looking for?"

They walked the rows of trees, from one end to the other, and Meg was glad she had worn the boots. The grass was wet, beaded with rain and dew, and brilliant green. They startled a rabbit, who darted away toward the edge of the orchard. Unseen birds sang from the branches around them. Meg had to keep reminding herself that this was a damage assessment, not a stroll in the summer fields, but it was hard to focus.

"So what's the overall verdict?" she asked.

"Like I said, you didn't suffer much. Maybe ten percent, but we can hope that thinning makes the remaining apples bigger and better. All things willing."

"Amen. I feel like we should create some sort of shrine up here, and make offerings to the gods of agriculture."

"The goddess — Ceres. Well, Saturn gets

all the PR, but Ceres was nicer. There are probably more female gods than males, in any case — more nurturing, you know. Like Fauna — she had some good parties."

"Let's go with goddesses. After all, we women are the ones running this show, right?"

"You got it."

"I told you I ran into Carl Frederickson once before, right? Do we need to worry about this hive problem?" Meg asked.

Bree nodded. "In a general way, yes. Colony collapse disorder is a real problem, all over. But for the moment, here, no. We can talk about that after harvest. Uh-oh."

"What?" Meg followed Bree's gaze, and saw Nicky's car pull into her driveway. Nicky got out of the car and waved to Meg, who waved back. "You don't much like Nicky, do you, Bree?"

Bree snorted. "She's okay, if you like the sunshine type, but she pisses me off sometimes. I mean, Daddy buys her a restaurant? What's that about? Me, I've had to work for everything I ever got."

"I know what you mean, but I think she's sincere — she doesn't shove it in your face. And she's had a rough time since she got here. Starting a marriage and a business at the same time, in an unfamiliar place, can't be easy, and then one of her best friends — not to mention a colleague — gets killed right under her nose. So cut her a little slack, will you? You can hate her later, when things settle down."

Bree looked contrite. "Sorry, I'm being petty. Look, I said I'd help her find staff for the place. That counts for something, doesn't it?"

"Of course it does, and I'm sure she'll thank you. Well, I guess I'd better go see what this is about. I hate to say it, but it usually isn't good news."

"I'll try not to say 'I told you so.' See you later."

When Meg reached the bottom of the hill, Nicky was still leaning against her car, looking upset. Meg sighed inwardly: she'd just dodged one bullet with the orchard, and she really didn't want to try to fix Nicky's most recent mess, whatever it was. "Hi, Nicky. What's up?"

"Hi, Meg. I'm sorry. This is stupid — you probably have a million things to do. Heck, I have a million things to do. But I just had to get out of there."

"Problems?"

"It's Brian. He's been acting really weird lately. I mean, he won't tell me what he's doing. He comes and goes. And he keeps

296

staring at me when he thinks I won't notice. But he won't talk to me! I don't know what I did . . ." Nicky looked like she was about to cry.

Meg rushed to forestall her. "Why don't we go inside and get something to drink? And we can sit down and try to figure this out."

Nicky obediently followed her into the kitchen. "I wonder if we'll ever have a house like this," she said wistfully, looking around the sunny kitchen. "I mean, not anytime soon. We can't afford to live anywhere except over the restaurant, at least for the first year or two."

Meg refrained from saying that Nicky had known that when they bought their place. And she could see that things might get kind of claustrophobic, living and working in the same place with your husband. "At least you've got a short commute," she said lightly. "Iced tea?"

"Sure, that's fine. I mean, I'm okay with the arrangement, for now. But I wonder if Brian is. Maybe he didn't think things through very well, or maybe I just steamrolled him and he went along with what I wanted. And we're both so busy, and so tired all the time. I thought this part of it would be fun. And . . ."

Meg set a glass in front of her and sat down. "Yes?"

"I miss Sam!" Nicky burst out. "I know it's hard to explain, and it's kind of odd, getting married and then having Sam move in with us right away. But we needed him. We were kind of like the Three Musketeers, you know? We all had different skills, but they meshed — we worked as a unit. And he was, like, my best friend. It would be one thing if he'd left, but he's dead!" Nicky finally gave in to the tears she had been fighting, covering her face with her hands.

Meg wondered what she was supposed to do now. Maybe doing nothing would work: Nicky seemed to need to vent more than anything else, and maybe giving her the chance to do that, coupled with a sympathetic ear, would be enough. She had to keep in mind that Nicky hadn't had a mother for quite a while. Did she have any other female friends? Not in Granford, certainly. So Meg resigned herself to playing surrogate mother and friend, rolled into one.

"It's okay, Nicky. You've taken on a lot in a short time, even before Sam died. I think you deserve some time to let it all out. Heck, if you want to scream and throw things, that's fine with me."

Nicky sniffed and produced a watery smile. "Thanks, Meg. I keep trying to be cheerful and upbeat for Brian, and somehow that just makes him grumpier. I wish he'd talk to me. Sam and I used to talk about everything, and it really helped."

"Nicky," Meg said slowly, "do you think Brian was jealous of Sam?"

"Huh? But Sam and I, we weren't that way. I mean, he was a friend."

"I know, but maybe Brian had a problem with the fact that you two were so close. You could talk to Sam in a way that you didn't talk to him, and maybe he felt left out. And he doesn't know how to change that, even though Sam is dead, so he feels guilty about resenting a dead man. Could that make any sense?"

Nicky stared at her, and then her expression changed. "You don't think . . . ? No, it's not possible."

"What?"

"That Brian had anything to do with Sam's death? I mean, Brian's not violent, or mean. But maybe they got into something and it just went wrong. Maybe they were both out there looking at pigs together. Maybe . . . Oh, I don't know!" Nicky melted into tears again, this time with a hint of hysteria.

The scenario seemed unlikely to Meg, but nevertheless she asked gently, "Nicky, have you talked to Brian about this?"

Nicky looked up at her. "I can't. I've tried, but half the time he's not around, and when he is, we're both so busy . . . or he just brushes me off. Meg, could you talk to him for me?"

Oh, hell. She should have seen this coming. Now she was supposed to be a go-between? "Nicky, I don't think that's appropriate . . ."

Nicky grabbed her wrist. "No, Meg, please! Just talk to him, find out what's bothering him. Maybe he'll talk to you. He just clams up with me."

Or maybe he'll tell me I'm a busybody and to get the hell out and mind my own business. Which I should. "All right, all right," she gave in, "I'll talk to him."

"Will you go now?" Nicky asked. "He's at the restaurant. That's one reason I had to get out. He wouldn't talk, but he kept watching me all the time with that droopy expression."

Well, she might as well get it over with. "All right. You want to stay here? Bree's around."

"Okay. Thank you, Meg. I know it's a lot to ask. But I'm afraid if I say the wrong

thing, everything will blow up — us, the restaurant. I don't want that to happen. I love Brian, and I really want this to work. So maybe he'll talk to you, or at least he'll be polite."

You are going to owe me a lot *of dinners, Nicky.* "Okay. If you see Bree, tell her where I went, will you?"

Nicky nodded. "Thank you, Meg. I really appreciate it."

21

For once Meg wished the ride to town took longer. She didn't want to talk to Brian. She didn't want to put herself in the middle of a messy situation, and if it did all blow up, she'd probably get blamed for something — the failure of the restaurant, or maybe the marriage. Or both. She wasn't good at this kind of thing; she was much happier ignoring personal crises until they either went away or resolved themselves. Not always for the better, she reminded herself. Well, she'd told Nicky she'd try, so here she was.

Meg parked and walked up to the front door and rapped. "Brian?" she called out.

"Back here. Hang on."

Brian emerged from the back of the building, wiping his hands on a rag. "Oh, hi, Meg. Nicky's not here."

"I know. She's at my place."

"Huh?" Brian looked confused, and Meg

302

wondered if he'd even realized that Nicky had left.

"She was upset. Actually, she was upset because she thinks *you're* upset, and she doesn't know what to ask you. Look, I'm sorry — I don't usually mess with other people's problems. But I know what it's like to be a stranger in town, to not know anybody, and I want you to know that I'm here if you're willing to talk about it. And if you're not, you can throw me out and I'll understand."

Brian tucked the towel under his belt and rubbed his hands over his face. "What did she tell you?"

"She said that you were acting odd, and not talking to her. Listen, can we sit down, somewhere that people aren't likely to walk in on us?"

"The kitchen, I guess." Brian led the way, then pointed toward a stool. Meg pulled it toward the table and sat.

"Brian, I'm sorry. I shouldn't be in the middle of this — you two need to work this out between yourselves. But the fact that your friend was murdered makes it kind of public, and unfortunately I've had a little experience with that sort of situation since I arrived here. Nicky says you're acting weird toward her, and it really upsets her, and she doesn't know what to do. Look, I know I have no right to butt in here, but . . . did you have a problem with Sam?"

Brian stared at her. "So she sent you," he said flatly. He scrubbed his fingers through his hair. "I *was* jealous. Sam and Nicky . . . sometimes I felt shut out. It's like they had their own language, their shorthand, and I couldn't share it with them." He shook his head. "Dumb, isn't it? I mean, Nicky married me, not Sam. And I have to say he was a pretty decent guy. And a good cook. Okay, let's cut to the chase. She's actually wondering if I had something to do with Sam's death? No. No way I would hurt him, or anybody else, for that matter."

"Brian, I believe you, and I'm pretty sure Nicky doesn't really think that. It's very clear that she loves you; it's just that you're both overworked and under a lot of stress. But why is Sam dead?"

Brian stood up and paced around the kitchen. "I don't know! I mean, if it had happened in Boston, I could almost understand it. Something random, like a mugging, a robbery — you kind of look out for it. But here? This place looks like something off a Christmas card. Why would anyone here want to kill him?"

"Can you think of *anything* that you

haven't already told the police?"

He shook his head. "I don't think so. I mean, we were all coming and going. I wasn't even sure where he was half the time, until he walked in carrying a bunch of something new. He was raised in a city, like Nicky. He didn't go around oohing and aahing over pretty landscapes, but he appreciated artisanal products. He was getting to know the neighborhood, you know? He was like a kid in a candy shop, only he was hauling home vegetables. You see anything there that would tick someone off? Enough to kill him?"

"No, I don't," Meg agreed. "What about Derek?"

Brian snorted. "Derek's a drama queen, but he couldn't kill a spider."

"So, from what you've said, and what we know, *nobody* had a motive to kill him," Meg said.

"Somebody did," Brian muttered bitterly.

They fell silent for a moment. Meg was pretty sure that whatever issues Brian had with Nicky, Sam wasn't one of them. What else would it be? "Brian, Nicky says you haven't been talking to her much lately. I know you've both been busy, but is there something more going on?"

Brian's shoulders sagged. "We're running

out of money."

Ah. "How bad?"

"The nice chunk Nicky's dad gave us as a wedding present made it possible to buy this place, and to fix it up. The stuff we've bought we paid for — the kitchen, the front of the house. In a couple of weeks we're going to have this great space all fitted out and ready to go, but . . . well, we can't afford to open."

"What do you mean?"

"Let's put it this way — we can either afford staff, serving empty plates, or we can fill the plates, but then we'll have to do everything ourselves — prep, cook, serve, and clean up. It's too much for two people to handle. I don't even know if we can keep Edna on."

"Nicky's father can't help out again?"

Brian shook his head. "Even if we could get up the nerve to ask him, he's been pretty hard hit by the market slump. He's tapped out."

"Have you talked to any banks about a loan?"

"Sure. At least, I have. Nicky doesn't know. That was our deal — she'd handle the cooking, I'd handle the management. And she's been so upset about Sam's death that I haven't wanted to dump anything

306

more on her. But the bank here more or less laughed at me, unfortunately. We have no capital, except what's in the building, we have no financial track record, we're starting up in a risky business in a depressed area. Heck, *I* wouldn't lend money to me if I were a banker."

"Is there anyone else you can ask? Family, friends, outside investors?"

"You're kidding, right? Everybody's hurting. I know, we were idiots to think we could start this up and make it work, just as the market went south."

"And you feel like it's your fault?" Meg prompted.

"Of course I do! I had it all mapped out, with spreadsheets and projections. A nice little business plan with color charts and everything. But nothing ever works out, right? Even with getting a decent deal on this place, and living here to save money, and buying half our equipment used, we're still short."

Meg could sympathize with their problems. They were young and hopeful — and they hadn't allowed much margin of error for their start-up. Understandable, but didn't make it easier for them to swallow. Meg sat, turning over in her mind what Brian had said. She had no money to lend even if she wanted to, and she couldn't think of any friends or colleagues to tap. Brian had done the right things, and gotten the predictable answers. It must be awful to face failure before you even started. No wonder he hadn't shared this with Nicky yet.

But there had to be some way out of this. Nicky and Brian had done so much, come so far. The place was lovely and ready to go. What could she do . . . ?

A vague idea started to take shape in her mind. "Brian, do you have to make any decisions right away? I mean, in the next few days?"

"Apart from deciding which one of our bills to pay with what we've got left? No. There aren't any orders we can stop, or changes we can make now. Why?"

"I may have an idea, but I want to check a few things before I say anything. If you can wait a few days, I might be able to give you more. But right now, will you please talk to Nicky? I think she suspects something is seriously wrong, but she's afraid to ask. You're married, and you're business partners — you need to let her know what's going on."

He sighed. "I know. Will you ask her to come back?"

"Soon as I get home." Meg stood up. "Brian, you two can work through this. Maybe you'll have to sacrifice this place, but you can move past it, if you love each other." Meg realized what she said and almost gagged. If Nicky had appointed her as wise mother, her subconscious mind seemed to have taken it to heart and was now spouting platitudes.

But it seemed to be working: Brian looked more cheerful than he had when she arrived. "Thanks, Meg. I'm sorry you had to get into our dirty laundry, but I think you're right."

Back in her car, Meg pulled out her cell phone and called Seth. When he answered, she said, "Where are you?"

"Eric's barn in Hadley. You miss me already?"

"Yes, but that's not why I'm calling. I need to talk to you about something. Can we meet for lunch?"

"Sure. How about that diner by the tracks in Northampton?"

"Sounds good. Half an hour?"

"See you then."

Meg started the car and realized she was smiling again. She pulled out of the driveway and headed for her own place.

Nicky and Bree were sitting at the kitchen

table with plates in front of them when Meg came in. "Wow, something smells good!"

"Nicky's been showing me how to make a frittata. We saved some for you," Bree said.

"Thanks, but I've got a lunch date. And Nicky, you should go home and talk to Brian."

"He's not hiding some awful secret?"

"Nothing to do with Sam, if that's what you're asking. But you two have things you need to talk about. Go, now."

"Thanks, Meg." Nicky gave her a quick hug on her way out the door.

Bree sighed. "You could have waited until she did the dishes. Where're you going?"

"Lunch with Seth, in Northampton."

"Ah. Should I plan to be somewhere else this afternoon?"

"No." Meg swatted her. "If you can believe it, this is actually a business lunch of sorts. I'll fill you in later. I'm still working things out in my head."

"Very mysterious. Well, you two have a nice time, and we can talk when you get back."

As she drove to Northampton, Meg's mind was occupied with trying to put her spur-of-the-moment idea into some sort of logical order. Seth was already waiting at the endearingly shabby diner when she

310

walked in. When he saw her, he stood up and smiled.

"Hi," she said as she slid into the booth. Suddenly she felt shy.

"Hi to you. Everything all right?" Seth asked a little anxiously.

Meg realized suddenly that she hadn't made it clear on the phone that what she wanted to talk about had nothing to do with what had happened the night before, but Seth didn't know that. "Oh, fine. Look, about last night . . ."

"Last night was great. Wasn't it? You're not having second thoughts?"

"About us? No, of course not."

He laid a hand over hers on the table. "Good. I just didn't want you to feel pressured. I know things could get awkward if it doesn't work out, and you're stuck with me in your backyard."

"Seth, I'm happy. You're great. We're great." She stopped, then burst out laughing. "This is ridiculous. Seth, last night was wonderful, and I hope there will be many more like it."

"Okay," Seth replied cautiously. The waitress appeared with tattered menus, and they ordered. "So what do we need to talk about?"

"This is just an idea I had, and it's pretty

sketchy, so hear me out. After you left this morning, Nicky came by all worked up because she thought Brian was holding something back from her. She asked me to go talk to Brian."

"So you did, I assume?"

"I did." Meg sighed. "How did I end up in the middle? Anyway, he told me that he was upset because they've more or less gone through all their money, and he didn't know how to tell her. Brian said they had enough money either to open without food, or to buy supplies but not be able to pay for staff. And I thought we might be in a position to do something about the food."

"How?"

"I'm pretty new in town, and I'm also pretty new to farming. I know my crop isn't big enough to sell to major chains, so I'm going to be talking to smaller places. And that started me thinking. My impression is — and correct me if I'm wrong — that there are a lot of people in Granford who live on farms that their parents and grandparents used to farm for a living. But that's not economically feasible anymore, so most of them have jobs somewhere else, and raise a small crop or a few head of livestock, more out of nostalgia than anything else. Jake Kellogg is a good example — when I met

312

him, he says he raises pigs because his father raised pigs before him, but it's not primarily for the income."

"I'm with you so far, but how does this apply to the restaurant?" Seth was following intently.

Meg chose her words carefully. "Do you think it would be possible to round up enough of these small farmers to provide the food for the restaurant?"

"For free?"

"No, I don't expect them to donate the food outright. But here's the part I'm trying to work out: say they enter into some sort of partnership agreement with Nicky and Brian — becoming, in effect, minority shareholders in the restaurant? They provide what they raise, under a contract with the restaurant, but they wait to be paid until the restaurant is on its feet and can pay them back? Maybe with interest, or a share of the profits, like a co-op? Does this make any sense? Would people go for it?"

Seth sat back and stared over Meg's head, thinking. He didn't answer immediately, and finally he said, "I like it. I think you're bang on about the people who are growing stuff around here — I can name quite a few off the top of my head. Some of them sell to farmers' markets or to some of the restaurants in Amherst and Northampton, but they could just as easily sell to the Czarneckis' restaurant, so they wouldn't lose financially in the long run. But wouldn't it be kind of feast or famine for the restaurant? Plenty of stuff from June to October, but what would they do over the winter?"

"I have no idea, but it's something we can all talk about. I mean, people survived for generations on whatever they grew in their backyards. Based on what Nicky has talked about before, I think it's more a question of making the case to the patrons — eat what's in season, not what we've shipped in from New Zealand."

"That makes sense, but it's a marketing question. We'd have to work out how much of what products, timing, some sort of legal agreement format."

Meg interrupted, "Should the town be involved? *Could* the town be involved, or should this be a private agreement?"

"Another good question." Seth nodded. "I'd have to run it by the Board, and maybe town counsel."

The waitress reappeared, slapped plates in front of them, sloshed coffee into cups. "Anything else?"

"Not right now," Seth said. He waited until she had returned to the counter, then

314

said, "Meg, I like the idea. I think it's doable, but we'll have to sit down with Nicky and Brian and see what they need and whether they're interested, and if they're willing to accept a partnership idea. And then we'd have to approach the local farmers and see if they want to participate in something like this, and what they've got to offer. I mean, you can't plan a menu around three months of green beans and pumpkins."

"Heck, I've seen more than that growing in Granford in the short time I've been here — I'm not worried about that. Can we go talk to Nicky and Brian after lunch?"

"Uh, sure. Is it that urgent?"

"Seth, they're supposed to open in less than two months. They've got to know that they'll be able to, and then we've got to talk to all the growers and get them on board, and then we've got to figure out a way to promote this — you know, this is a wonderful marketing idea, and maybe they can drum up some interest in the Boston food community — after all, Nicky and Brian must have some connections there — and —"

"Whoa, slow down! One step at a time."

Meg took a deep breath and smiled at Seth. "Works for me."

22

Meg followed Seth's car back to Granford and the restaurant. She was warmed that he hadn't dismissed her idea. She knew the concept needed some fine-tuning, but she believed the idea was sound. And her own orchard business would benefit, too, wouldn't it? She would have a reason to talk to the other small farmers in town, to get to know them — that would be a big plus. And she was uniquely qualified to pull something like this together, based on her analytical background. Brian could give her cost and income projections, and maybe she could figure out where he'd gone wrong, or been overly optimistic. She could help to determine what he and Nicky could afford to pay for food, which in turn would give a ball-park estimate for the value of a partnership share, if it came to such a formal agreement. Maybe that wouldn't even be necessary; maybe it could all be done with a handshake, with farmers extending credit along with goodwill. No, the restaurant was still an unknown quantity — a formal agreement would be a better idea. And she'd have to listen to what Seth and the farmers had to say, and see how interested they were. But the basic idea still sounded right. The rest was just detail. She hoped.

It wasn't until Meg pulled into the parking lot of the restaurant that she realized that she had let her enthusiasm carry her away and she hadn't even mentioned the idea to Brian yet. This might be an awkward conversation if Brian hadn't told Nicky about their financial mess; and even if he had, they might both be too upset to listen to her new plan.

Too late — Nicky and Brian had come out the door at the sound of their cars. Nicky's face looked a bit red and blotchy, but she summoned up a smile and waved. "You coming in or what?" she yelled.

"Is this a good time? I've got an idea I want you to hear, but we can come back later," Meg said, approaching the porch.

"It's okay — we're good. Brian told me what's been going on, and it's a whole lot better than what I was thinking. So come on in."

Meg climbed the porch stairs, with Seth

317

behind her. Brian held the door for them and Nicky led the way to the kitchen.

"You hungry?" she asked.

"We just ate lunch!" Meg protested. "Besides, when did you find time to cook anything?"

Nicky laughed. "I cook when I'm upset. It calms me down. Of course, I also cook when I'm happy. Guess that's why I'm a chef!" She smiled at Brian, and he smiled back.

Meg deduced that all was right, or at least a lot closer to it, in their little world. Nicky deposited a small china dish in front of her and Seth, and handed out spoons. "It's a mini-clafoutis — I found somebody who had some early cherries, and I didn't want to waste them. Taste it and tell me what you think."

Meg dipped into the golden batter and pulled out a bite studded with small red cherries. She tasted it: still warm, it was a perfect balance of sweet and tart, soft but with a little crunch from the coarse sugar sprinkled over the top, and from something else. "Almonds?" she asked.

Nicky beamed. "You got it! I added some ground almonds for texture — the flavor goes well with cherries. You like it?"

"It's great. Not too heavy, not too sweet.

Seth?" It was a good thing Meg was actively involved in running an orchard, or Nicky's food would be adding inches to her waist in no time.

"What she said," he answered, swallowing the last bite. "I know I've said it before, but — Nicky, you can *cook.*"

Nicky dimpled. "Thank you both. Now, what did you want to talk about?"

Meg looked at Brian, who had been hovering in the background, looking proud. "Brian, come sit down — this involves both of you."

Brian joined them at the table. "Is this about . . . what we talked about?"

"Brian, you can say it," Nicky said. "Our financial mess. Our empty pockets. The gaping hole in our budget."

Meg checked to see if Nicky was being snide, but she looked surprisingly sunny. "The difficult financial situation you're in, right. You said Brian told you what the problem is. Did you have any ideas? I mean, if you're thinking of selling out, or just shutting down, there's no point in getting into this."

Nicky and Brian exchanged glances, and Nicky answered, "If there is any way at all that we can keep this going, we're in. We can't just walk away. So what've you got?"

Meg looked at Seth before she began, "Brian, you said you didn't have the cash or credit to buy the food you need, right?"

"Not and do anything else."

"My thought was, why not see if you can interest local farmers in providing what you need?"

"But we've been doing that already. At least, Sam had started doing it, and Brian and I have been following up when we could. That's how I got the cherries," Nicky said.

"I know, but I was thinking of something more systematic. As you probably already know, most of the farmers around here don't produce much. In fact, calling them 'farmers' is kind of a stretch — they're more like hobby farmers. But if you put them all together, you might — heck, you'd probably have enough to provide for one restaurant, right?"

Brian sat back, looking thoughtful. "So you're saying we contract with them to provide exclusively to us?"

"Something like that. You have a formal agreement to buy some or even all of what they produce. I know, you're going to tell me you can't pay them, not now. But what about if you offered them shares in a partnership? You two would still hold controlling interest, but they would get what you owe them and a share of the profits, too. They'd have to understand that they're going to have to wait a bit for their money, particularly the profits part, but you'd have enough to get you started. What do you think?"

Brian and Nicky looked at each other, and then Brian spoke. "Off the top of my head, I see a few issues. The first is the legal basis for this — we'd have to get somebody to draw up an agreement, whatever form it takes. Second, we'd have to know that enough providers are interested, and what they can give us. Third — well, that's Nicky's territory. Nicky, can you cook from whatever you get locally?"

Nicky's eyes were shining. "Oh, Brian, don't worry about the nitpicky legal side. But sure, I've always planned to work with local products. That's what I want for this restaurant — food that hasn't traveled more than a few miles before it's served."

"If I can play the devil's advocate here," Seth interrupted, "what about during the winter? What do you do when all you've got is a lot of squash?"

Nicky smiled at him. "It's never that bad. You've got meat, chicken, and eggs year-round. Sure, there's squash, pumpkins, and the like. Some apple varieties keep well over the winter, or you can dry them. Cheeses. And you know what? You stock up on whatever you get in the summer and fall, and you preserve them. What do you think people did in the old days? They spent a heck of a lot of time in summer canning stuff for the winter. There's even an old storage pantry in the basement here, with shelves. We'd just be re-creating what they used to do in this very house. Ooh, I like this."

"Before you get too excited, you realize that you'd have to start canning right now, if you want to have anything to eat next winter," Meg said.

"I know, I know," Nicky said dreamily. "But think about it! Maybe we could gather people together here, before we open, and they could relearn how to preserve our foods. That's pretty much fallen by the wayside these days, right? Maybe we could hold a class here. I mean, it'd be a whole lot easier to do in a big kitchen like this than at home, and we could get a bunch of women together and they could all learn at once . . ."

"Sort of like a canning bee?" Meg volunteered, swept up in Nicky's enthusiasm.

"Exactly! Oh, this is really great. Do you

think it could work?"

"We'd have to get the farmers on board pretty quickly," Seth said, "but I've known most of them my whole life. I can tell you who to talk to. And I can talk to the other members of the Select Board. They might be willing to help with the legal side, if town counsel agrees, since this will benefit the community. There might be some sorts of community assistance grants available for a start-up like this. Lots of possibilities."

Nicky bounced out of her chair, too excited to sit still. "Oh, thank you, thank you both! How soon can we start?"

"Tomorrow?" Meg looked at Seth, and he nodded. "Why don't we put together a list of what we know is available, and what you want to look for?"

"Let me find something to write on," Brian said, and disappeared into the front room. Nicky threw herself back into her chair.

"Nicky," Meg said in a low voice, "are you two really okay? And don't let us steam-roll you into this idea if it's not right for you."

"Oh, Meg, thank you for worrying, but Brian and I are fine. I'm a lot tougher than he thinks I am, but it's sweet that he was trying to protect me. Anyway, your idea is exactly what this restaurant needs. I mean, there are more and more restaurants that advertise using local foods — bless them! — but the idea of having the whole community involved? That's a great twist. And that means that most of the people in town will show up at least once, just to see what we're doing with their produce. And if it's good, they'll keep coming back, right?"

Meg had to smile. "That would certainly be one benefit."

Brian reappeared with paper and pencils and sat down. "Okay, Nicky, what do you want?"

"Veggies are easy — let's wait on those. Meg, can we get apples from you, if you've got the right kinds?" When Meg nodded, she went on, "I think the most important thing is our proteins, right? Beef, pork, lamb, chicken, fish. Pork we know we can get locally." A brief shadow passed over her face, but she kept on. "Seth, anybody raise cattle here?"

"Sure — Elliott Deane, over toward South Hadley."

"Dairy or meat? Because we'd need both."

"Then you should talk to Mary Cole, too. She makes great cheeses, and butter, if you ask nicely. And you've already found Kibbee's."

"Fish, fish . . ." Nicky tapped her pencil on the pad. "There's a river near here, right?"

Seth smiled. "Yes, the Connecticut River, which is still good fishing. Particularly for shad, when it's in season."

"Wonderful. Then there's mushrooms. Fresh herbs. I hear the Hadley asparagus is good. Ooh, and how about local heirloom vegetable varieties? I'll bet we can find stuff that doesn't ever appear in stores."

Meg interrupted, "I can talk to Gail at the Historical Society, see if she has any old harvest fair listings and what was available in the past. You could have a nice tie-in that way."

"Oh, right, good, Meg. I love this! Seth, you have any other ideas?"

"I know a few people we could talk to tomorrow. It might be good to test the waters, see what they have to say, before we get too deep into this. But first you and Brian have got to figure out quantities and pricing, so at least we'll have some talking points."

Brian nodded. "We can do that. I've got some spreadsheets roughed out already. Nicky would have to tinker with the menus and ingredients."

"Why don't I touch base tomorrow morning and see what you've come up with? Nicky, maybe you could throw in some sample menus, so we can show people how you plan to use the food? You want to come along?"

Nicky suddenly looked less eager. "Seth," she said reluctantly, "I'm not real good meeting new people. I get kind of tongue-tied — you saw that at the meeting in town. These are your friends — could you talk to them first? Please?"

Meg avoided looking at Seth. She'd come up with a bright idea, dragged Seth into it, and now Nicky was asking him to give up more of his time. She resolved to ask him about it later. She'd be happy to help out — if Bree let her off the orchard leash long enough — but like Seth, she had her own business to attend to, she reminded herself.

"Yeah, I can do that. But just the first round. You're going to have to do the rest of it. Oh, and I'll lay it out at the Select Board working meeting on Tuesday — you don't have to be there for that. This is just exploratory, but Tom and Mrs. Goldthwaite may have some ideas of their own."

"Thank you, both of you. We owe you so much, and we'll make it up to you somehow."

They were startled out of their happy

mood by an abrupt pounding on the front door.

"Mr. Czarnecki? This is Detective Marcus."

The cheerful atmosphere in the kitchen evaporated like water on a hot griddle. Brian stood up abruptly and went to the front. Meg, Nicky, and Seth looked at each other.

"What's this about?" Meg asked.

Seth shrugged. "I have no idea."

Brian returned with Detective Marcus in tow, followed by Art Preston. Brian continued around the table to stand behind Nicky's chair. Meg glanced at Art, but his face gave nothing away.

"Ms. Corey, Chapin." Marcus nodded. "I have some more questions for you and your wife, Mr. Czarnecki."

Seth had stood up when Marcus entered. "Would you prefer that we leave?"

"Not necessary," Marcus said curtly. "The ME faxed me the autopsy results for your friend this morning. Turns out it was a little more complicated than we thought."

"You said Sam died from suffocation. Asphyxia. Right?" Brian asked.

"He did. But the ME also found evidence of anaphylactic shock. More specifically, it looks like he was stung by a bee and had a pretty strong reaction. Did either of you know if he was allergic?"

Nicky and Brian looked at each other, but it was Nicky who spoke first. "This is the first that I've heard of it, but Sam grew up in a city, like me. I don't know if he ever ran into any bees. Maybe even *he* didn't know he was allergic. Is that what killed him?"

"No, suffocation's still the primary cause of death. But if he was in anaphylactic shock, it would have made it a lot easier. You never saw him with an epinephrine pen?"

Nicky shook her head and swallowed before answering. "No, never. He was always completely healthy. I mean, he barely took aspirin. I can't think of any other allergies he had. Certainly no food allergies — I would have known about that."

"Was there anyone else he was close to, who might have known about it?"

Nicky was shaking her head. "I don't think so. I gave you all the personal information I had, so you could contact his family. I met his folks once or twice, when they came up to visit him, but we never talked about stuff like that. You could ask Derek, I guess. Maybe Sam told him. But it's news to me. Brian?"

"I didn't know anything either," Brian

said. "So what does that mean about Sam's death, Detective? He was stung by a bee, and then fell down and suffocated?"

Meg realized with a start that Marcus probably still hadn't broadcast the news about the footprint. She forced herself to meet Marcus's gaze.

Marcus looked briefly at Meg before going on. "There's one other item that we didn't release. Sam Anderson suffocated, but someone helped him die. There was a muddy footprint in the middle of his back." Marcus sat back in his chair and waited for responses.

"So you're definitely saying it was murder?" The words were out of Meg's mouth before she could stop them.

Marcus fixed her with a cold look. "Yes, it was. I guess that's no secret anymore."

"Detective," Meg said carefully, "that conclusion was hard to avoid based on the questions you've been asking."

Marcus looked tired. "Procedure, Ms. Corey." He turned back to Nicky, who was struggling with tears. Meg knew it must have been hard to hear it put into words, whatever she had suspected.

"Someone really killed him," Nicky whispered, and then her voice grew stronger. "Someone shoved him into the mud and held him there, while he tried to breathe and couldn't, and waited . . . and . . ." Finally she dissolved into tears, and Brian was quick to pull her close.

He looked over her head at Marcus. "I guess we kind of hoped it was an accident after all. You have any idea who did this?"

"It was a man's shoe," Marcus said without elaboration. He looked at Meg and Seth, but neither volunteered a comment. *Let him do his job,* Meg told herself. She avoided looking at Art.

Finally, Marcus stood up. "Let me know if you remember anything else." He nodded at the group and stalked out, leaving everyone stunned.

Art stayed behind. "Sorry to barge in on you like that. I think he wanted to catch you off guard, to see how you reacted. He asked me along as a courtesy."

"So what does this allergy tell us?" Seth asked.

"It widens the field of suspects," Art said. "It means that it wouldn't have taken a lot of strength to hold him down, if he was already in shock. A woman or even a child could have done it."

"Poor Sam," Nicky said softly, her head against Brian's shoulder. "What a terrible way to die."

"Is there a good one?" Art said. "Well, I'll leave you to whatever you were doing. Meg, Seth." He nodded, then left.

Seth followed him out, leaving Meg feeling like a third wheel in the kitchen.

She stood up. "Look, this is a difficult time, and I don't want to rush you into anything. Think about what we said. We can move forward if you want, but don't feel you have to. Talk it over tonight, and let me and Seth know."

Nicky brushed away a last tear and said, "Meg, we don't have to talk about it. I love your idea, and I want to see if it'll work. If it doesn't, at least we tried. So maybe you can stop by in the morning and we'll have a shopping list for you. I'll give you breakfast."

"How can I pass up an offer like that? See you tomorrow."

Seth was still talking to Art when Meg went out to the porch. "Art, Marcus didn't have anything more to share with you, did he?"

"Nope. They've got the size and make of the shoe, but it's a common one. It's hard to say how badly Sam was affected by the bee sting, and how easy it would have been to hold him down. So I guess we've got more information but still no answers. I wish there was more I could do."

"Seth and I will be talking to a lot of the local farmers, for the restaurant," Meg said, glancing at Seth. "We can keep our ears open, find out if any of them ever saw Sam. I know Carl Frederickson mentioned running into Sam, when I talked to him today."

"The beekeeper? Hmm. You never know what will turn out to be important, Meg. I'll pass on that bit of information. Well, I've gotta go. I'll keep you posted."

Meg moved closer to Seth, leaning her shoulder against his. "Nicky's right — it's a horrible image, someone holding him down and watching him struggle. I can't imagine anyone doing that. I hope Marcus finds something to go on."

"So do I, Meg."

23

Seth stopped by early the next morning to pick up Meg, who was waiting in the kitchen while Bree finished breakfast. "Hi, Bree," he said. "Did Meg tell you about our new scheme?"

Bree swept crumbs off the table into her hand, then went over to the sink to throw them away. "The rough idea. Interesting, if it works. You know, I could ask the pickers if they know of any other people who might want to sell small lots. They do get around, and they hear things."

"That would help. And ask Michael, too?" Meg said. "If you give me that list of small markets that Michael gave you, I can get started on that tomorrow."

"Done — I'll leave it on the table for you. You two have fun."

As Meg settled herself in Seth's car, she said, "Seth, do you see any holes in the idea, by the light of morning?"

"Nope," he responded cheerfully. "I think people would be happy to get involved — makes them feel part of the restaurant, which would be a big boost for Nicky and Brian. It's a win-win situation."

"You know, this *is* kind of fun. I'm not the type to walk up to strangers and introduce myself, but this is a terrific way to get to know people in town, both for me and for Nicky and Brian. You sure it won't take up too much of your time?"

"What time?" he joked. "Seriously, it's good for the town — I want the restaurant to work, and I want the people around here who still care about farming to have a reason to go on doing it. And heck, I get a free breakfast out of it."

"That you do, and it should be a good one." They had reached the town green. Meg gazed out over the green, where a few churchgoers were straggling into the tall white church. "It's so lovely. It *is* kind of like a postcard, and it's hard to accept that there are all sorts of problems lurking right under the surface."

"Like a killer?"

"You know, I can't get a handle on Sam's death. Nobody around here knew him, so why would anyone want him dead? It just keeps getting worse. I mean, if somebody

334

wanted to kill him, no way could they have counted on that bee sting and Sam going into shock. Which makes it sound like a random spur-of-the-moment thing. But who?"

"I wish I knew."

Nicky was waiting for them in the kitchen, with a lavish spread on the table. "I hope you're hungry!" she greeted them. "I can't seem to cook for small numbers. And every time I try a recipe, I think of something else I need to find. I added more maple syrup to the list just this morning."

Meg was surprised when Edna emerged from the pantry at the rear.

"Edna!" Seth exclaimed. "Good to see you here. Have you started already?"

"Part-time for now, just getting a feel for the place."

So Nicky and Brian were confident enough of their strategy that they had given Edna the go-ahead? Meg hoped that boded well. "You have a list ready for us, Nicky?" she asked.

"After you eat — pleasure before business, okay?"

They dug in happily. Halfway through her stack of pancakes with fresh strawberries, Meg said, "There will be some things you can't get locally, right? Like coffee. Please don't tell me you won't be offering coffee. And chocolate."

Nicky laughed. "No, we're not fanatics. And we'll have to buy liquor. Unless you know of a winery?"

"Not offhand. I've been told I could make hard cider eventually, but that takes special permits. Right, Seth?"

He nodded. "How about mead?" When Nicky cocked her head at him, he went on, "From honey. We'll talk to Carl — you know him, right, Meg?"

"Carl Frederickson, sure. He did say something about honey. But mead is alcoholic, right? Is that regulated, too?"

"Probably. I'd have to check, but it might be worth looking into. And from a business perspective, Meg, you should check out not only hard cider but applejack. Or apple vodka."

"Please! Can I at least get one crop picked before I start expanding? But I admire your zeal."

When all plates were empty, Nicky refilled their coffee cups and handed out sheaves of paper. "Here's what I'd like to find — a wish list — and I gave you some menus so you could see how the food we collect ends up in our dishes, and get a sense of the language we're using."

Meg riffled through her stack. "Wow. Very professional. You've got a good balance of simplicity and sophistication here. Seth?"

"Looks good." Seth drained his coffee, and scanned Nicky's wish list. "I think we should talk with Jane Morgan for chickens and eggs — you had one of her chickens at Mom's house, Meg. Nicky, you want veal?"

"If it's raised fairly."

"Strictly grass-fed — that'd be Elliott again," Seth muttered to himself. "Bill Matthews for fish — he fishes the river, but he lives in Granford. And Caleb Morton supplies vegetables to some of the farmers' markets — he'd be a good person to talk to about produce. Let's start out at Elliott's farm and the cattle — that'll cover several bases at once. Nicky, that was a great breakfast. We'll report back later. And remind Brian to put together those business plans, okay? We can pick them up later, too."

Outside the morning coolness was already giving way to summer humidity. Edna was sitting on the porch shelling something Meg didn't recognize. "Things working out so far, Edna?" Seth asked.

"Good enough. Those kids got lots of ideas, and I gotta pull 'em back now and then. But she sure can cook."

"Glad you think so, too. Listen, you heard

what we were talking about, right?"

"Hard not to."

"You think people in Granford will go for the idea? You've been serving food around here for a long time."

Edna stared out over the green. "I'd like to see it happen. Nicky's right — the food's better if you get it fresh. I'll leave the business plan to you folks. Me, I'm just happy to cook." She stiffened, and Meg followed her gaze. Caroline Goldthwaite was one of the last stragglers leaving the church building, her erect stance recognizable even from this distance. *What was that all about?* Meg wondered.

As they climbed into Seth's car, Meg said, "Does Edna have some problem with Caroline Goldthwaite?"

"Ancient history now, but yes. A lot of us think Mrs. Goldthwaite was behind denying Edna financing when she wanted to buy the diner."

I wonder why that would be? Meg thought, suspecting she already knew the answer. "I notice you didn't mention the pigs. Are we not going to talk to Jake Kellogg?"

"We can talk to him — I just didn't want to upset Nicky by bringing him up. He's the best around, no question."

"Would finding a dead chef on his land

338

put him off helping out the restaurant?"

"The pigs weren't upset, so he's good. I think Nicky will come around once she tastes his bacon."

"He makes his own? Is that hard?"

"Nope. Build yourself a smokehouse, which doesn't have to be more than a raised shed, and you're good to go. In fact, I helped Jake put his together. Only took a day."

Meg sighed. "The number of things I do not know continues to amaze me. I've got some unidentified foundations on my place. Do you know what they were?"

"One was a corn crib, I'd guess." When Meg looked blank, he explained, "People used to keep the corn up on stone piers, to keep the rats out."

Meg shuddered. "More than I wanted to know. I don't have rats now, do I?"

"I wouldn't worry. No corn, no rats. Okay, we're here."

The next several hours followed a pattern that quickly became familiar. They would drive up the long farm drive or, if a new house had been built on the land, pull in the driveway off the country road. Seth would knock, greet whoever answered by name, ask about the kids, the job, the boat, the fishing — any of a number of things.

339

More and more it seemed to Meg that Seth knew not only everybody in town, but also their entire life histories. He was careful to introduce her, and many of the people they talked with already knew who she was; she could tell from the way their eyes darted toward her quickly. Oh, yes, the one who moved into the old Warren place. But Meg smiled and chatted, and under Seth's umbrella, the sometimes-farmers warmed to her.

And without exception, they all reacted positively to their idea of a collaborative restaurant. No one was ready to commit to real numbers, but everyone expressed interest, with varying degrees of enthusiasm. As they ran through the spiel for the fifth or sixth time, even Meg thought it sounded pretty appealing. And it certainly made her hungry.

But after several hours, she was ready to call it a day. The day had been fine but hot, with little breeze. Meg had admired cows and calves and milking apparatuses. Apparati? She had discussed cheese, soft and hard. She had seen rows upon rows of crops that she couldn't identify, and had noted a few that Nicky hadn't mentioned. Would she want fennel? Leeks? She had been introduced to cherry trees, plum trees, even an errant fig tree growing in a sheltered corner. Meg had had no idea that there was so much food surrounding her — because she had never looked. She felt humbled by her ignorance, and secretly thrilled that she now had a part in it all, however small.

And now she was tired, sticky, and hungry, and they still had to stop back and debrief Nicky and Brian.

"Had enough?" Seth asked, starting the car.

"I hope you're joking."

"Hey, we've still got a few hours of daylight left."

Meg laughed. "I'm beat. You know, you're amazing — you never seem to slow down. It's hard to keep up with you."

"I'm just built that way — it used to drive Mom nuts. I always had a lot of energy — nowadays they'd probably label me ADD. Mom and Dad did their best to channel it to something useful. Anyway, you're not the first person to complain. Hey, I've got an idea."

"As long as it doesn't involve walking anywhere or talking to anyone, fine. But remember we've still got to stop at the restaurant."

"Don't worry — this won't take long."

Meg no longer had any idea where they

were, after following meandering farm lanes for hours, so she sat back and admired the passing landscape and enjoyed the air-conditioning in the car. They reached the base of the ridge that marked the northern end of Granford, and Seth followed a road barely two lanes wide, winding up the side of it until they came to a cleared area and a pull-out. He stopped the car, and they both stepped out. "There." He waved his hand at the vista. "There's Granford, laid out at your feet."

They were still shy of the top of the ridge, shaded by tall old trees, and a faint breeze cooled Meg's damp hair. "It is lovely, isn't it? It looks so peaceful." She could see the steeple of the church, scattered white houses, many still with adjoining barns, and plowed fields green with crops. She could hear the distant lowing of cows — how strange that the sound carried all the way up there. "Like it's never changed. At least, if you swap carriages for cars. But the roads are the same, aren't they?"

"Yup, most of them were laid out in the eighteenth century, like the one in front of your house."

"Like the orchard — that's probably been there about as long, in one form or another. Why is it everything around here seems to have a long history except me?" *And what is it about this lovely view that's making me feel melancholy?* Meg wondered.

"You still worried about fitting in?" Seth tilted her chin up so he could look in her eyes.

"Less so than I was, maybe. But I saw the way some of the people today reacted when you introduced me."

"Meg, give them time. They're good people."

"I'm trying. You know, I wonder if being with you makes it too easy — they accept me by proxy. I get the Seth Chapin stamp of approval."

"Is that a problem?"

"No, of course not. I'm grateful. As long as I'm not just one of your fix-it projects."

"Do you have to ask?"

She studied his face. "No."

He pulled her closer and kissed her, and she forgot her surroundings, and her fatigue, and her worries about being accepted by the population of Granford. The kiss ended gradually, and she found herself leaning against Seth, her mind entirely empty. Her body, on the other hand, was very much alive, but now wasn't the time to do anything about that. This was good, this was nice. This could work. And then maybe

343

someday soon there would be a restaurant where they could celebrate the special occasions of their lives. She sighed.

"What?" he said into her hair.

"I like this. Do we have to go back to the real world?"

"This isn't real?"

"Well, yes, it is. But we have other things we need to do."

"I know," he said, but he didn't let go immediately. "We'll stop by the restaurant on the way home."

"Right." She peeled herself away reluctantly, then turned to take one last look at the vista, gilded by the sinking sun. "How sad to think there's a murderer down there somewhere."

"Not for long."

"You really think Marcus will find the killer?"

"I think he'll give it his best shot. Unsolved murders don't look good on his résumé, and this one is sensitive. I think he'll want to get this cleared up as fast as he can."

"I hope so," Meg said dubiously. Trouble was, she'd seen Marcus at work before, and she wasn't convinced.

24

Nicky and Brian had been suitably impressed with their progress, but neither Meg nor Seth had time to call on anyone else over the next day or two. Meg was working her way through the list of small markets that Michael had provided, and met with mixed success. Some already had contracts for as many apples as they needed; others were willing to accept some orders on trial, with the promise of accepting more if the first batch proved satisfactory. Since Meg was still puzzling over what kinds of apples she had, when they would ripen, and how many she could expect, she was grateful for any hint of support. It was a start.

Tuesday morning she sat down to review the financial projections that Brian had provided. He had done a competent job, she decided, even though the details of this particular business were unfamiliar to her. Financial statements were more or less rsal, and boiled down to expenses us income. Of course, for a start-up that volved a lot of guessing, but from what Meg could tell, Brian's guesses had been conservative and reasonable. She had seen for herself that he had kept the build-out simple, concentrating resources in bringing the systems — plumbing and electrical — up to code for this new use. Interior decoration had been held to a minimum, with Brian and Nicky doing a lot of the painting themselves. Obviously they had had to invest in kitchen equipment, but much of that had been acquired secondhand (located, checked over, and approved by Seth). There had been no way to avoid buying tables and chairs, and the numbers there had been dictated by the space available combined with the number of covers Brian projected that they needed to break even. Add to that the linens, china, glassware, cookware, and the other inescapable necessities of running a restaurant, and it was clear where the money had gone. There had been no waste, no extravagance.

They'd started with the generous gift from Nicky's father, but that was spent now. With no demonstrable cash flow until September at the earliest, the bank wasn't about to give them a loan. And in any case, under current economic conditions, everybody was tightening belts. Small business loans were simply not happening these days. Not that it really would've been a good idea for Brian and Nicky to take on debt at this point anyway.

Which left the gaping hole of inventory: food, beverages, and disposable supplies. Liquor was nonnegotiable, according to Brian, and Meg wasn't going to disagree. Brian had walked her through the principles behind pricing an entrée, and the target cost seemed reasonable to her, if he wanted to attract a broad mix of customers. So, failing a lottery win, Meg's plan for a collaborative effort was the best hope if this restaurant was going to open in September — or ever.

She had promised to brief Seth on her off-the-cuff analysis before he talked to the Select Board. She wasn't sure if running this by the Board was a courtesy, to keep them informed, or whether there was something tangible the Board members could contribute — like funding the services of the town's attorney to draw up whatever partnership documents might be needed. Of course, a town might have access to grants and external funding that individuals might not, but so much of that funding had dried up that it was more or less moot.

Seth rapped on her screen door at six before letting himself in. "How's it look?"

Meg sighed. "They did everything right. I can't fault the decisions they made. They just underestimated, and ran out of money. Heck, I'd support them for a loan if I were a local banker. You don't happen to have any pull there, do you?"

"Even if I did, there are a lot of people in the queue ahead of them. Are you having second thoughts about this collaborative idea?"

"No, not at all. The more I think about it, the more I like it. And I keep thinking of ways to promote it — it could serve as a great blueprint for any number of small local businesses. My friend Lauren might be able to help there." When Seth opened his mouth to speak, Meg hurried to forestall him. "I know, I know — I'm getting ahead of myself. I'm just lining up arguments to support this. It's good for the town. It's good for everyone involved."

"Hey, I agree with you. I don't see much downside. Were we going to eat something before we headed to the meeting?"

"Oh, right, food. I think I've got sandwich makings in there somewhere. I've been so busy the last couple of days, trying to line up buyers for myself, that I haven't had time to think about food." She smiled. "It might be easier to persuade the Board if we took some of Nicky's cookies along."

Seth went to the refrigerator and started foraging. He emerged with packages of cold cuts, bread tucked under his arm. "I like the cookie idea. Nicky's cooking is definitely one of the best selling points we've got. Maybe we should be bringing goodies along to everyone we call on."

"Now you're thinking like a promoter! You're right, and I'm sure Nicky would be happy to whip up some stuff. Are you making the sandwiches?"

"Sure." As Seth peeled the wrapping off the cold cuts, Lolly appeared from somewhere and stationed herself at his feet. "Hi there, you. You like turkey?"

"As far as I can tell, she likes everything. I've caught her eating green beans."

Seth dropped a small shred of turkey at his feet, and Lolly pounced on it, then waited eagerly for more. "Pig." He ignored her as he assembled two sandwiches. Meg went back to the refrigerator, pulled out a pitcher of iced tea, and located two glasses.

"Speaking of pigs," she said as they sat down on opposite sides of the table, with Lolly taking the seat between them, "you haven't talked to Jake Kellogg yet, have you?"

Seth shook his head, his mouth full of sandwich. After he'd swallowed, he said, "Haven't had time. Probably won't have time this week. You want to handle it?"

"I think I can. After all, I've met him already. Although I'm not sure what questions to ask, but at least I can give him the general idea. What kind of pigs does he have? I've seen them, but I don't know one pig from another."

"Berkshires. They're good eating."

"Okay. Maybe I'll stop by tomorrow — he works somewhere else, right?"

"Yeah, but he should be home between five and six." Seth's sandwich had disappeared. "Anything else we need to go over?"

Meg handed him a folder. "I've boiled down the numbers there. I've tried to make it a simple snapshot. The bottom line is, I think the restaurant plan is sound, with one more infusion of funding — that's the farmers, with in-kind contributions, and long-term participation. I would support it as a good investment on their part. And I think the idea has appeal beyond the numbers."

"No argument here. You ready?"

Meg gathered up her own folder and her

purse. "Let's go."

When Meg and Seth arrived at Town Hall, Tom Moody and Caroline Goldthwaite were already seated, along with a man Meg didn't recognize. Tom stood up when they entered. "Hey, thought you'd gotten lost, Seth. Hi, Meg. This is Fred Weatherly, Granford town counsel. Among other things."

Fred clambered to his feet and reached across the table to shake Meg's hand. He was a short and rather round man, and his hand was damp. "Good to meet you, at last. Tom here doesn't give me enough work, so I have to hold down a real day job."

Mrs. Goldthwaite gave what sounded suspiciously like a sniff, avoiding Meg's eyes. "I don't see why we need Miss Corey here. This is a working meeting, not a public meeting."

"Mrs. Goldthwaite, I invited Meg," Seth said mildly. "She's better equipped than I am to talk about what we want to present to you."

Mrs. Goldthwaite looked at him as though he were a guilty schoolboy. "I for one don't see what there is to discuss."

Tom interrupted. "Mrs. Goldthwaite, let them speak their piece, okay? After all, this restaurant does affect the town, so it's relevant." When she didn't answer, he went on, "Okay, we have any old business to get out of the way?"

Meg sat quietly as the Board dealt with a short list of local issues covering waste disposal, zoning, and funding for an unexpected repair to one of the town schools. Finally Tom looked around the room and said, "Okay, if there's nothing else — Seth, why don't you tell us about your pet project? And keep it short, will you? I promised to be home before midnight."

"Tom, I know there's another baseball game on. I'll give you the highlights, and you can go home and think about what questions you have. In a nutshell, Nicky and Brian have come up short of money for the restaurant."

Mrs. Goldthwaite interrupted. "No surprise there. The project was poorly conceived from the beginning."

Seth responded quickly. "Mrs. Goldthwaite, I don't think that's true. I think they've done a great job working within their resources, but admittedly they're young and inexperienced, so they underestimated — though not by much, I might add. And I think we've found a way to help them out."

"Is this going to cost the town anything,

Seth?" Tom asked.

"No. Hey, I know how little we have. But I would like the town's endorsement for the plan, and public support. Heck, we might even get some publicity out of it."

Tom sat back in his chair. "Okay, Seth, the ball's in your court."

Fifteen minutes later Seth had laid out the history of the restaurant and its current problems. Meg had contributed a brief analysis of the numbers and projections. Together they had sketched out the idea for a collaborative venture that they had come up with.

Mrs. Goldthwaite listened in stony silence, avoiding everyone's eyes. Tom nodded and said little for most of it. Finally he spoke. "Who've you talked to?"

"Several farmers." Seth rattled off names.

"What's their take on it?" Tom went on.

"Overall, they like it. Of course, we've still got to work out an acceptable legal structure — that's where you come in, right, Fred?"

Fred's eyed jerked open. "Um, yeah, right. Happy to help." Meg wondered if he knew what he'd just volunteered for.

"And we're under some time pressure," Seth continued, "because they want to open at the beginning of September. That would give them a shot at snagging the parents bringing all their kids to school, and also take advantage of the late summer crops."

Tom turned to Fred. "Is that a reasonable time line for you to work out the details? Assuming we have something like oral agreements in place?"

Fred nodded. "If you keep it simple. How many partners you talking about?"

"Does it matter, up front? I'm guessing twenty, but we'd like to keep it flexible, so we can add on if we find someone new. Or so that people can drop out if it doesn't work for them."

Fred nodded. "Let me see what I can put together. Tom, am I billing you on this one?"

Tom and Seth exchanged a glance. "Yeah, but we should put a cap on it. Say ten hours? If you can't get something cobbled together in that time, let me know."

"I don't suppose anyone is going to ask my opinion?" Mrs. Goldthwaite said, speaking for the first time in several minutes.

"I'm sorry, Mrs. Goldthwaite. What's on your mind?" Tom asked.

Mrs. Goldthwaite straightened her already-straight back and smoothed down her skirt. "I think this whole discussion is absurd. Seth, you're asking us to condone poor business management, and support a pair of strangers who have made some faulty decisions. What kind of message does that send? I know that bailouts are popular in some circles, but I don't see why Granford need follow that model. And do we have any reason to believe that they're here to stay? Or will they get tired of their new toy and go back to wherever they came from, leaving that building unusable as a home?"

"Mrs. Goldthwaite," Seth began patiently, "I think the restaurant will be a real asset to Granford, as well as a source of revenue for us ultimately. You've met Nicky and Brian — they're good people, the kind we want to attract and keep. And we're not asking the farmers to give up anything. They'll get paid, and they'll get a share of the profits. What's more, they'll be directly involved in bringing new financial and social life to the town. What's wrong with that?"

"I do not see that the commercialization of the town center is desirable. I'm not convinced that the attention such a restaurant attracts is what we want for Granford."

"And I disagree," Seth replied. "All the people I've talked to have welcomed the idea, whether or not they plan to provide any food. We need a place like this here. And Nicky and Brian need some help to make it happen. Of course, the plan is to make it a profitable business, once they get over the first hurdles."

"Then we must agree to disagree." Mrs. Goldthwaite shut her mouth with finality.

Seth turned to Tom. "Tom, do you support this project?"

"Sure, and for all the reasons you outlined. We need new life, and we need new revenues. The town isn't going to be out of pocket for this — unless Fred here goes wild. And I like the owners. So, sorry, Mrs. Goldthwaite, but I'm with Seth on this."

"That doesn't surprise me," she said, and Meg was startled at the bitterness in her tone. "Have we finished our business here? Because I'm tired and I would like to go home."

"I think we're done." Tom stood up. "Meg, thanks for coming tonight. And thanks for your input regarding the finances. Maybe we can count on your expertise on a few other matters?"

"Tom, I'm happy to help out any way I can."

Tom rubbed his hands together. "Great. Well, I guess we're adjourned. Thanks for coming, Fred. Why don't you send us all what you pull together on the partnership structure? Say, by the end of the week."

"Yeah, okay, fine. 'Night, all." Fred made his escape, and Meg wondered if he would produce anything at all. Still, it was a start.

Mrs. Goldthwaite stalked out next, without saying good night to anyone. "She's not happy," Seth said to Tom.

Tom sighed. "When is she ever? She wants everything in Granford to stay just the way it's always been. I hope I'm not that stuffy when I get to be her age."

"It's her home, and it always has been. Do you know if she plans to run for selectman again?"

"She hasn't said, and I haven't asked. Besides, that's months away. But if anything comes to a vote, and I'm not even sure it will, then I'm on your side, Seth. Meg, good to see you again. Good luck talking with the rest of the farmers — let me know how it goes."

They went out the front door, with Tom turning off the lights behind them. He waved as he headed toward his car.

Meg looked around the town. It was still light, but there weren't many people around, on foot or in cars. There were lights on in the restaurant: apparently Nicky and Brian were barreling ahead at full speed.

"Seth, is Mrs. Goldthwaite going to be a problem?"

"I don't think so. She's usually pretty reasonable, even if she's kind of out of step with the world. And worst case, Tom and I outnumber her. But I hope it doesn't come to a real confrontation. You ready to go home?"

"I guess. I've got more markets to call on over the next few days, but I think I've made a good start. Now all I need is apples to sell them."

"All in good time."

25

The next week passed in a blur. Pickers came and went, bringing boxes, shifting things around in the barn — doing almost anything but actually picking. Meg was becoming accustomed to the sound of voices outside the house at odd hours, but there was no rushing the apples. Monday morning she woke with a start and realized she hadn't seen Professor Christopher Ramsdell since her class had ended in May. She knew he was busy. This was, after all, peak growing season, and he had many commitments to field research. Add to that the new integrated pest management project that the pharmaceutical company DeBroCo had proudly announced earlier in the year, and the construction of a new building on the UMass campus to house it, and Christopher must have been run off his feet. She knew that Bree had consulted him periodically. Still, she felt she should check in with him, report on Bree's admirable progress, and make sure she was on track. She needed to ask him what equipment she still needed, who had bought the crop before this, and what if any spraying was still necessary. In fact, the list kept growing, and Meg sprang out of bed just to stop the spinning in her head.

Downstairs she fed Lolly and pottered around fixing breakfast until she thought it was reasonably late enough to call Christopher. Of course, he should be keeping farmers' hours these days, right? Just after eight she called his office and was happily surprised to hear his voice.

"Christopher, it's Meg. Have I caught you at a bad time?"

"Meg, how delightful to hear your voice. I'm about to head out to oversee a spraying, but I can spare a moment. Was there something on your mind?"

"Nothing urgent — I just realized that we hadn't talked for a while and I wanted to make sure I was doing things right."

"And is young Briona working out well?"

"She is indeed, and I bless your name daily for sending her my way. Though she doesn't have your wealth of experience."

"Ah, Meg, you flatter me."

"I do. Do you have time to get together

today? I know it's short notice."

"Let me check my calendar," he replied, and Meg could hear the riffling of papers in the background. "I'm over in Hadley this morning, but that shouldn't take more than a couple of hours. I'm meeting with the building contractor at two. Could you possibly squeeze in lunch?"

"Perfect. I'll meet you at your office at noon? Does that work?"

"Excellent. See you then, my dear."

Meg hung up smiling. Christopher was a sweetheart. His early years in England had left him with a courtly charm that seemed incongruous in an agricultural scientist, but he was a delight to spend time with — in addition to being knowledgeable about both orchards and human character. Meg was happy to have Bree managing her orchard, but she missed the more frequent contact with Christopher that she had enjoyed earlier in the year.

Meg spent her morning talking to still more food vendors — luckily Amherst and Northampton were well supplied with them — and she rapped on Christopher's office door just before noon and found him at his desk, poring over what appeared to be blueprints, his silvery hair rumpled, reading glasses perched on the end of his nose. He looked up and beamed at her. "Meg, please come in. I've just been going over the De-BroCo plans. I must say they aren't trying to cut corners, but I have some quibbles about space allocation — some of the labs are a bit cramped. But I'm sure we'll be able to work out the details. Shall we go to that lunch spot we've been to before?"

"Sounds good. Why don't you let me drive?"

Once they had parked in Amherst, a feat made easier by the reduced summer population of the university and the college, and ordered, Christopher sat back and looked at Meg. "You appear to be thriving. So the life of an orchardist agrees with you?"

"So far. I'm enjoying it, between moments of panic. I assume Bree filled you in about the hailstorm?"

"She did indeed. You were lucky, but maybe the gods are on your side — you deserve some luck. And she reports that the trees are doing well. I'm sorry I haven't been by more frequently, but this new center is consuming all of the time I can spare from research activities."

"Is everything going well?"

"Surprisingly so, touch wood. I was concerned that the corporation might have a hidden agenda, but so far they have made no demands. I could not ask for more, although I fear that my skills as an administrator may be inadequate to the task. And I shall miss the fieldwork." He took a swallow of his iced tea. "So tell me about your latest scandal. A young man associated with this proposed restaurant, I hear?"

"You *are* well informed. Yes, he was going to be the sous chef there, except he ended up dead in a pigsty."

"Heavens, how dramatic. Not, I take it, on your land?"

"No, thank goodness. But I've been working with the restaurant owners — a really nice pair of newlyweds from Boston — and we've come up with a plan . . ." Meg proceeded to outline her collaborative scheme, and was gratified that Christopher paid close attention.

When she'd finished, he said, "You might think of talking to someone at the Department of Hospitality at the university. I would imagine they might have some ideas, and it would be a good opportunity to affiliate with the university — as a source of advice, or even staffing."

"That's an excellent idea, Christopher. I'll tell them to look into that," Meg said. "So, regarding my potential purchasers, who has bought the apple crop in past years?"

"As I recall, one of the local farmers' groups. Once the crop was harvested, I had no further oversight. But I might have records in my files."

"Bree has contracted with the pickers you've used before."

"The Jamaicans. Excellent. They'll do good work for you. Have you met them yet?"

"I have — Bree brought them by. She does have things well in hand, I think."

"I'm glad. I have every faith in that young woman. And in you, Meg."

"Why, thank you. I'm just trying to muddle through."

"Ah, but it's more than that. You found yourself thrown into a difficult situation, and you had no compelling reason to stay. And yet you did, and here you are. I admire your tenacity, especially in the face of adversity. I hope the gods of harvest are kind to you this year."

"So do I. But I can't control that, can I?"

"Alas, no. But it does help to take a long-range view. If this year's crop fails, there will always be another year."

"Oh please, don't mention the term 'fail.' I don't want to hear it. Though I am lining up contingency plans if the crop is, shall we say, less than perfect. I understand there's a collective cider mill in the vicinity."

"You see? You're already thinking like a true farmer. Hope for the best, but plan for the worst." Christopher glanced at his watch. "Heavens, I must get back."

As Meg drove back to Granford after depositing Christopher in front of his office, she reflected that in fact she probably *would* have turned tail and run if it hadn't been for him. And Seth, of course. But it was Christopher who had assured her that she could handle running the orchard. He had taken the time to explain each step along the way. He had found Bree for her. And he had proven to be a true and supportive friend. Maybe that was what had inspired her to act as guardian angel to Nicky and Brian, since she knew how much that kind of help mattered.

Maybe there was something to making your own luck. In fact, she had been lucky about a lot of things since she'd arrived in Granford: good friends, a sense of community. And Seth. He was definitely on the luck list.

26

By early August, Meg felt as though she was running up to the orchard every few hours, to make sure nothing had changed. Bree had instructed her on the various means of testing for ripeness, but it wasn't the same as actually touching or even tasting an apple. Or slicing into it to see if the seeds had turned brown, a simple but reasonably accurate indicator of ripeness. Of course, she felt a pang of guilt every time she pulled — correction, gently twisted, since pulling damaged the branch — an apple from the tree and bit into it. Each apple was precious, and she couldn't afford to waste any, at least not knowingly. So far, unfortunately, nothing was ripe enough to pick, which meant she had to wait. The pickers had to wait. It was frustrating.

Lauren called occasionally from Boston — far more often than she had been calling before. Could it have anything to do with

Detective Marcus, who, much to Meg's regret, had yet to make any significant progress on solving Sam's murder? The last time she had spoken to Lauren, Meg had probed a little — discreetly, she hoped.

"Have you heard anything from your detective lately?"

"Oh, so now he's 'my' detective?" Lauren had said with a laugh.

"You know what I mean. Have you seen him lately?"

Lauren seemed to hesitate for a fraction of a second. "Uh, yes."

Meg was surprised, and possibly hurt. Did that mean Lauren had been in town, but hadn't stopped by? Hadn't even confided in her? But, well, if Lauren didn't want to tell her about it, Meg wasn't going to press. "Did he happen to say anything about the murder?"

"Meg, he wouldn't do that — it's not professional. But I think it's fair to tell you that he's frustrated."

"Aren't we all? Are you coming back this way anytime soon?"

"Um, let me get back to you on that, okay? But I'll definitely be there for the restaurant opening. I love this idea you've cooked up — ooh, look, I made a pun. I put in a word to a friend at the *Globe,* and she said they might do an article."

"Oh, Lauren, that would be terrific."

"Well, you know the kinds of problems newspapers have been having lately, so don't get your hopes up. I'll let you know. And see you soon!" She hung up before Meg could garner any more details from her.

If Marcus was showing his frustration to a stranger like Lauren, Meg reflected, he must really have hit a wall. Meg was torn between hoping that the killer would be found, and hoping that the whole nasty event would fade quietly away and leave the path clear for the successful opening of the restaurant.

She was fidgeting around the house when her gaze lit upon the stack of boxes full of materials belonging to the Historical Society, which she was cataloging for Gail in her spare time. She squelched her guilt about not having made much progress recently; she'd been too restless to concentrate, especially when the weather was fine. The cataloging task was better suited to long winter nights, when her lamp cast a pool of light over the fragile documents she was trying to identify.

But, she realized, she *had* finished one box, and she really ought to return that one to Gail (and hope that Gail didn't hand her another one, or worse, two, in its place).

Resisting the local tradition of just showing up, she called first. "Gail? Hi, it's Meg."

"Oh, hey, Meg. You picking yet?"

"Nope. I feel like an expectant mother. Right now all I can do is go visit the trees and say encouraging things to them. But I've finished going through one of the boxes you gave me, and I thought maybe I could drop it off. It also occurred to me a while ago that we never followed up on looking into the history of the restaurant. And Nicky's looking for old recipes and food preparation info, so we could kill several birds with one stone."

"Great idea! The kids are both in day camp, and I could be in town in, say, fifteen minutes. That work for you?"

"Sounds good. See you in fifteen."

When Meg pulled up, Gail was already waiting, sitting on the granite stoop of the Historical Society building on the green. She didn't get up, but called out, "Did you find any treasures?"

"No specific things, but cumulatively there are all sorts of goodies. I'm getting a real sense of how the town used to operate a century or more ago — how people got around, how and when they worked, how they socialized. I'm going to have to look up a few things to make sense of them, like

369

what the religious and social organizations were back then. But I do love it, and I can feel useful while I learn."

"Be careful or you'll get sucked in just the way I did. History can be addictive."

"So I've noticed. Have you had a chance to look for anything on the Stebbins house?"

"Now you're doing it, too."

"What?"

"Calling a place by the name of a prior owner. Or in this case, a century-plus of prior owners."

Meg laughed. "Like my place is the Warren farm. I don't mind. I guess I'm a Warren, several generations removed."

"Come on inside — but brace yourself. It's pretty stifling." Gail pulled out a set of keys and opened the front door. "There's no air-conditioning."

Meg laughed. "There's none at my place either — hard to retrofit a true colonial, even if I could afford it."

Meg had been inside the Historical Society building months earlier, but then the problem had been a near-complete lack of heat, and she had been wearing at least three layers of clothes. Now she was blasted with a wave of hot air, and broke out in an instant sweat. She followed Gail into the dim interior — all the ancient roller shades were drawn. The peculiar collection of stuffed dead animals, a gift from a long-deceased taxidermist, looked less moth-eaten in this light, but no less ominous — all those beady glass eyes staring. Gail made a beeline to her desk in the far corner and retrieved a fat and tattered folder.

"I pulled some stuff, but I'm sure there's more. The only problem is, it's scattered through all the houses the Society owns, and I'd have to track the records down. But this is enough to get you started, right?"

"I'm sure. It's not like we're going to write a book about it. Are there any pictures?"

"Sure. Let's take this back outside before we melt," Gail said, and headed for the door.

The air outside, a mere eighty, felt delightfully cool as they made their escape from the building. Gail headed for a maple-shaded bench in the middle of the green, with Meg trailing behind. When they were settled, Meg said, "Let me get this straight: in winter it's too cold in there to do anything, and in summer it's too hot. When do you get anything done?"

"There's a week in April, unless it's the kids' spring break. And a few days in October, after the Harvest Fair. You're coming to that, right?"

"I haven't even thought about it," Meg answered.

"A lot of it is aimed at the kids, but it's fun. You should come."

"I will. Now, what about those records?"

"We'll have to be careful. I'm breaking every archival rule known to humankind, to be treating them like this. But it's for a good cause, right? How're things going? I hear you're trying to gather the farmers together to help out the restaurant."

"My, news travels fast."

"It's a small town, Meg. I can tell you what Doris Jacobs planted in her kitchen garden a month back, in part because she's planted the same thing for years, but also because she ordered a new kind of sunflower she saw in a seed catalog, and she was talking about it in the pharmacy the other day."

"Wow. I guess I'll have to watch what I say. Even to the trees."

"You talk to the trees?" Gail asked with a half smile.

"Doesn't everyone? And now do I have to wonder if they've been bugged?"

Gail stared at her a moment, then threw her head back and laughed wholeheartedly. "My God, a pun. I didn't know you had it in you. I knew I liked you."

She wiped her eyes and opened the folder

in her lap.

"Okay, here we go. From what I can tell, the place was built around 1820 by Joshua Stebbins. He was a merchant, with business dealings in Springfield, and he wanted to impress people, hence the brick, which was more expensive than wood back in those days. The house stayed in the family for quite a while, I think — you could find out more from property records, or maybe there's a title search for when the kids bought the property. As I remember it, they bought it from one of the Stebbins descendants, but no one who'd ever lived here."

"You call them 'kids,' too?"

"They just seem so young to me. In a good way. They're fresh, and eager, and hopeful — everything's in front of them."

"As long as they get past the murder of a friend."

"I think they can survive that, as long as it gets solved sometime soon. Any word on that?"

Meg thought briefly about sharing the information about the bee sting and the muddy footprint and vetoed it. "Nothing new. So show me what else you've got about the house."

"There are a good number of pictures, because it's right on the green, and it got included as background for a lot of fairs and events here." She handed Meg a sheaf of pictures, and Meg leafed through them. The house lurked in the background, behind the crowds and tents and booths, with its distinctive gable line and flanking chimneys. Clearly little had changed over the last fifty or a hundred years, save that the bushes in the front of the porch had grown. The road in front went from graveled to paved, then paved again.

Meg handed the stack back to Gail. "Nothing with the house alone?"

"Not that I've found yet. You know, you really ought to talk to Caroline Goldthwaite."

"Why? Has she worked with the Historical Society?"

"On and off, but more importantly, she used to live there."

"Mrs. Goldthwaite? Really? She never said anything about that."

Gail shrugged. "She's got to be, what, eighty? Actually, I think she was born in the house — probably literally, back in those days, maybe 1925? She lived there until she married, which would have been around 1945. So it's been a while."

"She didn't inherit?"

"No, she definitely wasn't the one the kids

bought it from. When she married, it was expected that she would live on her husband's property, end of story. She's pretty much into following the rules, you know?"

Meg nodded. "I certainly got that impression. There is only one way to do things, and Mrs. Goldthwaite's the one with the rule book — which is out of date. You know, though, the fact that it was her family home could explain why she's so opposed to it becoming a restaurant."

"Because of fond memories of the house? Not necessarily. More like, she doesn't want to see Granford change, ever. But even she can't stop it. It's kind of sad."

"Does she have any real constituency in town? I mean, she *was* elected."

"More out of respect for her, I think, than any kind of agreement with her political views. Heck, it's not political anyway, not in the standard sense. She's a local institution, but she can't really stand in the way of progress, can she?"

"Seth says no, since Tom Moody's on his side if it comes to a vote. Poor Mrs. Goldthwaite — it must be hard for her. Her husband's dead?"

"A few years ago, yes. And they never had kids — too bad, since I think that might have mellowed her a bit. Anyway, you can think about talking to her, although since you're allied with the side of darkness, she might not cooperate."

"I'll think about it." Meg leafed through more of the documents. "You have anything specifically on food? Weren't there ever any places to eat around here?"

"Ah, Meg, most people didn't have the money to spend eating out. This town has never been rich. Nobody's starving either, but there's not a lot of extra cash. You know about the diner, where Edna used to work? There was that, and if you go back further, there was an inn, over there where the store is. Tavern downstairs, a couple of beds for travelers upstairs — nothing fancy."

"Okay, so there's at least a tradition of an inn on the green here. We could play that up."

"We? How did you get so involved in this?"

"I wish I knew. I feel kind of responsible for the kids — I was the one who suggested Granford, when they had just started looking. And I like them. But I've got an orchard to run, and it's my first time for everything. Thank goodness I found Bree."

"She working out?"

"Definitely. She's smart, and she works hard. She's got the pickers lined up, and I've sorted out markets for the crop. Now we just need the apples."

"Hurry up and wait, eh? That's farming for you. So, how are you and Seth doing?"

Meg was startled by Gail's abrupt change of subject. "Is this more of the Granford 'everybody knows everything' phenomenon? Is there a website where you all pool your information?"

Gail laughed. "Website? Heck, no — we use smoke signals, or carrier pigeons. Seriously, if I'm intruding, just tell me to mind my own business. But if things are good, I'm happy for you. Both of you."

"Thank you," Meg said primly. "Things *are* good, and that's all I'm going to say."

"Gotcha." Gail's cell phone rang, and she rummaged through her pockets to find it. "What's the problem, sweetie? Oh, dang, you're right. I can run it right over to you. See you." She hung up with a grimace. "I forgot to give the kids their bag lunches this morning, so I'd better go drop them off. Listen, you keep that material for now. You can share it with Nicky and Brian, and I'll keep looking, both for the house and for any food-related stuff. I'm sure we've got something."

"Sounds good. I won't keep you. Besides, I haven't checked my trees for at least an hour, and maybe something will have changed."

Gail laughed. "Right. You do that. I'll talk to you soon." She set off for her car — carefully parked in the shade of the church building — at a brisk trot.

Meg went back to her car more slowly, thinking. Funny that Mrs. Goldthwaite had never mentioned her association with the Stebbins place. Or maybe she just assumed that everyone already knew? Insider information took on a whole new meaning in a small town like this. Had Mrs. Goldthwaite even been inside the house since she had left decades ago? Had she seen the changes that Nicky and Brian had made? The whole way home, Meg mulled over this new view into Mrs. Goldthwaite's resistance to the restaurant.

27

After a haphazard lunch, Meg was still restless. She could go through the rest of the materials Gail had given her, but that was inside work, and she really wanted to be outside, moving. She had talked to small markets between Granford and Amherst; maybe she should cross the river and try the rest on Michael's list, and then she could tell Bree she had finished with it. And if she had any time left, she could stop by some of the Granford farmers' homes, after they got back from work.

Energized, she grabbed her bag and keys and headed out. After several hours, with a few more tentative commitments from markets in hand, Meg decided to quit while she was ahead. She had to admit she had come to enjoy the process, which surprised her. The country roads were beautiful and far from busy, and she was beginning to recognize some of them and could get from one place to another without getting lost. Maybe she'd hate it in winter, when these same roads were piled high with snow, but right now it was lovely. She was learning so much, and found herself looking at produce displays quite differently than she would have only a month or two earlier.

She checked her watch: it was after five. Seth had said Jake Kellogg might be home at this hour. Maybe it was worth a trip by his place to talk with him.

She found the farm with no trouble, but when she knocked on the door, it wasn't Jake but his wife who opened it. The sound of a radio blared behind her. "Oh, hi — Meg, is it?" she said, looking harried. "You looking for Jake? He might be out back with the pigs. Is his car here? Oh, right, there it is — he can't have gone far. Maybe you could check the barn out back? I don't know." She yelled back over her shoulder, "Jessica! Turn that thing down!" Then she turned back to Meg. "Sorry. Look, if you don't find him, stop by here on your way out, and you can leave him a message." She shut the door before Meg could respond.

The sun was lower now and a cool breeze had sprung up, and Meg had spent too much of the day either in the car or standing around and talking, so a walk might do her good. She set off along the lane that led toward the pig field.

It was, she decided, a good day for a stroll. She was pleasantly tired but satisfied with what she had accomplished. The air was warm but not hot, thick with pollen, and lots of colorful weeds she couldn't identify bloomed wildly in the ditches that flanked the lane. She rounded the gentle curve that hid the house from the pigs, or vice versa, and almost stopped: there was someone there already, leaning against the fence, apparently deep in communion with the pigs, and it wasn't Jake. As she drew closer, she realized it was Caroline Goldthwaite.

Mrs. Goldthwaite looked up when she noticed Meg approaching, but her stance didn't change. Up close, Meg realized that she held what looked like a long walking stick, and she was using it to scratch the back of the nearest pig, who looked ecstatic.

"Hello, Mrs. Goldthwaite. That pig looks happy."

Mrs. Goldthwaite's rhythm didn't slow. "I believe she is. Aren't you, Lulu?"

Lulu appeared to be grinning. "What brings you out here?" Meg asked, mainly to forestall being asked the same question. Knowing how Mrs. Goldthwaite felt, she didn't want to bring up the restaurant and set off a new round of unpleasantness, unless she had to.

"I live at the other end of the lane — the house is on East Road. I don't think this lane has a name, as is the case for many farm roads hereabouts. I walk over this way whenever I have the opportunity, weather permitting, of course. My daily constitutional." She gave one of her characteristic sniffs. "I assume you're here to talk to Jake about his pigs, for . . . that place."

There was no avoiding it now. "Yes, for the restaurant. You never mentioned that you used to live in the Stebbins house, Mrs. Goldthwaite."

"Didn't I?" Mrs. Goldthwaite kept her eyes on the pigs. Lulu had wandered off, but a smaller pig had trotted over and was begging for attention. "That's right, you're a newcomer. You wouldn't know the history of a place, would you?"

"I'm doing the best I can to learn about it. I asked Gail Selden about the history of the building. She said I should talk to you."

Mrs. Goldthwaite nodded silently, still watching the pigs.

When she didn't volunteer any additional details, Meg cast about for a change of topic. "Did you know the Warren sisters? The ones who left the house to my mother?"

"Yes, although I was a child at the time. My father bought apples from them, if I remember correctly. We lived in town, and we didn't farm, but my father believed in supporting the community. He was on the Select Board for a time, years ago. Although then they called it the Board of Selectmen. It was, in fact, all men in that era."

"When did you first run?"

"After my husband died, a few years ago. I was . . . bored, I suppose. I thought it would be wise to seek out an activity that demanded that I get out of the house now and then, or I would turn into one of those crazy old ladies that children used to call witches. Heaven only knows what they call them now. Children have become quite rude, which I think reflects poorly on their parents. I'm sorry I never had the chance to set a better example, but Herbert and I were not blessed."

"Did you and your husband farm?"

Mrs. Goldthwaite shook her head. "We didn't have enough land for that — Herbert's parents were forced to divide their holdings to accommodate several sons. Herbert managed the hay and feed store on the highway outside of town, not far from your place."

Meg struggled to find something else to

say. She assumed she was probably already in Mrs. Goldthwaite's condemned column for her public association with the restaurant project — and for her implicit criticism that Granford needed the money that a restaurant or any other commercial project would bring in, thereby sullying the historical purity of the place.

Meg noticed that Mrs. Goldthwaite was quite content to let the silence between them lengthen. She seemed focused on the pigs. Obviously she had visited them before, maybe had been doing so for years. Had the pigs always been in this field?

A faint alarm bell rang in Meg's mind. This was Mrs. Goldthwaite's regular walking route, she had said. Did the state police know that? Had they questioned her about Sam's death? She could have seen something, heard something, when Sam died. Someone could have come through from her end of the lane, and few people would have made the connection.

Or maybe she hadn't just seen something. Maybe she had done something.

No. That was absurd. Meg studied Mrs. Goldthwaite out of the corner of her eye. She was a tall woman, although age had bowed her back, despite her erect carriage. Meg realized that she hadn't realized how tall Mrs. Goldthwaite was, since generally she had been seated at the meetings Meg had attended. Mrs. Goldthwaite also did not move like an eighty-year-old woman — clearly a recommendation for regular exercise, fresh air, and clean living. Meg tried to imagine the scene: Sam had been stung by a bee and he was woozy, going into shock, unsure of what was happening to him. He would have leaned on the fence for support — because the fence was the only support at hand. He was tall, and the top of the fence would have reached his waist. He could have fallen — or it would have been easy for someone to give him a push and topple him over the fence to join the pigs.

If — and it was a big if — he *had* been pushed, wouldn't Sam have been surprised? Wouldn't he have struggled? But she had no way of knowing how incapacitated Sam had been. No one did.

Meg realized she was dancing around a thought that she didn't want to put into words: Mrs. Goldthwaite might have killed Sam, or at least facilitated his death. Surely she hadn't sicced a bee on him, but she could have been there when it happened. She would then have been faced with a choice: seeing Sam in trouble, she could have sought help, hurried back to her place

385

or to Jake's and called for an ambulance. Maybe it would have been too late, but she could have tried. That would have been the right thing to do.

Or she could have stood where she was standing now and looked at Sam, gasping and wheezing, maybe pleading for help, and taken advantage of the unexpected situation. She could have given him a nudge — just the smallest nudge — and knocked him over into the pigsty. And then what? Clambered over the fence? Meg looked more carefully around the perimeter of the field. Of course: there on the perpendicular side was a gate. Mrs. Goldthwaite could simply have walked over and let herself in. She knew the pigs, and they were accustomed to her.

Meg looked at Mrs. Goldthwaite's shoes. Sturdy, supportive boots, suitable for walking over rough ground. With a thick, heavy sole. They could easily have been her late husband's. Would that tread match the footprint found on Sam's back? Had prim and proper Caroline Goldthwaite stood over prostrate Sam as he fought to breathe, placed one foot on his back, and waited until his struggles stopped?

It was a horrifying thought, and Meg wondered if she had finally gone over the edge. She forced herself to look directly at Mrs. Goldthwaite, who was regarding her with a faint smile.

"Are you feeling well, Meg? You look a bit pale. Perhaps you aren't quite accustomed to the physical demands of farming, especially in the summer heat. It must be a challenge, to take on that house and the orchard, all at once. And still you find time to involve yourself in other activities in the town."

Meg swallowed. "I believe in contributing to any community I belong to — surely you approve of that. I have expertise that may be helpful, and I'm happy to volunteer my time."

"I do indeed. I wish only that you had chosen a more worthy undertaking."

"You still believe the restaurant is a bad idea?"

"I do. It cheapens the character of the town. Oh, I acknowledge that people will need to eat, and often they like to go out for a pleasant evening, but surely there are other suitable locations, out along the highway perhaps. There is no reason why it must be in the heart of town."

In the house that you must have loved at some point in your life. "Plans are going forward, you know."

"Are they? That remains to be seen. I still

have some supporters in this town, you know. And those young people may yet fail. Your Mr. Chapin does not always get his way."

Meg no longer knew what to believe. Had her fantasies gotten out of hand? Mrs. Goldthwaite appeared as she always had, a proper old lady. A little stiff, perhaps, and set in her ways, but a pillar of the community. Not a murderer.

But maybe, just maybe, Mrs. Goldthwaite had been more deeply dismayed than anyone had realized about what she perceived as unwanted changes coming to her beloved town, to what was once her own home. Perhaps she had found herself presented with an opportunity to eliminate one of the three partners involved, and perhaps she had hoped that by eliminating Sam, the others would lose heart and leave town. It would have been a risk, and one that had not anticipated Nicky and Brian's response.

Well, there was no way Meg was going to confront Mrs. Goldthwaite here and now. She needed to think this through. And she should talk to Seth. He would know what to do. Meg was surprised by the wave of relief that swept through her at that thought.

Mrs. Goldthwaite's voice woke her from her trance. "You shouldn't depend too much on Seth Chapin."

Was she a mind-reader? "What? Me? Why?"

"I would guess he is what one might call 'interested' in you, if that's the appropriate term. But Seth has a tendency to spread himself too thin, while at the same time he has a soft heart for those in need. I'm sure he's pleased to act the gallant knight on your behalf, but that may not last."

Meg bristled. Mrs. Goldthwaite was presuming to give her advice on her love life? And worse, implying that Meg was some sort of charity case in Seth's eyes? It took her a few moments before she could say in a reasonably level tone, "I'll keep that in mind. Thank you for your concern, Mrs. Goldthwaite."

Mrs. Goldthwaite straightened up carefully and stepped back into the middle of the lane. "You think I'm meddling. But I've seen a lot in my eighty years. I've watched children like Seth grow up, become men. I'm glad he's stayed in Granford, because we've already lost too many good young people, to college and to jobs elsewhere. That does not mean I approve of his opinions. I believe that he is misguided in his commitment to this restaurant idea, but for that I blame you. I do not think he would be half so supportive of it were you not involved. But apparently there is little I can do to change his mind, which saddens me. Forgive me, but I should be getting home. If I don't keep moving, my joints stiffen up a bit."

But before she turned away, she met Meg's gaze and held it. "Meg Corey, you're an intelligent young woman. I think we understand each other."

Mrs. Goldthwaite turned and began to make her deliberate way toward home, leaving Meg standing flabbergasted, watching her retreating back. No, she most definitely did not understand what had just happened. What had Caroline Goldthwaite been trying to tell her?

"Meg!" A voice called out from behind her, and Meg turned to see Jake Kellogg walking toward her. "My wife said you were here somewhere, looking for me. What's up?"

"Hi, Jake. I wanted to talk to you . . ." Mechanically Meg went through her now-rehearsed spiel about the restaurant co-operative. "And I wondered if you could provide pork. Seth also said you had a smokehouse?"

Jake cocked an eyebrow at her. "You sure those kids are going to want my pigs, after what happened here?"

Meg had wondered how to bring that up, and was glad that Jake had opened the door. "Maybe not right away, but down the road I'd say so. Seth says your pigs are the best around, and I think they're looking for quality."

"He's right about that. Sure, I'd be happy to consider the idea, when you get the details hammered out. Let me know."

Meg smiled at him. "I'll do that, and thanks. Listen, Jake . . ."

"What? You still thinking about that boy, Sam?"

"It's hard not to, standing here. You're the one who found him, right? What time of day was it?"

"I came out here in the morning, after breakfast."

"You come out here every day?"

"Pretty much. I like talking to the pigs. Easier than talking to my daughter. She's sixteen."

"Caroline Goldthwaite likes chatting to your pigs as well. She was here when I arrived."

"Yeah, she's out here almost every day. She's one tough old dame."

"Did you mention that to the police?"

Jake looked at Meg with consternation.

"You think Mrs. Goldthwaite saw something? The killer, maybe?"

Funny how he'd jumped to the more benign conclusion, Meg thought. "It's possible. I'll bet the state police don't know that this lane runs right to her property, and that she likes to take walks."

"Huh. You might have something there. You think I should tell someone?" He looked honestly concerned.

"I'll do it," Meg said. "It probably doesn't matter much. Well, I should let you get back to your pigs, and I've got to get home myself. I'll let you know when we get some sort of agreement put together with the restaurant."

They said their good-byes and parted ways, as Meg turned to go back to her car. Maybe it was nothing, she thought as she walked along the dusty lane. Maybe she was reading too much into a coincidence, or maybe she just didn't like Mrs. Goldthwaite and was happy to remove her as an obstacle to this restaurant project. Meg had to admit that she felt very proprietary about it, and she resented Mrs. Goldthwaite's stubborn resistance. She had to be careful to separate her own personal hostility from the facts. Still, someone in authority should talk to Mrs. Goldthwaite about what she might have seen, or not seen, and when.

If she was lucky, Seth would tell her she was wrong about Caroline Goldthwaite. Caroline Goldthwaite could not be a killer. Could she?

28

Meg had been waiting for ten minutes, sitting on Seth's back stoop and staring at nothing in particular, when he came home. She hadn't known where else to go. She didn't want to go home and face Bree, so she had sought out Seth's house and had settled herself to wait for as long as it took. She had spent the time turning over in her mind what Mrs. Goldthwaite had said. Their conversation might have been brief, but it was the longest personal exchange they'd ever had. On the surface, everything Mrs. Goldthwaite said had been innocuous. So why couldn't Meg shake the nagging feeling that there was something off-key?

"Hey there," Seth said as he joined her on the stoop. "You look upset. Something wrong?"

She fought the urge to lean against him, to seek out personal comfort through the contact. "I'm not sure. I may be going nuts, so I want you to listen and tell me if I'm off track."

"Okay. What's this about?"

"Well" — she took a deep breath — "I went calling on the rest of the local markets, and after I got done, I had a little time left, so I thought I'd go talk to Jake Kellogg. He wasn't at the house, but his wife said he might be out feeding the pigs, so I went looking for him. He wasn't there, but Caroline Goldthwaite was."

"Yeah, she lives out there," Seth said absently, and then his expression changed. "Ah. You think she might have seen something? Did she mention anything like that?"

"No. She said she liked to take walks along the lane by the pigs, but that was all."

"And?"

"Seth," Meg said slowly, "I'm wondering why she didn't come forward and talk to Art, or Marcus. She said she walked that way regularly, so she probably did the day Sam died — it was a nice day, right? Even if she hadn't seen him or anyone else, she should have mentioned it, because it could narrow the time line down. Art might not have thought about it, and am I right in thinking that Marcus wouldn't know how all the lanes connect around here? So he could have addresses for neighbors, but if he looks at a map, he'd have seen that Mrs. Goldthwaite's house is maybe a mile or two away from where Sam was found. And the farm lane wouldn't show up on the map, so he might not know it went all the way through."

Seth wasn't looking at her, but staring at the path at his feet. "I'm with you so far. But what are you saying? That Mrs. Goldthwaite had something to do with Sam's death? Because she *didn't* say anything?"

"This is where it feels like I'm out on a limb. But follow my thinking. One, I just found out from Gail that Mrs. Goldthwaite was born and raised in the former Stebbins house, now Nicky and Brian's place. Two, she's set in her ways and doesn't like modern changes. She's argued publicly against the restaurant."

"I'd forgotten that she grew up there — before my time," Seth mused. "Go on."

"So Mrs. Goldthwaite doesn't want to see a restaurant in her childhood home. Say she goes out for her constitutional, as she does every day, and she comes upon Sam admiring the pigs. She'd feel that he was invading her personal territory, wouldn't she? First he and his friends take over her former home, and now he's in her backyard, too."

"Meg, where are you going with this?"

Seth turned to look at her now.

"I think you can guess. Mrs. Goldthwaite runs into Sam, whom she already hates, even though she's never met him. He's been stung by a bee, and he's in shock. She would recognize that. And she's faced with a choice: she can go for help, or she can do nothing and see if Sam recovers. If he recovers and wonders why she didn't act, she can just claim that she got flustered."

"But that's not what happened," Seth said flatly.

"No, it's worse. Remember the footprint? Oh, Seth — I think she helped him die." She waited for his reaction. She was accusing his fellow board member, and a revered local citizen, of murder. It sounded crazy even to her.

Seth took his time in responding. "Say that's true. Then, how? She can't weigh more than half of what Sam did."

At least he hadn't dismissed her theory outright. "It wouldn't have taken strength. Look, I was standing there today, and I could visualize it. Sam was tall, and he was weakened by the bee sting. It would have been easy to topple him into the pigsty." Maybe with that walking stick she had seen her carrying?

"And he could have climbed out again."

"Not if he was seriously weakened . . . and someone held him down."

Seth studied her face. "You're saying that Caroline Goldthwaite pushed Sam over the fence and then held him down until he died."

Meg met his look squarely. "I think so. It's possible. And I think at the very least someone has to talk to Mrs. Goldthwaite about it."

Seth went on, "And she never told anyone anything."

"No one ever asked. Everyone treats her as if she is beyond reproach. Seth, I know how unlikely this sounds, but it makes sense. Has Marcus identified any other suspects? No. Sam's ex, Derek, has a solid alibi — plus, he wouldn't have known the way to Jake's farm or the pigsty. Nicky and Brian claim they don't know where Sam was, and they didn't know the farms around here any more than Derek did. Besides, Sam was a friend and they needed him for the restaurant, so what motive would they have had? Jake was the nearest person, but he and his wife were at work. But Mrs. Goldthwaite had motive and opportunity, and because Sam was already weakened, she had the means." Meg took a breath. "Seth, tell me I'm crazy. Because I don't want it to be

Mrs. Goldthwaite."

Seth put an arm around her and pulled her close, and she didn't resist. She was surprised that her case had sounded stronger as she laid it out, and she was also surprised to realize that she hoped she was wrong. Accusing Caroline Goldthwaite of murder would send ripples through Granford, and it wouldn't make Meg any more popular. She pulled away and looked up at Seth's face. He looked . . . what? Sad? Grim? Angry? "Say something," she said.

He sighed. "I hate that what you say makes sense. Still, I've served on the Board and on committees with Mrs. Goldthwaite for years. She may be old-fashioned, and she's definitely strong-willed, but I have trouble seeing her as a murderer."

"I'm not saying she planned it. Maybe she just acted without thinking."

"The Caroline Goldthwaite I knew would have turned herself in afterwards. She believes in the law, in right and wrong, and in personal responsibility." Seth sighed again. "Let's talk to Art before we throw Mrs. Goldthwaite to the wolves. I owe her that much."

Seth made the call, and he and Meg sat in silence together until Art drove up.

"You two look cozy," Art said as he

climbed out of his car. "What's up?"

Seth stood up to greet him. "Pull up a chair. Meg's got a theory about the murder, and you need to hear it."

Art sighed. "So this really is business. Here I was looking forward to a beer." He located a lawn chair and dragged it closer to the door. "Okay, let me have it."

Meg repeated what she had told Seth, and Seth didn't interrupt her. When she'd finished, Art didn't say anything for several beats, watching a barn swallow diving for insects behind the house. When he finally spoke, he said, "Meg, you sure do make my life more interesting. I can't say I buy all your assumptions, but there's enough there that I have to check it out. I need to talk to Caroline Goldthwaite."

"What about Marcus?" Seth asked.

"I'd rather see what Mrs. Goldthwaite has to say before I drag him into this. Maybe Meg's read too much into this."

"You want to do it now?" Seth pressed.

Art looked pained. "Won't it keep until morning, Seth? You think she's going anywhere?"

"Maybe there's no rush, but I'd like to see this settled sooner rather than later. For all our sakes." Seth stood up. "I should come with you."

Art rose to his feet as well, with a sigh. "I guess you're right. You coming, too, Meg?"

Meg also got up. "I'd rather not. You don't need me there, do you?"

"No, we'll be fine," Seth said. "You go on home. I'll come by later and tell you what happened." He gave her a quick kiss, then climbed into Art's car.

Meg watched them leave with mixed emotions. Part of her thought she should have gone with them. After all, she was the accuser, and she felt some obligation to confront Mrs. Goldthwaite directly. And maybe if she watched her deny it, she would believe her and everything would be all right. Which would leave them back where they had started, with no suspects and no resolution in sight. But if it turned out that Mrs. Goldthwaite was involved — Meg shied away from calling her a killer — what impact would that have on the town, and on the restaurant? And on her? She didn't know; she couldn't guess.

Slowly she made her way to her car and drove home. When she walked into the kitchen, Bree was there, cooking something that smelled good. Meg realized she hadn't eaten since breakfast. "Hey, Bree. That smells great."

Bree turned from the stove. "Hi. I didn't

know if you'd be back for dinner, but I made plenty. Where've you been?"

Meg went to the refrigerator and pulled out a bottle of wine. "I went over toward Hadley to talk to the last of the markets about stocking our apples. I need to put all this together, but if you add it all up, I think we're in pretty good shape. I'll let you look at the list, and you can tell me if I'm off." *Please don't tell me that right now, though — I'm not sure I can handle anything more today.* "And I'm starving, if you don't mind sharing." She poured a glass of wine and sat down. Lolly emerged from somewhere and wrapped herself around Meg's ankles. "Hello, you silly cat. Do I smell interesting?" Maybe it was from the pigs: Lolly was definitely entranced by the scent of something on Meg's pants.

"No problem." Bree filled two plates and set one in front of Meg before sitting down across from her. Then she took a harder look at Meg. "You look lousy. Something wrong between you and Seth?"

"No, nothing like that. And I don't think I can talk about the rest, not just yet. Can we eat first? I think Seth will be by a little later, and I'll know more then."

Bree shrugged but didn't argue. Instead she launched into a description of what

402

she'd done that day, and Meg was content just to listen.

Seth arrived as they were finishing the washing up. Meg took one look at his face and went to him, and he grabbed her and held on. This had to be bad news.

Bree was watching, and said, "You want me to go somewhere else?"

"No," Seth replied, "this is going to be public soon enough, so you might as well stay. Meg, you have anything to drink?"

"There's beer and wine."

"Beer's good."

Meg peeled herself away from him to retrieve a bottle from the fridge; and while she was there, she pulled out the wine bottle and refilled her glass. It looked like she might need it.

When they were all settled around the table, Seth said bluntly, "There's no pretty way to put it. Caroline Goldthwaite's dead."

Meg went cold. "What? How?"

"Pills. Must have been right after she got home. She left a note."

Bree interrupted. "Who? Is Caroline Goldthwaite the old lady on the town Board?"

Meg took a deep breath and told Bree, "I was out at Kellogg's farm today to talk about the pigs, and I ran into Mrs. Goldthwaite — I hadn't known she lived near there. And while we were talking, I realized that she could easily have killed Sam. It seemed crazy, but I told Seth, and he and Art went out to her place to talk to her." She turned back to Seth. "Was I right?"

Seth looked ten years older than he had when he left. "Unfortunately, yes. Art and I got out there and knocked. No answer, but the door wasn't locked. We went in and found her laid out on the bed, with the pill bottle on the table next to her. I think she'd been saving them for a while. In her note she claims she had cancer, pretty advanced, apparently. That took a toll on her, and she had plenty of pills. Art took the note with him, but I can tell you what she said." Seth took another pull on his bottle. "She kept it short and bitter. You had it about right, Meg. She hadn't planned to hurt anyone, but when she ran into Sam when she was out walking that day, she just snapped. She claimed that he'd already fallen into the pigsty, and by the time she had made her way to the gate and back, he was unconscious. She wrestled with her conscience, but then . . . she decided to hold him down. She admitted that, as well as saying that she'd hoped that his death would derail the project, drive Nicky and Brian away, and

404

that Granford would remain just as it has always been — at least for the time she had left."

"How awful." Meg shut her eyes and pictured Caroline Goldthwaite as she had been only hours before, her head held high, her gait steady, walking away to her death. And that parting comment. She'd been right: Meg *had* understood — too much. Meg felt the beginning of tears.

"Wow," Bree said. "So she killed herself and left a confession. I thought things like that happened only in movies."

Meg and Seth exchanged a glance, then Seth said, "Unfortunately this was quite real. It's an awful thing she did. And it's a shame that that's what people will remember about her, rather than her long history with this town."

Bree had seen the look that passed between them, and she stood up. "Listen, I think I'm going to head upstairs. See you in the morning." She beat a hasty retreat, leaving Seth and Meg alone in the kitchen.

"Well," Meg began, then stopped. Seth looked terrible — drained and sad.

"Yeah, well," he answered. His bottle was empty.

"I'm sorry, Seth. I wish I'd been wrong. I admired her, in a way. She stood by what

405

she believed in."

He shook his head. "Don't be sorry, Meg. She made a choice — one choice that ran counter to everything else she had ever done in her long life. Thank goodness she left that note. I'd rather know for certain than have this murder hanging over the town."

"But I still feel awful. And you must feel worse — you've known her all your life."

"I have. Doesn't make it easy." He stood up slowly. "I should go."

Meg stood quickly and walked around the table to stand in front of him. "Why?"

"I don't think I'd be very good company."

"Oh, Seth, do you think I care about that? You're hurting, I'm hurting. Stay, please. We can comfort each other."

He studied her face. "I guess I'm not used to having anyone worry about me."

"Neither am I. But we could get used to it, couldn't we?"

He sighed. "Meg, I would really like that."

She went to him, and he pulled her close.

EPILOGUE

Meg pulled into the parking lot at the restaurant and stopped the car. This early in the morning, there were few other vehicles in the lot — most, she surmised, there to deliver produce fresh from the field, just as she was. She walked around the car to haul the bushel basket full of apples from the front seat, where she had carefully strapped it in.

She had picked them herself only an hour earlier, and she had reveled in every minute of it. If there hadn't been other pickers around, she would have talked to each apple, apologized for tearing it away from the tree, promising it a happy afterlife. She had come to understand the truly primitive need to celebrate each harvest, because it was such an uncertain and wondrous event each year.

And this was the official "debut" for her apples, so she wanted to make sure they were perfect, each and every one. They were Gravensteins, a variety that she now knew had originated in Denmark in the seventeenth century. They ripened early and were good for cooking, but didn't hold well. They were the ideal choice for the recipes that Nicky had concocted for this special day, or so she said — Nicky hadn't shared the details of the menu with anyone except Brian and Edna.

Meg walked around to the kitchen entrance on the opposite side of the building. She could see through the screen door that the kitchen was a hive of activity. Nicky was directing traffic; Edna was at the stove, checking something in a steaming pot; and a couple of what looked like high school students were busy chopping all sorts of colorful things.

Meg rapped on the screen door. "Nicky?" she called out.

Nicky looked over and let out a squeal of glee. "Meg! You've brought your apples! Come on in."

Meg wrestled her way through the door with her basket and stood uncertainly on the other side. "Where do you want them?"

Nicky looked around the kitchen, where almost every surface was covered with food. "Here, just give them to me. Oh, they look gorgeous!"

"Picked them myself, this morning. So far the crop looks great."

"Oh, Meg, I'm so happy for you. And for me! I feel so lucky. Look, I don't have time to chat now, but you'll be at the dinner, right?"

"You know I wouldn't miss it. I'll get out of your hair and let you work."

"Thanks! Later!" Nicky whirled away.

Meg nodded at Edna and tilted her head toward the back door. Edna nodded in return. When Meg left, Edna joined her a few moments later.

"Hey, Meg," she said.

"Hi, Edna. Look, I know you're busy, but I just wanted to be sure there weren't any problems. How's Nicky holding up?"

"What, you wanna fix something else? Everything's going great, don't you worry. All the folk have delivered their stuff — one lady even brought some flowers for the tables. Nicky's having a grand time, and can that girl cook! She's even giving me ideas, and I been cooking since before she was born. So you just take yourself home and come back looking pretty later."

"Thanks, Edna. That's what I plan to do."

As she drove away, Meg told herself to stop worrying. Everything had come together beyond her best hopes. And her orchard was doing well — Bree predicted a bumper crop.

September. How had it arrived so fast? And everyone told her that time was going to move even faster, as different apples ripened and needed tending. Sort and grade, ship and hold. She assumed there was a rhythm to the whole process, but this was her first time through it. She was determined to observe every part of it — and if she was lucky, to enjoy it.

When she got home, Bree was standing in the driveway talking to a couple of the pickers. As they trekked off toward the orchard, Meg said, "All good?"

"Yup," Bree answered. "Oh, Seth stopped by and said he'd pick you up around six."

"You need a ride, or is Michael bringing you?"

"I'm good — I'll come with Michael, to make sure he doesn't change his mind. Hey, listen, I wasn't quite sure what to wear. This isn't going to be fancy, is it?"

Meg laughed. "You know these people — half of them will show up in jeans. It really doesn't matter. We're here to celebrate the restaurant opening, not to impress anyone. And I'd wear something with a comfortable waist, so you can enjoy the food. Not that you have to worry."

"You're looking pretty trim yourself — all this exercise, hauling bushels and baskets and whatnot around. You deliver the apples?"

"I did. It was controlled chaos in the kitchen. Thanks for finding some kitchen staff for them."

"Pickers' kids — they can always use the money."

"Anything else I need to do?"

"Nope. It's all under control."

Despite her protestations to Bree, Meg debated long and hard about what to wear, standing in front of her closet. She couldn't remember the last time she had dressed up; probably before she had moved to Granford. She hadn't even unpacked more than one of her "nice" business outfits. But still, she wanted to honor the restaurant. And if she admitted it, she wanted to remind herself that she was female, not just a farmer who wore muddy jeans and muck boots. A little corner of her mind wanted to show Seth that she cleaned up pretty good.

In the end she pulled out a simple dress with fluid lines, which slipped over her head and fell to her knees. Bree was right — she'd lost weight, not surprising with all the unfamiliar physical work she had been putting in. The dress skimmed her body, and she felt loose and free in it. She scrabbled through the dark closet looking for shoes and came up with a pair of strappy low-heeled sandals that would do — after she blew the dust off them. A shawl against the cool night air of September completed the outfit.

"I'm leaving now!" Bree called out from downstairs, and she heard the slam of the screen door, and a car pull out of the driveway.

Meg ran a comb through her hair and dashed on some makeup, just in time to hear Seth's voice. "Meg? You ready?"

"Coming," she replied. One last look, and she added a pendant on a silver chain before heading down the stairs.

She picked up her bag in the hall and made her way to the kitchen, where Seth waited at the back door. Fishing her keys from her bag, she pulled the kitchen door shut behind her and locked it, then turned to face Seth. "I'm . . ."

She was stopped by the expression on his face, one that she couldn't identify. It was something like yearning, with a hint of surprise.

"You look . . . wonderful," he said.

Oh. For all the time they had spent together, he had never seen her dressed up.
And she had dressed up, for Granford, for
the restaurant — and for him. She swallowed a shallow "oh, this old thing" response and managed to say, "Thank you."
For a long moment they didn't move, and
then she stepped off the stoop. "We should
go." It was time to christen the restaurant.

He took her elbow to escort her to the
car. Driving to town, Seth was silent.
Tongue-tied? she wondered, and smiled out
the window. She didn't break the silence
until they neared the restaurant, approaching from the opposite end of the green. The
building sat like a dowager queen, its windows glowing. A small crowd of people
stood in clusters on the porch, glasses in
their hands, while two young servers circu-
lated with trays of hors d'oeuvres. "It looks
just like I imagined it," she said.

"It looks terrific. I wonder why we didn't
think of this years ago — it looks like it's
always been here. Here we go," he said, pulling into the already-crowded lot and parking. He hurried to open the door for her,
and once again took a gentle grasp of her
elbow to guide her up the walk and the front
stairs. Was he worried that she might trip in
her modest heels? Or was he staking a

public claim to her, in front of what looked like half the citizens of Granford? Either way, Meg felt warmed by his gesture.

Once on the porch, they were approached by one of the young servers, dressed in a white shirt and dark pants, who proffered a tray laden with wineglasses. They each took one, but there was no time to drink before another server arrived with a tray covered with all sorts of bite-sized baked goodies. Meg said, "You know, I'm a sucker for these things. The problem is, they're all so beautiful that I hate to bite into one."

Gail Selden approached. "Hi, Seth. You look great, Meg!"

"What about me?" Seth asked in mock dismay.

"You?" Gail looked him up and down teasingly. "I'll give you a B-plus. Anyway — Meg, did you hear about Caroline Goldthwaite's will?"

"No. Why?"

"She left everything she had to the Historical Society! I doubt it's a whole lot, but it means we might actually be able to install a decent heating and cooling system."

"Gail, that's great! I'm so glad for you." At least one good thing had come out of the whole sad mess, but Meg wasn't about to say that. It made sense: Caroline Goldthwaite had cared about Granford, or at least the Granford she had known throughout her long life, and she had left her estate to preserve its memory.

"Oops, gotta go," Gail said. "I made my husband come, and he hates this kind of thing, so I've got to keep him company before someone corners him and wants to talk about sheep or chickens."

"We can talk later." Meg laughed. She turned to Seth. "Did you know?"

He shook his head. "Nope. Maybe Mrs. Goldthwaite wanted the Historical Society to clean up its act so the restaurant didn't outshine it on the green."

"Fair enough. The old and the new, sharing the space."

There was a discreet tinkle of chimes, and people began drifting into the building. For the event this evening, Nicky and Brian had chosen to use the big room that had once been a front parlor. The fireplace with its ornate mantle was filled with a riotous bouquet of chrysanthemums and other fall flowers, matched by smaller bouquets on the table. Brian stood in front of the fireplace, looking surprisingly dignified — and nervous. "Please, come in, sit wherever you like."

By some unspoken mutual agreement,

Meg and Seth gravitated toward a table in the far corner, from which they could watch the other guests arriving. Meg did a quick count: the tables were clustered to provide seating for six at each. There was plenty of room to circulate between the tables; the tables were small enough to permit easy conversation. The crisp white tablecloths were accented with autumn-colored napkins, and the silverware, glassware, and simple white china gleamed. *Well done,* Meg thought.

Seth's sister, Rachel, followed by her husband, Noah, appeared at the front door. They scanned the room and, spying Meg and Seth, made their way to their corner, although Rachel greeted several people along the way. She threw herself in a chair next to Meg. "Whew! The sitter was late, and I thought we wouldn't make it. Isn't this terrific? I love the look of the place."

"I agree. It just feels right. I didn't know you were coming, Rachel."

"Didn't I tell you? Nicky invited me — we've been swapping recipes."

"I've been busy trying to get the harvest rolling, and I haven't even talked to them for a week or two. I assume she's invited all the growers in the partnership?"

"Of course. You know, I really love that

idea — everybody's in it together. Since it's their investment, they're going to have to come back and eat, right?"

"Yes, that was part of the thinking. That, and the quality of the food itself should keep them coming."

Seth at her side gave Meg a nudge, and nodded toward the door. She followed his gaze to see Lauren Converse — with Detective Bill Marcus in tow, looking stiff and uncomfortable. Lauren spied Meg and dragged him toward them.

"I swear, she didn't tell me she was coming," Meg hissed to Seth, keeping a smile plastered on her face. "Well, hang on to your socks — this should be interesting."

Seth stood up reluctantly, and Meg kept one hand on his arm.

Lauren and her companion had arrived at their table. "Hi, Meg, I thought I'd surprise you. And before you and Seth jump all over me, I've told Bill that he can't talk business tonight, and he has to make nice and promise not to arrest anyone. At least until after dinner's over."

Marcus looked as though he'd rather be anywhere else. "Meg, Seth," he said, his teeth clenched.

"Bill," Seth replied in a similar tone.

"Please, sit down," Meg said with as much

grace as she could muster. "Later," she mouthed at Lauren. Lauren smiled sweetly. "Bill, do you know Seth's sister, Rachel, and her husband?"

The polite amenities carried them over the next few minutes, and Meg could sense Seth gradually relaxing beside her. She wondered if she would have to kill Lauren later. No, that would not be a good idea, since it would confirm Bill Marcus's worst suspicions about her. She smiled at him, and received something resembling a smile back.

Small talk established, Meg kept an eye on new arrivals and observed Frances Clark walk in — with Christopher Ramsdell? How did the realtor and the professor know each other? She was going to have to ask Frances about that later. Jake Kellogg came with his wife, as did Tom Moody. She saw Bree slip in, followed by a sheepish Michael in a slightly shabby corduroy sports jacket. The room filled quickly, and when all the guests had found seats, Nicky emerged from the kitchen, looking flushed and joyous, and Brian went over to stand by her. They exchanged a look, and she nodded.

Brian cleared his throat, and gradually the hubbub subsided. "Welcome, and thank you all for coming. We wanted to bring you here this evening to thank you for helping us every step of the way. Without you, we wouldn't be standing here tonight. We owe special thanks to Meg Corey and Seth Chapin, who dreamed up this idea of partnering with you, but you're all important to us and to the success of the restaurant, and I hope we'll be seeing you again and again, at both the front and the back door. Tonight's meal is made entirely from the food that you've brought us, including the first Warren's Grove apples — although maybe we cheated a little on the wine, but we're working on that, too. And if Seth Chapin didn't actually grow anything, well, he made sure we had water and fuel to cook it all."

A laugh followed this comment, and with a smile, Seth raised a hand to wave at the crowd.

Brian went on, "One more thing. You might have noticed we haven't put up a sign for the restaurant, because we hadn't decided on a name for the place until recently. We've decided to call it Gran's, first of all because it's Granford's restaurant, second because it suggests good home cooking, and third because it's short and easy to remember." Another laugh followed, and Brian smiled. "Nicky, you want to add anything?"

Nicky stepped forward shyly. "I want to welcome you, too. I'm much more comfortable in the kitchen than out here talking to people, but I need to thank all of you for helping us. You've taught me something very important about what it means to be part of a real community, and I hope our food is everything you hoped it would be. And if it isn't, tell me and I'll fix it! Thank you again!" With a duck of her head, Nicky retreated to the kitchen.

"All of you, our partners and our friends, please enjoy your first meal at Gran's!" Brian said, beaming, and signaled to his wait staff, who poured out of the kitchen like a flock of swallows bearing trays laden with the first course.

Three hours later, the crowd reluctantly rose from their tables in ones and twos and drifted toward the doors, looking somehow plumper than when they had arrived, and thoroughly pleased. Meg and Seth remained in their corner, waiting for those nearer the front to clear out.

"Lauren, you have a place to stay?" Meg asked, hoping silently that she did.

Lauren winked at her. "Don't worry about me. I'll give you a call in the morning, okay?"

"Fine." Meg didn't want to know anything

420

more about Lauren's plans, especially i. they included Bill Marcus. Although, Meg had to admit, he had been surprisingly pleasant for the entire evening.

Rachel stood up and dragged her drowsy-looking husband to his feet. "Great food, great company. I'll be sending all our guests here, believe me. Talk to you soon, Meg. Come on, Noah — home." And they, too, swept out the door.

"Should we say good-bye to Brian and Nicky?" Meg asked, reluctant to move.

They had managed to get to their feet when Nicky appeared at the doorway to the kitchen and searched the room. Finding them, her face lit up and she hurried over, trailed by Brian, and flung her arms around Meg. "Oh, Meg, it was everything I hoped it would be. Wasn't it great? Didn't everybody look happy? And they ate everything! I don't know how I can ever thank you. And Seth. We couldn't have done it without you." Out of the corner of her eye, Meg noticed Brian and Seth swapping manly handshakes and back pats, but they looked happy, too.

Meg laughed and returned Nicky's hug. "You two did a wonderful job. The food was terrific, and I think everybody was impressed. I'm proud to be a part of it. Well, ve should let you relax — it's been a long day."

"But a good one. Thank you, thank you, thank you!"

It took a few additional minutes before Meg and Seth could extricate themselves, and make it out onto the now-empty porch. The air was cool, with a suggestion of fall, and a few lights glinted from across the green.

"I wasn't just being polite, you know — I think they hit just the right note: perfect food, plenty of it, and not too fancy. I didn't see a single unhappy face in the room." Meg leaned back against Seth. "We did something good here, didn't we?"

"That we did. I think you can be proud of what you started. About this, and a lot of other things."

"Mmmm?" Meg said vaguely. She felt far too good to ask for details, especially while Seth was nuzzling her neck.

"Look what you've accomplished in the last eight months. Look at how far you've come."

"You've been a big part of that, Seth."

"Happy to help, lady. We make a good team. Shall we head home?"

"Yes. I think Bree said something about staying with Michael . . ."

The drive home was short, made in comfortable silence. But when they pulled into Meg's driveway, she laid a hand on Seth's arm. "Seth, there's somebody in the front."

He pulled forward and stopped the car. "Stay here, I'll check."

Meg ignored his instructions and got out of the car — after all, this was her place, and her trespasser. By the time she had made it around the car, the intruder had stepped forward, followed by a bewildered Seth.

"It's about time! Your cell phone's off, you know."

"Mother?"

WELCOME AND THANK-YOU MENU

All ingredients were grown sustainably in Granford

FIRST COURSE

Chilled zucchini buttermilk soup
with fresh herbs
Buttermilk from Cole's Dairy

Mesclun salad

Local greens and marinated vegetables
with mustard-maple vinaigrette
Greens and vegetables from Morton's Farm

MAIN COURSE

Crown roast of pork with apple-sage
stuffing, fingerling potatoes,
and green and yellow beans
Pork from Kellogg's Farm

Apples from Warren's Grove

Morgan's Farm roast chicken with shallots
and thyme, wild mushroom risotto
Chicken from Morgan's Farm

House-made pasta with summer vegetables
Vegetables from Morton's Farm

DESSERT

Goat cheese mini cheesecakes with
hazelnut crust and apple-blossom honey
Cheese from Kibbee's Farm
Honey from Carl Frederickson

Open-face berry tart with crème fraîche
Berries from Kizior's Farm

RECIPES

APPLE SLAW

If you're tired of the same old cabbage slaw, apples go surprisingly well with other vegetables in this crunchy, colorful dish.

2 apples, peeled and cored, then chopped or shredded (Granny Smiths work well — you want a tart, firm apple)
4 carrots, shredded
3 small parsnips (the big ones get too tough), shredded
1/4 head red cabbage, shredded
1 small red onion, sliced (optional)
2 tablespoons chopped parsley
2/3 cup mayonnaise
2/3 cup sour cream
1 tablespoon ketchup
1 teaspoon sugar
salt and pepper to taste

Combine the apples and vegetables in a

large bowl and toss. In another bowl, mix the mayonnaise, sour cream, ketchup, sugar, and salt and pepper. Add to the vegetable mixture (you may not want to add it all at once — you don't want it to be soupy). If you're not going to eat the slaw quickly, chill.

You can experiment with other vegetables as well. Try celery root or jicama!

GOAT CHEESE MINI CHEESECAKES

You can make these as tangy or as mild as you like, depending on your choice of goat cheese.

Makes 1 dozen

1/2 cup crumbled sugar cookies (homemade or purchased)
1/4 cup finely chopped hazelnuts
1 tablespoon plus 1 teaspoon sugar
3 tablespoons unsalted butter, melted
1 8-ounce package cream cheese, at room temperature
8 ounces goat cheese of your choice, at room temperature
1/2 cup sugar
1/2 teaspoon vanilla extract
2 large eggs, lightly beaten
1/2 cup sour cream

pinch of salt

Preheat oven to 350 degrees.

Line standard muffin tins with paper liners. Combine the cookie crumbs, hazelnuts, and sugar, then stir in the melted butter. Press 1 tablespoon crumb mixture firmly in the bottom of each lined cup (the bottom of a glass works well for this). Bake until set, about 7 minutes.

Lower oven temperature to 275 degrees.

With an electric mixer on medium-high speed, beat the cream cheese and goat cheese together until smooth. Gradually add the sugar, followed by the vanilla. Beat until well combined, about 3 minutes. Drizzle in the eggs slowly, stopping often to scrape down the sides of the bowl. Beat in the sour cream and salt.

Pour the batter into the lined cups, filling almost to the very top. Bake 20–22 minutes. Cool completely on wire racks. Refrigerate in the muffin tins at least 4 hours or overnight.

To serve, you may drizzle honey or a berry syrup lightly over the cakes.

RACHEL'S STRAWBERRY MUFFINS

This recipe is best made with small, ripe strawberries. And the muffins should be eaten quickly!

Makes 12 muffins

1 cup flour
1 cup cornmeal (fine ground)
1/2 cup sugar
1 tablespoon baking powder
1/2 teaspoon salt
11/2 tablespoons grated lemon zest
1/4 cup butter, melted
1 cup buttermilk or yogurt
1 egg
11/2 cups coarsely chopped strawberries
coarse sugar for topping

Preheat oven to 350 degrees.

Grease or line standard muffin tins. Sift together the flour, cornmeal, sugar, baking powder, salt, and lemon zest. Chop the berries roughly and toss with 1/2 cup of the dry ingredients (this keeps the berries from sinking to the bottom of the muffin).

Whisk together the melted butter, buttermilk or yogurt, and egg. Mix the liquid mixture into the dry ingredients (do not overmix). Fold in the strawberries.

Spoon the batter into the muffin cups, filling 2/3 full. Sprinkle the coarse sugar lightly over the tops.

Bake 20–25 minutes. Turn out and cool on a rack.

ABOUT THE AUTHOR

Sheila Connolly has been nominated for an Agatha award for the Glassblowing Mysteries she writes as Sarah Atwell. She has taught art history, structured and marketed municipal bonds for major cities, worked as a staff member on two statewide political campaigns, and served as a fundraiser for several nonprofit organizations. She also managed her own consulting company, providing genealogical research services. In addition to genealogy, Sheila loves restoring old houses, visiting cemeteries, and traveling. Now a full-time writer, she thinks writing mysteries is a lot more fun than any of her previous occupations.

She is married and has one daughter and three cats. Visit her website at www.sheila connolly.com.